BEYOND THE WEST SEA

A STRIPLING WARRIOR NOVEL
MISTY MONCUR

BEYOND THE WEST SEA

A STRIPLING WARRIOR NOVEL
MISTY MONCUR

Eden Books – Stansbury Park, Utah

© 2016 Misty Moncur
All Rights Reserved

Cover photo © 2015 Heather Waegner
Cover design by Misty Moncur

This novel is a work of fiction. Characters, names, places, dialogues, and incidents are products of the author's imagination or are used fictitiously and are not to be interpreted as real. Any resemblance to actual persons is coincidental.

This is not an official publication of the Church of Jesus Christ of Latter-Day Saints. The opinions and ideas expressed belong solely to the author.

With the exception of short excerpts for review purposes, this book may not be reproduced, in full or in part, by any means or in any form without prior written permission. To do so is unlawful piracy and theft of intellectual property.

Published by Eden Books, Stansbury Park, UT

ISBN-10: 0-9898959-6-3
ISBN-13: 978-0-9898959-6-5

Moncur, Misty Leigh, 1978-
Beyond the West Sea/ Misty Moncur
Summary: Miriam's life takes a turn when she tries to follow the promptings of her heart.

ISBN: 978-0-9898959-6-5

Library of Congress Catalog Control Number

2015951734

This one's for

ZACH

You make raising a son a veritable piece of cake.
#motherboy2017?

And with thanks to myopic, socially awkward boys everywhere.
#you'recuterthanyouthinkyouare
#LibwouldhavelikedStarWarstoo

CHAPTER 1

I woke to shouting workmen and incessant hammering. Yawning, I rubbed the sleep from my eyes and rose. I was eager to see the ship in daylight, but it was not why I had come to the coast and had nothing to do with my lodging aboard the large sailing vessel.

I rolled my sleeping mat and set it in the corner. Turning slowly toward the door, I wished there was something more to do, but there was nothing. So I took a breath, tucked my hair behind my ear, and stepped from the dim cabins.

"It is the sun's reflection off the water," one of the crewmen explained when he saw me squinting. I didn't stop to listen, just flashed him a tight smile and picked my way across the cluttered and unfinished deck toward the far end where I hoped I would be out of the way. I glanced around. It was probably wise to stay away from the men, many of whom had ceased their work to stare at me. I stepped over some wood blocks, found a seat on a pile of ropes, and watched the carpenters and craftsmen while I waited for Ethanim to come for me.

It had been nearly dark when we had arrived, and he awakened me before dawn to tell me he meant to go inland to the market to replenish our supplies. Certainly we had used them up on our journey from Orihah, but I knew it was an excuse to go exploring. He hadn't thought he would be back before the morning meal.

"You get some more rest," he had said, even his whispered voice unable to conceal his eagerness to explore the coastal town where his best friend had been living for months.

I had smiled into the dark after he stole silently from my room. I didn't mind him leaving me alone for the morning. He had been kind to bring me here and such a pleasant companion on the journey. And besides, I was tired from the journey and had willingly laid my head back down.

A man who looked to be in charge was scrutinizing some drawings and directing the placement of a large beam. It looked like a complicated job that required the strength of many men, but it was all happening down at the other end of the ship. If the work moved to this end, I would have to move. Hopefully, Ethanim would find me first, but though I waited patiently and the work was interesting, Ethanim did not appear and I eventually tired of watching the workmen. I lay back in the ropes, made myself as comfortable as I could, and settled in to wait.

I became gradually aware of two men speaking near me and realized I must have fallen back to sleep.

"I think we have a stowaway."

I blinked my eyes open and looked for the position of the sun. It was nearly noon!

Two men worked near me. I recognized them both. One was the man I had seen holding the plans and giving orders to the work crew. The other one was Lib, Ethanim's friend, but a quick glance around did not produce Ethanim. Lib was tall, blond, slender with strong and square shoulders, and looked to be preoccupied with building the ship. When the other man spoke, Lib stopped what he was doing to lean back and peer at me around a stack of lumber, but clearly with little interest.

"I'm not," I said sharply. "A stowaway, I mean. I'm not."

The man laughed and smiled kindly. He was older than Lib, maybe in his thirties. I took in his strong shoulders, thick arms, rough hands, wide nose, and smiling eyes. He looked excited. Happy. Exuberant even. He either loved this boat or he loved me, and I was betting it was the boat.

"I know," he admitted in a kind of apology. "Just looking for some solace, eh?" he asked, going back to his work. It looked like he and Lib were making an adjustment to the rigging for the large sail. "It can be nigh unto impossible to find peace and solace around here."

"Something like that," I mumbled, tucking a piece of hair behind my ear and gazing out at the sea—shimmering blue as far as I could see.

I thought the man intended to leave me alone then, but after a few moments I heard him ask, "She your sister?"

Lib barely glanced at me and didn't bother with a response beyond a shake of his head and humorless laugh, as if to say that someone like me could not possibly be related to someone like him.

I could see how the man might think it, though. My hair was nearly the same rare, golden color as Lib's, and while he was tall and broad-shouldered and I was small and thin, we did share other similar features—long fingers with bony knuckles, light skin that tanned easily, freckles on our arms, and eyebrows darker than our hair. I would have thought the same thing.

"Lib is a terrible brother," I said.

That got both of their attention.

The other man laughed. "Teases you mercilessly, I suspect."

I shot an assessing look at Lib. He looked like he could take a joke. "Once when I was small, he held me upside down by my ankle over the latrine, and when I tried to spit at him, it ended up in my hair." I stood and stepped toward the man. "I'm Miriam," I said.

His grin was quick. "Hagoth."

"Oh?" I had heard of Hagoth, the shipbuilder and adventurer. "You're younger than I thought you would be," I said.

"Did this young pup tell you I was old?" he laughed as he gave a last hard pull on the rope he held. Turning to Lib, he said, "I didn't know your sister was visiting."

Lib stared at me for a long moment, his eyes dark and suspicious. "Neither did I."

"I didn't even know you had a sister," Hagoth pressed.

Suddenly looking from me to Hagoth, Lib said, "I don't. Miriam and I are not acquainted."

Clearly, I had misjudged him, and he couldn't take a joke.

"We met last night," I said.

Lib's eyes narrowed as he looked back to me.

"I came with Ethanim," I told him, hurt that he didn't remember. It wasn't like there were other visitors sleeping in the new cabins, and from what I had observed, there were no other women on board, either. I sighed and turned to Hagoth. "I guess I am the one who teases. Lib speaks the truth. We are not related, but I did grow up in Orihah, not far from Lib." Not far from Lib's childhood home, anyway. Lib hadn't lived there for years.

I felt Lib's eyes on me. He was studying my face, trying to decide if he recognized me or not, but he obviously didn't.

Hagoth observed us both for a moment, his bright eyes darting between us, and then he sort of smiled to himself and winked at me.

I thought Lib, a boy I had looked up to when I was young, a boy whose bravery and faithfulness I had heard tell of, was just this side of rude. He was not living up to the stories I had heard of him.

Sighing to myself, I wondered, and not for the first time, what I was doing there.

Hagoth made some excuse and said he had to go, and before I knew it, he was gone and I was standing awkwardly alone with Lib.

He brushed some imaginary dirt off a pallet, kicked it lightly, rubbed the side of his nose, and looked longingly over my shoulder at his friend's retreating back.

Not knowing what to say, I clasped my hands together and looked out at the sea.

"I was preoccupied last night," Lib said at last, maybe a little apologetically.

"Ethanim says you have been very busy."

Actually, what Ethanim had said was that Lib was too busy for his friends. I tucked my hair behind my ear again when the sea breeze blew it free.

"Yeah." He bent and picked up the thick rope. He wound it into a tidy coil as he said, "I can't wait until she's ready to sail."

"How long will it take?"

"Many months."

"Months? But it looks almost finished!"

I might have imagined it, but I thought his eyes lit up. "There's—" He broke off and shook his head. "There's a lot to do still," he finished. Then he started to edge away. "I guess I will see you later," he said and followed Hagoth across the deck.

"I guess you will," I said, letting my eyes follow him.

I watched as he approached Hagoth, watched Hagoth grin and say something that made Lib's face turn red. He turned away from Hagoth and checked the strength of a knot that did not seem to be loose.

"I think he's a snob," I told Ethanim later when we were eating the food he had brought from the market.

Ethanim chewed thoughtfully and finally pushed the food

to the side of his mouth. "That will make being married to him hard." He took another bite of his fish stew, scooping it into his mouth with his fingers.

I took another bite, too. It was good, but I thought it was seasoned too heavily. "You still think I'm crazy."

"To want to be Lib's wife? No, not at all. To travel all this way to snare the heart of a man you've never met? Yeah." He chewed for a minute and then added, "Really crazy."

"That's pretty much what my parents said."

"What did Noah think?"

My oldest brother. I squirmed a little on my seat. "He talked you into taking me, didn't he?"

He grinned. "It didn't take much talking, Miriam. Escort a pretty girl on a week long journey to the sea? I had to think on it for about a second."

I flushed and squirmed again.

He took another bite, chewed for a moment, but then pushed the food to the side of his mouth and said, "I'm all for Lib getting married. I just think you might have your work cut out for you."

"Because of Keturah, you mean?"

His face hardened and he looked down into his stew. "Yeah."

I didn't know much about the situation, only what I had pieced together from bits of Noah's conversations and a little from David. Lib had fallen in love with the only female warrior in Helaman's army during the war, and Ethanim did not approve of his friend's feelings. "I met Hagoth, today," I said to change the subject.

"I haven't met him yet. What is he like?"

"He loves this boat."

"Did you know Lib helped him design it?"

"David told me." I looked around. "This has been in the works for a long time."

Ethanim nodded. "Lib has a very gifted mind for engineering. He has been drawing plans for things like this since we were kids." I detected a note of pride in his voice. "He knows everything about everything."

"He doesn't know much about being polite."

Ethanim barked out a laugh, but more generously allowed, "He is hurting, but I can't believe he was impolite—especially to a little girl."

"I'm not a little girl," I argued.

"Okay." But his amused smile said he thought differently.

"I'm sure getting this ship seaworthy has been very stressful for him."

"I'm sure it has been like a fun game for him," he disagreed, still looking amused, "but even if it was stressful, it would be no excuse to be rude to a girl."

"He wasn't exactly rude," I admitted, wishing I hadn't brought it up. "He wasn't impolite."

He just didn't like me. Didn't like the way I looked, the way I smelled or walked. He didn't like me on his magnificent boat.

"Hey, listen." Ethanim waited until I looked over at him. "I think what you're doing here, well, it's good. Inspired and brave. The holy spirit impressed you to come here and marry a man you hardly know. You acted on it. You did it. You're here. The

8

Lord wouldn't lead you astray. I don't see Lib's disposition getting sweeter anytime soon, but then, I don't have the wiles of a pretty little girl with which to sweeten it."

Warmed by his words and the wink that accompanied them, I only said, "I am not a little girl."

He cleared his throat. "About that," he said. He leaned forward, putting his elbows on his knees and regarding me with a frown. "I can see as well as any man that you are not a little girl."

I swallowed hard and looked down at my hands.

"When I refer to you that way, I'm not trying to insult you or put you in your place. I'm trying to keep an appropriate distance." I could hear the earnestness, almost tenderness, in his voice. "I need to think of you as my friend's little sister, not as the beautiful woman I can see you are, not as a woman who is prepared to become a man's wife."

Oh Ethanim, I thought. I felt suddenly very naïve, but I was grateful for his blunt speaking and also for his faith in what I was doing.

"I will help you with Lib as much as I can," he went on, a soft determination in his voice. "I'll help you do what you feel is right, but I must ask you to help me, too." He caught my eye. "Alright?"

I lifted my chin. "Alright."

That night, the fatigue of the journey had apparently worn off, and I couldn't sleep.

I was silly not to have realized Ethanim wouldn't see me the way Noah did, wouldn't think of me the same way. I wasn't his sister, and bringing me here had been hard for him in ways I didn't understand, but should have.

I sighed and slipped out of my bedroll. Glancing back at it as I made my way from the room, I thought of how much trust Noah had placed in Ethanim and felt foolish all over again.

The air was cool and salty on the deck, and I wondered that the boys could sleep in the stuffy hold, which was where Lib and Ethanim and several of the work crew had gone at dusk. It had been stifling down there when Hagoth had given us a tour, and that had been with both traps open.

It was no wonder they were open now, and I stepped softly around the openings so I wouldn't wake any of those who slept below.

I couldn't see the waves in the dark, but their soft rhythmic crash against the shore told me the sea was not calm. It was stirring, and it matched my mood.

I knew my first impression of Lib had been a bad one. I had tried not to have any expectations of him. I had thought I didn't. But how could I not? Keturah and Gid said he was wonderful. My brother, Noah, always spoken very highly of him and had the utmost respect for him. Ethanim was his best friend and, though frustrated with his recent depression, loved him like a brother.

I looked at the stars, small bright lights in an otherwise very dark night.

How can I do this thing? He doesn't even see me, and he is ever so much more hurt than I was prepared for. I smiled. *But heavens, is he ever handsome.*

I had only vague recollections of Lib as a boy. I had been only seven when he had gone to war, but he had made enough of an impression on me that I remembered him. But to be fair, I had memories of all Noah's friends. Noah, my oldest brother, was eight years older than me and had joined Helaman's army when he was just fifteen. I recalled that time vividly—the messenger who came to recruit the boys from Orihah, their excitement and determination to go, the words about their departure during the Sabbath meeting, the other boys who walked out of the town with Noah headed north to a training field near the city Melek. Both Lib and Ethanim had been among them.

Noah was home now, married to Sarah, a girl who had grown up near us. He worked with my father on the farm, and he was content there. He would have brought me here to the coast himself, but Sarah would soon give birth to their first child—any day now. There was Jed, my other brother, but he had his work to tend to and was newly betrothed. Still, he had been willing, but Noah had thought to ask Ethanim, Lib's best friend, to bring me to the coast. Ethanim was glad for the excuse to visit his friend and had agreed quite readily.

And so I was here, and I was wondering what my next step should be. I had felt so strongly of the holy spirit that I needed to come here and marry Lib, but just showing up and stepping onto his boat was not accomplishing the task. So far, it wasn't even accomplishing a simple friendship. It actually seemed that Lib was deliberately looking through me like I didn't exist.

But I secretly took heart in that because ignoring me so

thoroughly had to be taking a deliberate effort and a certain level of awareness of my presence.

I pulled my wrap tighter around my shoulders, and considered the pile of rope I had napped in earlier. Perhaps it could offer me sleep again. It was silly. I didn't plan to spend the night in the ropes, but I made myself comfortable on them again, reclining to look at the stars.

I sensed more than heard someone else on the deck, and realized that I *had* fallen asleep in the ropes again. The sea had calmed, and a cold mist had crept into the air. Slowly turning my head toward the rail, I saw Lib standing there, his fair hair unmistakable in the moonlight.

My breath caught in my throat, and he turned at the soft sound.

He scanned the darkness, his eyes passing over me in the shadows. When he was satisfied there was nothing amiss on deck, he turned back to the rail. After a long time of staring out into the blackness of the sea, only moonlight on the calm, quiet ripples to show it was there at all, he sighed, pounded his fist lightly on the rail, and went down into the hold.

Maybe I had been expecting too much, thinking Lib would take an interest in me like I had taken an interest in him, thinking he would at least see me.

I took a deep breath of the humid night air. I needed some kind of plan. I needed to make him see me, and the things that interested Lib, the things he did see, were all related to the engineering and construction of that big ship.

CHAPTER 2

I only knew of one way to get information about the ship and how it worked.

Dawn had come and gone, but the fog had not yet burned off the beach. Ethanim had gone fishing with Lib, and I was waiting silently in the lee of the ship. When I saw Hagoth trot down the boarding plank and turn toward the town, I stole after him, feeling furtive but determined. It wasn't good of me to follow him, spying on his activities—he only went to take his meal with some friends—but I needed his help.

He met two other men and one woman at an inn on the far side of the town. I edged behind the corner of a building as I watched him laughing with his jovial friends. Once, when he looked in my direction, I slid back behind the wall. I had no business in this part of the town, and he would know it. He seemed to have a nice time, but he didn't stay long. When he left the town and walked the path back out to the docks, I drew on my boldness and ran to catch up with him.

"Hagoth!" I called. "Hello!"

He turned. His smile was quick and open. "Miriam, hello," he replied, stopping to wait for me.

At least I was not forgettable to every man.

"Are you going back to the ship?" I asked, feeling stupid because there was no other place he would be going on this path.

But he looked at me for a moment, and said, "Actually, no. I thought I would take a walk along the beach."

"Oh," I said, disappointed, but I didn't want to keep him from his work.

"Would you like to join me?"

I tucked my hair behind my ear, thinking I shouldn't, and also thinking it was exactly what I wanted. It was perfect.

"Yes, thank you. Have you always lived here on the sea?" I asked as we turned to cut south across the beach.

"No. I visited the sea with my parents once when I was little, and as soon as I became old enough, I brought myself back."

"Was it the ships or the sea that drew you?" I asked, liking the idea of him being a little boy.

He grinned and looked down at his feet as he walked. "The sea. I admit I am intrigued by where it can take me. The world is vast. It is filled with wonders and other peoples, exotic goods, knowledge." He looked up at me, and his eyes glinted.

"Have you been to many places?"

"Oh, aye. But it is never enough."

"So you have designed a ship to take you around the world."

He shook his head. "Lib designed it."

"But you have built it?"

"Yes. And I will sail it."

I looked up at him and saw the self-assurance in his eyes. "Do you feel compelled to sail? As if it is something you cannot resist?"

He was silent for a moment. The question wasn't a surprise. I could tell it was something he had thought of before.

"Oh, aye," he said, this time much more quietly.

I wanted to tell him I was here at the sea because the Spirit had whispered to me, too, but it just sounded ridiculous.

"I could tell that about you," I said instead.

"You could, could you?" he laughed.

I gestured to the ship in the distance. "That is a lot to accomplish on a whim."

He looked toward the ship for a moment and slowly nodded his head. Then he changed the subject. "And what brings you to the sea, Miriam, with that Ethanim? He is not your husband."

He might have tried to hide the deep curiosity in his voice, but I heard it.

"He is a friend of my brother's. Noah asked him to do me this favor, and he agreed."

"But do you wish to sail somewhere? The large ship won't be seaworthy for a while yet."

"I came here to meet up with someone." It was mostly the truth. Lib just didn't know it yet.

He hummed, confirming he had heard me, but he was quiet for a time and we walked along together as the waves lapped at the shore. He knew I was not being fully honest with him, and I could see him trying to put the pieces together. Suddenly, he turned to me. "How old are you, Miriam?"

"Nineteen."

"Not married?"

"No."

"Not betrothed? Not to that Ethanim?"

I giggled. "No."

"You have not got a string of men at home who vie for your attention?"

I shook my head. "There is boy who courts me. He is a good friend, but," I shrugged, "it has been some time and has not amounted to much more than friendship."

"Friendship is important in a marriage."

"It is," I agreed. "But it does not feel right. I think he feels the same. Otherwise, the courtship would surely have gone somewhere by now. And are you?"

"Married? No."

"Why not?"

He shrugged, a wide grin on his handsome face. "I've been busy." He cast me a sidelong glance, but didn't ask me any more personal questions about what I was doing there.

I would have answered them honestly, but I knew my answers would sound ridiculous. If not ridiculous, then foolhardy, and if not foolhardy, then impulsive. He wouldn't understand—that I felt compelled to find, befriend, and marry Lib, that I felt inadequate in every way to do it. But I had to do it. I had to make Lib fall in love with me.

Noah and my parents understood, to a degree, or said they did, but I was sure they all expected me to return home alone.

Ethanim understood, too, but just thinking of the things he had said the previous night made my face feel warm.

I can see as well as any man that you're not a little girl.

"I think you've gotten too much sun," Hagoth said, concern clouding his normally happy countenance.

My hands went to my cheeks.

"You should wear a hat. Your skin is so fair."

"We can't all be grizzled old sailors like you," I said.

He laughed, but when he spoke, his voice was gentle. "Miriam, did I say something to cause that blush?"

When I shook my head, it only caused him to laugh again, a warm chuckle that made me smile too. I should dispense with this small-talk and just get down to business.

"Tell me about the ship, Hagoth. How do the sails work? How might one sail if the wind does not blow in the direction he wishes to go?"

"Magic," he said without hesitation.

"Tell me true," I laughed.

He laughed too. He was such a pleasant man to be with, easy and obliging. "Alright, Miriam. It is called lift, and it works like magic."

"Lift," I said, trying out the word. "Explain it to me."

He gave me a funny look—not like he thought I wouldn't understand, more like he didn't know why I would care—but he told me.

"Lift happens when the sail redirects the wind in the opposite direction of the way in which one wishes to travel."

"But how?"

17

"Not entirely sure, to tell you the truth. Lib understands it better."

"But you are the sailor."

"And he is the scientist. I can work it in life. He can work in on paper. If you wish, I can show you what I have learned by experience, but I cannot explain it in technical terms."

"I shouldn't think I require the technical terms. You could show me on real sails?"

"Sure. I've a small sailboat I take out for fishing and the like. If you want, I will take you out into the bay in the morning."

"Truly? I would love to see how the sails work."

"Alright then," he said, looking down at me.

"Alright then," I repeated, trying not to catch his very contagious smile.

Ethanim was helping Lib smooth some wood planks when Hagoth and I walked onto the deck, boarding the ship together. He looked up at us, and his smile was instant, genuine, and maybe a little relieved. It was nice that he felt that way about me—protective and responsible. How I would accomplish my task here was so uncertain that Ethanim's steadfastness was a comfort.

Lib looked up too, and right at me. His gaze lingered for a moment, but then he glanced at Ethanim before turning back to his work, and I got the impression they had been talking about me.

Hagoth touched my elbow and led me toward them. The touch was unexpected, but after our talk on the beach, it didn't surprise me.

"Hello," I said when we stood before them. I turned to Hagoth. "Thank you for the walk."

"My pleasure," he replied. He stayed by my side for a moment more until Ethanim looked between us and frowned. Then Hagoth gave a start and found a plank to smooth for himself.

I watched the three of them working for a moment. "What is that you're doing?" I asked, directing my question between Ethanim and Hagoth. "Can I be of help?"

"Sure," Hagoth said.

"Sit right here," Ethanim added.

"We don't need your help."

There was a sudden, uncomfortable silence. Hagoth frowned and Ethanim glared at his friend. He stood slowly and came to stand by me.

"I mean, no thank you," Lib said. He tried to meet my eye, but looked quickly away. "We would never ask you to help. You are a guest here."

I wondered what Ethanim had told Lib about why he had brought me with him. It occurred to me for the first time that Lib would think the same thing Hagoth had—that Ethanim and I intended to become betrothed. That we perhaps loved each other, or at the very least, that we were much better friends than we actually were. Would I travel overnight with someone I did not intend to marry? I frowned. I hadn't thought ahead to how this might look to him.

"Of course you can help," Ethanim was saying. "It's easy. The sanding blocks are there, and you just run one along the

19

plank until it's smooth." His voice held so much enthusiasm, I could tell he was overcompensating for the rudeness of his friend.

But I wasn't here to make Lib uncomfortable. The opposite. I shook my head, and my hair came out from behind my ear. I tucked it back. "You're busy. I've interrupted." I started to back away. "I will go to my room now and see you for the evening meal."

With that, I turned away from them. I could easily imagine the looks the others leveled on Lib. I cringed. I didn't want them to coerce him into paying me attention. That seemed ploying and desperate, and I wasn't either of those things.

As I walked away, I noticed the drawings, the design plans for the whole ship, laid over a barrel. The drawing was detailed and exquisite, even embellished. I stopped to finger an embellishment at the corner. Had Lib done that?

My eyes followed the beautiful lines, the arcs and curves and angles, but my eyes kept catching on one particular line. I stared at the plans for a moment, aware that Hagoth was regaling the others with some story from town.

"You've got this angle wrong," I called over my shoulder.

They ceased talking.

"What?" It was Lib.

I pointed to the plans. "Right here."

I heard a snort behind me and a light tread on the planks as one of them approached me. I felt prickles go up my neck as Lib drew up behind my right shoulder.

"Right here." I traced my finger along a line that would not work, not if the way Hagoth had described it all to me were to work, not if this ship was sailing into the wind.

Lib studied the lines that he had drawn on the linen.

"Isn't it?" I looked up at him over my shoulder. I knew I sounded unsure, but unless I had completely misunderstood Hagoth, the line was drawn wrong.

Lib looked up from the drawing, and it was like he was seeing me for the first time. It might have been flattering, but it wasn't. I was the exact same girl he had been ignoring for days.

"It should be at a steeper angle," I said, and just in case he didn't get it, just to pound it home, just because I couldn't help it, I added, "You did it wrong."

"I did not do it wrong," he said calmly, but he worried his bottom lip between his teeth and turned back to the drawings.

I shifted my weight. "Well look. If you are traveling due north and the wind is blowing from the north east and your sail does not have the ability to turn this direction, the whole thing will capsize." I curved my hand above his where it was spread over the linen.

He finally looked up at me, and his lip fell from his teeth.

I shrugged. "The ship will sink." I subdued a smile of any kind and started toward the cabins on the upper deck, but I turned, leaned around him, and gave a small wave to Ethanim and Hagoth who had both stopped sanding the planks to stare at us.

I had taken a few steps before Lib lurched after me. "Wait!" I turned.

"If you're so smart, how do I fix it?"

21

Was he patronizing me? Or was he…teasing?

"You're the engineer," I said and let a small smile touch my lips. Then I went to my cabin, lay down on my bedroll, and grinned at the ceiling. I hoped I had not just made an enemy of the man who would be my husband.

The next morning, Lib approached Ethanim and me while we ate our morning meal. He held the plans for the ship rolled up in front of him.

"You were right," he said with a forthcoming that surprised me as he went to a knee and unrolled the linen. "But look at this."

"Right here," I said, pointing out the changes he had made before he could.

He halted for a moment surprised maybe, but asked, "What do you think?"

Glancing around and spying a spare piece of wood, I picked it up. "Have you got a graphite stick?"

He reached up and handed me the one he had placed above his ear.

I began making calculations on the wood. The two boys were quiet while I worked, but I gradually realized they were stone silent.

"You're wondering where I learned to do this," I said.

I kept my head down to my work but heard Ethanim laugh. "Yeah, actually."

I smiled. His great laugh was so contagious.

But Lib didn't join in.

I took my time with the calculations—not because I needed the time, but because I was nervous about what Lib's silence was saying. When I was done, when I had gathered my courage, I looked up and passed him the wood.

He merely glanced at it before tossing it down on the plans. They caught the breeze and billowed lightly.

"There is only one way you could have learned to do this in Orihah," he said, poking a finger at the wood, his voice flat. He glanced at his friend. "Only one person who could have taught you this."

I glanced guiltily at Ethanim as I passed the charcoal back to Lib. "Your father puts his graphite behind his ear, too," I said.

It was the wrong thing to say. Lib dropped the graphite by the discarded wood and clamped his mouth shut.

"He said he misses you," I told Lib. "He says it all the time."

"I miss him too."

His candor surprised me. David had given me the impression that his son didn't like to spend time at home in Orihah, but I thought I knew why, even if David didn't.

I studied Lib's face. He reminded me of his father, but with his light features, he didn't resemble David in looks. It was in the way he held his mouth, the way he squinted one eye in suspicion. It was in the things that were written in his eyes.

"So are my calculations right?" I asked when Ethanim didn't say anything and Lib just stared blankly down at the building plans.

Lib sighed and picked up the wood. "If my father taught you, I'm sure they are." But he looked them over and eventually reached for the discarded graphite. He began making figures of his own.

"I've never seen it done that way," I told him as I watched over his shoulder.

"I am just checking the accuracy of the calculations."

Ethanim got up, and I thought I caught a wink. "I'm going to go work with the crew and let you two talk sums," he said.

He started to go, but I said, "No, wait." My heart sank when I realized what I had to say. "I have to leave. Hagoth is taking me out on his boat." When I saw Ethanim's disapproving frown, I added, "To show me how the sails work."

Still lost in the calculations, Lib absently told me mine were correct and, perhaps sensing the levity in his friend, he rolled up the plans and made haste to leave me alone with Ethanim, who didn't waste time giving me his opinion.

"What are you doing?" he almost hissed. "If you're trying to make him jealous or something—" He folded his arms and leaned back on his heels. "I really think he's had enough of that."

"I'm not."

His eyebrow shot up skeptically.

It was like arguing with my brother.

"At least now he won't think I'm in love with you."

His other brow shot up. "Why would he think that?"

"That's what Hagoth thought. That's what it looks like. Why else would I have traveled here with you? Why else would you have brought me here to introduce me to a friend who is like a brother to you?"

He twisted his lips and glanced at Lib, who had joined the work crew. "For two smart people, we certainly didn't anticipate that."

"Maybe you could set him straight," I suggested.

"How can I do that without telling him why you're really here? Do we still agree it's best if he doesn't know?"

I nodded. "We agree."

"Miriam."

We looked up to see Hagoth striding toward us, strong and handsome, and I couldn't help returning his broad smile.

"Are you ready to go?"

I nodded. "I am."

He glanced at Ethanim. "No problems?"

"No," I replied quickly. I gave a small wave to Ethanim who wasn't exactly scowling, but wasn't exactly not scowling either. I ignored it and turned back to Hagoth, feeling the weight of Ethanim's glare as we walked away.

CHAPTER 3

At the time I had left Orihah, I wouldn't have said I was interested in sailing, but I got lost in Hagoth's descriptions of the boats and the open sea and the exotic lands he had been to. His knowledge and explanations were engaging, and his enthusiasm was contagious.

His small sailboat was in a calm cove up the coast, a distance away from the busy fishing docks and the flurry of building.

"My home is there." He pointed up the beach through some trees where I could see the outline of a small beach shack. "I have a friend who watches the place when I'm away. Not much to watch, though."

"It's very charming," I said honestly. "I bet your sunsets are fantastic."

"They are. Now, watch your step."

He helped me onto the boat which was moored to a small dock.

"Can you swim?" he asked.

I shook my head.

"We'll have to be sure not to heel too much then."

"Is that likely?" I asked, staring at the sparkling, calm sea.

"Always a possibility," he said, but he was smiling to himself.

I sat in the boat and watched while Hagoth untied the moorings. We headed out into the small bay and Hagoth set our course for the larger sea. After he had shown me how he could manipulate the two small sails to move the boat in the direction we wished to go, which was south, he directed me to push the rudder in, and we just sailed for a time along the beautiful coastline.

"We'll get into hostile waters if we don't turn around," my companion said when the sun topped the middle of the sky and started to descend.

I didn't have time to think about that before he pulled the rudder to turn the boat and said, "Man the sails, my dear. Let's see how well you have learned."

"Let's see how well you have taught me," I corrected, and he chuckled.

I got up and made my way to the sails. Turning them as I had seen him do, struggling a little with the knots he had put in the lines, I set the sails in place. I knew I had done it right when the wind caught them and I nearly fell over backward, but Hagoth caught me with rough sailor's hands on my shoulders.

I looked up at him over my shoulder. I wasn't able to hold his gaze. And what was more, I didn't want to. I didn't want to invite feelings between us. I remembered the look Ethanim had given me, and I knew that being on this boat was sending the entirely wrong message to Hagoth—to all three of them actually—Hagoth, Lib and Ethanim.

Hagoth must have caught my grimace, because he said, "Miriam. You are not promised to Ethanim."

He said it as a statement, but I knew it was a question.

"I told you. No." I had to put an end to this, though. He was still standing behind me, still had his hands on my shoulders, making me feel safe, and I liked the feeling. I liked him. And that was a problem, because I knew in my heart what God wanted me to do. I took a breath. "But to be quite honest," I said, "I came here to marry Lib."

His hands tightened slightly on my shoulders.

"That surprises you," I said, sensing he had not expected me to say that.

"Aye, it does, in a way. Not that I blame you. Lib will make someone a fine husband. It is only that he—"

"Doesn't think much of me," I filled in for him.

He laughed a little and turned me to face him. He was shaking his head. "I was going to say he doesn't seem much interested in marrying at all. And also," he peered down at me, "I thought you two were not acquainted."

The boat shifted and I lost my balance again, but Hagoth held me up.

"Need to get your sea legs," he said.

I nodded and then took a seat. "Lib and I were not acquainted before I arrived, and he does not know why I have come."

Hagoth folded his arms over his chest. He looked at me as if he was waiting for a good tale.

"Please sit down," I said, and when he leaned a hip against the side, I told him the whole story. The promptings I had felt, explaining them to my parents and brothers, traveling here with Ethanim, and wondering how to accomplish the Lord's will.

"But is it your will?" Hagoth asked after he had sat quietly and listened to everything I said, getting up once to adjust the sails when the wind changed. "Do you even want to marry him?"

"I want to do as the Lord commands," I said.

"It was a prompting, not a commandment."

I frowned. "Is a prompting not a commandment just for me? I desire to do God's will, and so do you, Hagoth, so don't give me that look."

"You don't even know him."

"That is why I am here—to come to know him."

"And what do you think of him so far?"

"I think he is distracted and cold," I said before I could stop myself. "And handsome," I added, though I could see it did not make a difference in what he thought of my plans. I reached over and covered one of his hands with mine. "Hagoth, can I be very honest with you?"

"Of course you may."

I took another breath. "I have loved our day together on this boat. I love your vision and your drive, and to be frank, I am quite taken with your sense of romance and adventure."

He raised both brows.

"But I will do as the Lord commands."

The wind blew my hair around my face as I waited for his response. He stared thoughtfully at me, and finally, when I wanted him to say something and he didn't, I said, "You think I am foolish—to trust so much in a feeling."

His lips did not smile, but his eyes did. "I was thinking that I admire you. I admire your conviction."

I could see the large ship in the distance now, and I gestured to it. "It is not as if I have built a ship."

"You're right." The water hitting against the hull of the sailboat made a dull splashing sound. The boat tipped and bobbed over waves that were becoming larger. "But, building the foundation for a life with someone is much more complicated, and I fear Lib will not be easy to persuade."

I laughed. "Ethanim said my womanly wiles would be helpful."

Hagoth turned the rudder so the bow tipped toward shore. "I doubt he is immune," he agreed with a smile.

Hagoth said he would help me with Lib, but the way he went about it was exasperating. He flirted with me outrageously when Lib was present, and when he wasn't present, Hagoth treated me like an old lady—respectful, but barely friendly. I didn't think the flirting was doing anything but pushing Lib away and giving him the wrong opinion of me. And I didn't like Hagoth treating me like his elderly aunt either.

Ethanim and I had been staying on the boat a week when I told the men I wanted to see more of the ships that were docked in the bay. "I would like to see a finished one," I said, "and see the goods they have carried back from other lands."

"You can come into the market with me today," Ethanim said. "There are goods in plenty all along the stalls."

Lib had accepted that Ethanim did not intend to take me to wife, but Hagoth's flirting had him still keeping his distance.

Hagoth shook his head and surprised us all when he said, "Let Lib take her to see the trade ships and the merchant sailors."

"Miriam doesn't need to see the sailors," Lib said. "They are crude and bawdy to the last one. Take her fishing with you on the bay or that pool in the gorge."

Hagoth gave his head a shake and then took a drink from a large mug. "Can't."

I watched their exchange with interest.

"Why not?" Lib still spoke with indifference. He didn't care where I went or who I went with.

"She did not come here to fish with me."

All four of us fell silent. I flushed. Ethanim looked from Hagoth to me with curiosity. Hagoth took another drink. And Lib wondered for perhaps the first time just what I had come there for.

Ethanim, always quick, said, "I have to get to the market," and he left abruptly.

Hagoth finished his drink and slowly put his mug down. Giving Lib a hard look, he ambled toward him. He clapped a large hand onto Lib's shoulder and shook him gently so he had his full attention. "A word of advice from an old sailor, Pup." Hagoth shot a glance back at me over his shoulder. "Start seeing beyond this ship."

Hagoth gave Lib a last small shake, as if to wake him up, and then he left, too.

I wanted to say something before it became uncomfortable, but Lib looked right at me and said, "What did he mean?"

I stared at him, reluctant to speak. I was not afraid for me, but for him. Was he ready to hear any of it? I made a quick and fervent prayer in my heart. What was I to say?

Lib was hurting, or rumored to be hurting, but he was not incapable of comprehending my mission here. He wasn't blind. He certainly wasn't stupid. His best friends both knew.

I owed him the truth. I intended for him to become my husband. I owed him the honor of being honest with him.

But before I could get the words out, Lib slowly straightened and set down the chisel and hammer he had been using. Wiping his hands on his tunic, he said, "Come on. Let's go see those ships."

"Are you sure? You're busy," I demurred.

In answer he just gestured to the ramp that led to the ground. He let me go down first and waited until we were walking up the beach toward the main docks before he asked, "Did my father send you here?"

"No, of course not." I licked my lips. "I came of my own accord."

"I suppose he wants you to persuade me to come home."

I shook my head. "He would not dream of asking that of you. He is so proud of what you are doing here. He doesn't want you to end up like him."

"He said that? That he doesn't want me to end up like him?"

"Oh yes. More than once."

"What's so wrong with him? I've spent my life trying to be like him."

"He's lonely."

Lib squinted into the distance.

"He doesn't want that for you."

"I'm not lonely."

"Then you should tell him. He can't help worrying. He loves you."

"And how do you know what my father feels?"

I looked up at his face. He wasn't angry, but there was definitely a challenge in his voice.

"My mother sent me to take him his evening meal once, and we started talking. We have become friends."

"Don't you have friends your own age?"

"Of course I do."

"And why did he start teaching you mathematics?"

"He told me how gifted you were at it. I wasn't very familiar with complex mathematics, so I asked him to show me what he meant."

"And he took that as an invitation."

"He said I had a good head for it."

He was quiet for a moment. The gulls cried up and down the beach—so different from the sounds of the forest at home.

"You do."

I smiled down at the sand. That sounded suspiciously like a compliment.

"Does he talk about me a lot?" Lib asked.

I looked up at his profile. "You are the sun and the moon to him."

And now I see why.

He huffed and rubbed the back of his neck, but I could see my words pleased him.

We had come to the docks where six large ships were moored in the harbor. A flurry of activity went on around them. It appeared one had just arrived and men were offloading cargo using ropes and oxen.

Lib turned to me. "Which one would you like to see?"

I looked around at the ships, the people coming and going, the sailors shouting and laughing, and I pointed to the ship that had just arrived. "The others look boring."

I thought a half a smile touched his lips, but it was gone before I could confirm it.

Unlike Lib's ship that was still under construction, the ship we boarded had women on it. Mostly they were disembarking, but in their presence, I didn't feel as conspicuous as I sometimes felt down the beach on the unfinished ship.

No one stopped us or prevented us from boarding the deck, so Lib led me around and pointed out the things I had seen unfinished on the other ship.

"Where has this ship been?" I asked him, wondering if, for the rest of my life, I would be asking my questions to him, drawing insights from him, seeking his advice and counsel. "Where did it sail from?"

He looked around, seeming to study the crew, but he didn't make a conjecture. Instead, he stopped one of them and asked.

"Thessalonica," said the burley crewmember. His eyes grew warm and he spoke for a time in a language I did not understand.

I didn't know if Lib understood it or not, but he thanked the man, and when the man nodded and went back to his work, Lib turned to me.

"Have you heard of Rome?"

"I have," I told him.

"This ship comes from the kingdom of Rome and brings with it goods from the warm climate of The Great Sea. Silk, hemp, spices, incense."

"Is it a long journey?"

"It depends on what you consider to be a long time."

Was he teasing me?"

"The time it took for you to look at me without seeing through me as if I wasn't there."

"I never saw through you!" he protested, feigning innocence.

I laughed. "Then you just didn't see me at all."

"I saw you," he said quietly. Then he cleared his throat. "Let's get off this boat. I don't feel good about being here."

I hadn't realized it until he said those words, but I didn't feel good about being there either.

When we disembarked together I saw a family with small children who looked tired and miserable. It looked like they had just come from the ship. The children all sat listlessly in the dirt as their mother looked anxiously around and their father questioned one of the men from the docks. As we passed them, the oldest child began coughing. It was a violent cough that racked his little body. Without thinking, I knelt to him and held his stooped shoulders until the spasm was over.

Lib grabbed my elbow and jerked me up. "No!"

I gave an involuntary shriek. He pulled me away, but not before he nodded to the child's parents in what appeared to be a kind of apology.

"The child is sick," he breathed. I could hardly keep up with his long strides as he rushed me away.

"He needed comfort and no one was offering it. He was such a small, pathetic little thing."

Lib stopped abruptly and looked—really looked—into my eyes. Then he turned to look back at the ship.

"Why did Ethanim bring you here?" he asked.

"Noah asked him to."

Lib started walking away, this time at a more reasonable pace. "Noah?"

"Noah is my brother. Didn't Ethanim tell you?"

"Ethanim," he said, "has told me precious little."

"I would have asked Noah to bring me, but he couldn't come. I might have come alone, though no one approved of that, but Noah asked Ethanim to make the journey."

"What was so all important here that you would have come alone for it?"

Obedience.

"I can travel alone."

"It's dangerous."

"I know."

"So why the urgency to get here?"

The whisperings of the Spirit.

"Why?" he asked again, not sharply but demanding nonetheless. "Because, I'm sorry, but I don't remember you, and I don't see how you can remember me either. Why should you even think to come here to this place?"

A knot formed in my throat. Why couldn't I just say it?

"Miriam."

"Because of the feelings in my heart. Because of the whisperings of the Spirit to my heart, Lib."

"Miriam," he said again, but his tone had softened.

I had been bold enough to come here. I could be bold enough to look him in the eye. I stopped, and, noticing it, he stopped too. I raised my chin until I could see into his face.

"Can you not feel them too?" My brows knit as I sought the answer in his curious eyes.

He didn't look away from me, and in fact stared at me for so long I became uncomfortable. Finally, slowly, he shook his head.

"I'm not sure I understand," he said.

"Then despite all your learning, you are quite stupid."

He smiled slightly, and his eyes sparked with amusement as if he might challenge me on that.

Forcing myself not to hesitate, willing my hand not to shake, I lifted it and caressed his cheek.

His eyes were the color of his father's, green like a new leaf. They showed his surprise. They showed his intelligence. And they showed a numbness, a coolness, a wariness I didn't know for certain how to break through.

But I did have some ideas.

I let my hand drop and looked around. "Are you taking me to the market?"

"I thought to, yes. It is time to eat." He started again in the direction we had been walking.

"I could cook for you—for you all." I knew he heard me, and I could see him considering the offer, but he didn't respond so I said, "I really liked what Hagoth showed me about the sails."

"It's even more astounding on a large scale. You will love seeing it on a large ship, especially ours—Hagoth's and mine."

"I don't know that I'll be around for that," I said, a disappointment I couldn't quite mask sneaking into my voice.

Lib folded his arms over his chest. "You could come back."

"Maybe."

"Ethanim will come again, I'm sure of it. You could come then."

"You could come home."

"No, I couldn't."

"Because of Keturah?"

He stopped walking. "Did Ethanim tell you about that?"

He wasn't mad, wasn't incensed or crazy with grief. He wasn't really showing any kind of emotion at all.

"Give me some credit for having eyes and ears," I said.

He took a deep breath and ran a hand through his loose hair, then smoothed it back down into place. "Well, that was a long time ago."

"I know. Sometimes when you've been hurt, it can take a long time to heal."

"And have you, Miriam? Been hurt?"

I thought of Shad, of the cold river, of soldiers and longing and heartbreaking honesty.

"No. Never."

He shrugged and started again toward the market. "I think I know what you're doing here."

"I doubt it."

"Give me some credit for having eyes and ears."

He was disconsolate, wry, self-deprecating, but I smiled, nearly laughing.

"That will make it much easier."

"Don't count on it," he replied, but I caught his smile too.

CHAPTER 4

"Here," Lib said as he passed me a folded flatbread filled with an aromatic mixture of cooked fish and vegetables. "Be careful or it will burn your tongue."

I hummed as I took a bite. It was hot, and I uselessly fanned my mouth with my hand. When I could talk again, I said, "You speak from experience, I think."

He grinned, showing me more of the side of himself he had been slowly sharing with me over the afternoon. "Maybe."

"Do you do much cooking of your own?" I asked after another bite.

He shrugged again. He had a way of doing it more with the subtle tilt of his head than with his shoulders. He had eaten his food in maybe two swallows—it was no wonder he had gotten burned—and his eyes were scanning the people around us.

"You sure you don't want a betrothal to Ethanim?" he asked abruptly.

"No, I told you—"

"Well, then look at that." He pointed.

Under the branches of a tree at the far end of the lane, where the people were not so numerous, Ethanim sat on his heels next to a girl—a slick-haired, olive-skinned, beautiful girl. Just one look at her elegantly curved nose and dark, captivating eyes made me jealous of her.

Jealousy was not a feeling I was very familiar with. I had of course experienced it before, but I had always been satisfied, happy even, with what I had—including my looks. But I would look like a pale scrap of linen to her dramatic fine purple silk.

I asked the obvious question. "Who is she?"

"No idea. Let's go find out."

"No!" I exclaimed. When Lib turned a questioning look to me, I licked my lips and said more reasonably, "No."

"Why not?"

I don't want to stand next to her, that's why not.

"Privacy. They may want their privacy."

Lib looked around at the people.

"I mean, just look at him. She is gazing at him from under her lashes and he's falling for it."

Lib let out a bark of laughter. "Falling for it?"

"She is beguiling him."

That made him really laugh. "All the more reason we should go to his rescue."

"Oh, alright," I groaned and followed him toward his friend and the beautiful girl.

Ethanim looked up when we approached, and the girl shyly followed his gaze.

"Who is this?" Lib asked, giving the girl a friendly smile.

"I'm trying to find out. We seem to have a language barrier."

Lib gave a small nod and began speaking to the girl in a language I did not understand. The girl's face brightened and she responded with a maelstrom of words. Lib went to his heels next to her and continued the conversation. He nodded as she talked and smiled, but it was a sad kind of smile.

After watching for a moment, I went to stand near Ethanim. When he glanced up at me with the same pensive look I felt on my own face, I just stared at him.

It took me a moment to register when Lib was talking to us again.

"This is Adreana. She is from Thessolonica." He gestured back toward the docks. "She came on that boat that just moored."

Ethanim and I had both turned to look at him. "Why is she alone?" Ethanim asked quietly.

"Her father and uncle died on the voyage. She is alone in the world now."

"Tell her she's not," Ethanim urged. "We can care for her."

"I did. I told her she could rely on your strong arm."

Ethanim tried to subdue his grin, but his eyes were bright as he looked Adreana over. "Can you teach me her language?" he asked as he forced his eyes back to Lib.

"Yes. But I think it would be better if she learned yours. She has a trunk filled with belongings and provisions at the dock."

"Can she stay on board the ship?" Ethanim's apprehension showed in his eyes.

Lib's straightforward reply was toned with a compassion I hadn't yet seen in him. "Of course she can." He paused. "Just don't give it out widely that we take in the needy. We can't house everyone."

Ethanim frowned like he didn't like thinking of Adreana as needy, but when he turned back to Adreana his smile returned. He held out his hand, motioning for her to rise, and told us, "I will take her to retrieve her belongings."

Lib spoke to Adreana, and then he and I watched Ethanim lead her away.

"How do you know that language?" I asked him.

He shrugged. "I have spent a lot of time on the docks."

"Do people from many lands come here?"

"Not so many. Some."

"But why?"

"Trade."

"Do we have goods they want?"

"It would be a useless voyage if we didn't. They arrive with cargo stored in their holds and return with goods from our lands. Are you ready to go back to the ship?"

"Oh yes. Thank you for showing me the docks and the boats today. And thank you for the flatbread. I know you had better things to do."

"I'm sorry I gave you that impression," he admitted quietly. "I was thinking. If you wanted to go up into the hills tomorrow, there is a good view of the narrow neck of land that leads to the north country. I could take you to see it."

The answer was yes, but I asked, "Is it far?"

"A morning's walk."

"I would like to see it."

"But you would like the walk with me more."

I was finding that Lib had a way of speaking directly that took a lot of the uncertainty out of communicating.

"It would be a useless walk if you were not there, yes."

He grinned and jerked his head in the direction of the sea. "Let's go."

When I arrived back in my room on board the ship, I saw Adreana's trunk in the corner. I guessed I was sharing my space with the beautiful Thessalonian girl. It wasn't like me to be jealous of things that others had—in Adreana's case it was exotic beauty—and I didn't have a right to, but I hadn't liked the way Ethanim looked at her. Lib either, for that matter.

I sat on my pallet and read a scroll filled with the words of the prophets until the light that slanted through the small window became too dim. The window was a luxury on board a ship like this, one that made me think Lib had taken more notice of me that night we arrived than he admitted to. Finally, I yawned, stood, stretched, and decided I had better go out and prepare an evening meal for the men.

I walked down the long plank that led to the ground where we cooked. Hagoth and Lib both were adamant that we not light fires on board, even within the stone fire rounds.

I could see before I stepped foot on the long grasses of the beach that Adreana was already cooking, and the entire crew surrounded her. The men talked and laughed and vied for her attention.

I took a deep breath and approached.

"Ask her if I may help her," I said to Lib's back.

He turned to look at me over his shoulder, and I was pathetically grateful when he offered a genuine smile.

"She has enough help."

I glanced around and rolled my eyes.

Lib regarded me for a moment, his eyes narrowing the way his father's did, his head tilting as if he were thinking about something. Suddenly, he moved away from the crowd, clearly intending for me to follow. We walked out toward the shore where the shimmering water touched the sand. The sun was beginning to set, and under other circumstances, it might have been a touch romantic.

"Don't you need to translate for her?" I asked.

"Many of the men speak Greek."

"Oh."

"Is something wrong, Miriam?"

I took a deep breath and stared out to sea. "I think I am missing my home." I smiled up at him. "I have never been away."

"I'm familiar with the feeling," he said.

"You left home a boy of but fifteen. I am much older than that."

"You're can't be so very old," he said. Then he cleared his throat. "I'm sure Ethanim will take you home any time you wish to go."

I shook my head slowly. "I have not done what I came here to do."

"And what exactly did you come here to do, Miriam?"

I swallowed. I briefly met his eyes, but shook my head. "It's complicated. It requires a finesse I'm afraid I don't have. And anyway, I think Ethanim has just found a reason to stay."

He glanced over his shoulder at the crowd of people. "I am not a good enough reason for him to stay?"

"Excuse me. I meant a prettier reason."

"Miriam, I think you're jealous." He chucked me under the chin with his fist.

It wasn't a personal touch, but I felt myself making too much of it. My cheeks got hot, and I knew I would not be able to blame it on the sun as Hagoth had done. All I could do was try to hide it by looking away toward the sea.

"I am not comfortable with jealousy. Do you think prayer will take it away?"

"Oh, aye," he said softly. It was one of Hagoth's sailor expressions, and I smiled when Lib used it.

"I don't understand it. I do not want anything she has, and I think her great beauty may do her more harm than good." I gestured to the men that surrounded her. "Nor would I wish to be without kin in a foreign land. And yet, I don't like the way you all look at her."

"You share homesickness with her. Perhaps that can be a place to start."

For a moment, he let me see the understanding in his eyes.

"And I don't think she will be alone for long," Lib continued. "Look at all those men."

"I do not want all those men, either." Despite her smile, I doubted Adreana liked the attention much more than I would.

He looked at me as if he didn't believe me.

I shook my head. "As if I would want one of those scroungey builders or tattered and grimy sailors!"

It might not have been the wrong thing to say, but it hung in the air between us for a long time until finally Lib brushed his hair out of his eyes and said, "I think the food is ready."

Adreana's meal was good, I had to admit it, and being able to cook for so many was quite a skill.

"What grain is this made from," I asked Hagoth when Lib and I were sitting at the fire with the others.

"It's wheat. Haven't you eaten wheat before?"

"Oh, yes, but not like this."

He nodded. The bread was quite different than anything I had ever cooked.

I looked at Lib. "Mostly we eat barley from Liam's farm. Some corn. Only a little wheat when we can get it in the market."

Ethanim spoke up. "The girl Jashon married grows wheat in her village, but they don't trade on the trade route. They keep themselves separate from other peoples. But who knows, now that Jashon is Ardon's father, perhaps he will open trade with Orihah."

Ardon was Salome's son. He was to be the next chief of their clan.

Was it my imagination, or did Lib color at the mention of Salome?

"I met her when they came to visit Liam and Naomi," I said. "I liked her very much."

"Are you close to Liam's family?" Lib asked.

I caught the look Ethanim sent to him. Guarded, exasperated, a little angry perhaps, and hesitant, as if waiting to see what else Lib would say. He was poised to interrupt if necessary. I put it together quickly. He didn't want the conversation to turn to Keturah.

"I only know them from church," I said. "Is there much wheat on the docks?" I asked, quickly returning the subject to grains. "I did not see any wheat fields after Hermounts."

"And how would you recognize a wheat field?" Lib asked, a smile touching his lips as he leaned back and folded his arms.

There were no wheat fields in Orihah. He was challenging my knowledge. To someone like me, who valued knowledge and sought earnestly for it, a challenge was barely short of an insult. And I was sure someone like Lib knew that very well.

But Ethanim raised his brows and shot me a secret grin. Then he got up and moved to the opposite side of the fire, leaving Lib and me in relative privacy.

Lib leaned down and murmured, "You forgot to tuck your hair behind your ear."

What?

I searched my lap for the reason he had said that.

"You do that when I make you nervous."

It was impossible not to tuck my hair behind my ear then, and when I did, we both laughed.

I remembered everything about that moment. The sand I couldn't seem to keep out of my sandals. The salty smell of the sea. The darting glances Hagoth kept sending us. The ones Ethanim didn't.

"I noticed Adreana's trunk is in my room," I said.

"I hope that's alright," he replied and added apologetically, "It's the biggest room on board and the only finished one."

"Of course it's alright. We are both here on your hospitality."

He might have blushed.

"I gather you don't like her. I can move the trunk if want."

But it wasn't as if I knew enough of her to like or dislike her. "Of course you shouldn't do that."

It surprised me very much that he offered, the more so because I thought he was serious—he would move it if I wanted him to.

"Ethanim seems quite taken with her," I noted.

He hummed his agreement.

"Perhaps that is why I became jealous so immediately," I mused quietly. I noticed most of the men were leaving the fire. Some headed off toward the town. Some headed up the long plank to find their beds in the hold. Some made camp on the beach.

Lib was silent for a long moment.

"I thought you said...I thought Ethanim was not..."

I watched him as he faltered, was charmed by the way he halted, as if he could not quite form the words that would get him the answer he sought.

"You forgot to run your hand through your hair," I said.

His discomfort vanished when I bumped him with my shoulder.

"That is what you do when I make you doubt your logic."

"Miriam." He looked away to hide his smile.

"There is nothing between Ethanim and me. He is only my friend, and he wasn't even that before we started this journey together."

"Traveling together alone has a way of bringing people closer."

I thought of all the things we had done to help each other on our journey. I had cooked what he had hunted. We had filled each other's water skins, slept on opposite sides of the fire, stayed awake talking under the stars. He had trusted me to take a watch so he could sleep. We had been everything to each other for those days of travel.

Ethanim, my brother's friend, a man I had hardly known beyond sight, had become the person I knew best here, and that included Lib, the man I intended to marry.

"I know we have perhaps given that impression. He is easy to be with, and we did become close," I admitted. "But Ethanim guards his heart very well."

We both turned our eyes to Ethanim, where he sat across the fire trying to learn Adreana's language.

"What I meant," I said, "was that I am used to having his full attention for myself. I let myself rely on him too much. I shouldn't have." I bit my lip. "I think of him like a brother, but the truth is, it is not quite like that."

"I understand," he said quietly.

But I wasn't sure he did.

I wasn't even sure I did. I should have waited until Noah could bring me. Or I should have come alone.

Lib and Hagoth lit lanterns from the fire before they put it out and led us all up into the ship. Lib gave me his and they wished us goodnight. I bid Ethanim a good night as Hagoth and Lib said a few last words to Adreana.

"I never thought you would fall for such a pretty face," I teased him.

"I fell for you yours."

As we stood together in an uncomfortable silence, I thought of all the things he might have said instead—that Adreana was good or sweet or kind, that she was alone, made him laugh, gave him something to think about. Anything but what he said.

"Don't say that."

In the quiet that followed, I only heard the strange words the others were speaking.

"Alright," he said at last. "I shouldn't have…" But he just shook his head and didn't finish the sentence as if he could not bring himself to lie.

But it had to be a lie, and if it wasn't, we had to turn it into one.

Adreana was moving off toward our room. The men were looking at me, waiting for me to join her. I raised my lantern and turned to follow, to light her way, but I licked my lips and turned back to Ethanim.

"Thank you for what you have done for me," I said.

His eyes shifted from me to his best and oldest friend. The moment was charged as everyone stopped and utter silence fell over us. Even Adreana knew something was happening. I heard a burst of jolly laughter from the men below in the hold. The waves crashed onto the shore and lapped against the big ship.

"Anything to help you find peace," he said, but his eyes never moved from Lib, and nobody thought he was talking to me.

I was the first to move, and Adreana quietly followed me to our quarters. She quickly set up a bedroll on the other side of the room. We both lay down and fell asleep.

Something woke me. It was still the dead of night, pitch dark but for the small light of the moon that lay in a square on the floor between us. I listened to the soft sobs until my eyes adjusted and I could see that Adreana's whole body was shaking with them.

I didn't debate whether or not I should, whether I knew her well enough, or whether I liked her. I just crawled across the floor and touched her shoulder. She jerked and rolled up onto her elbow, but she wouldn't look at me.

"Adreana," I whispered, the only word in her language I knew.

Then I wrapped my arms around her and as I rocked her into sleep, even though I knew she wouldn't understand the words, I prayed for her in soft, soothing whispers that turned into the soft tones of every lullaby I knew.

CHAPTER 5

I was groggy in the morning and my muscles ached, but I had spent half the night comforting Adreana and I couldn't be sorry for it.

She gave me a shy smile as I gathered my satchel and water skin and prepared to leave with Lib. I wanted to tell her she did not need to feel shy around me.

"Why did Adreana make this journey with her father and uncle?" I asked Lib when we were well on our way. "Did they plan to live here?"

"To tell you the truth, I don't think she set sail with her father. I think it was more like…a betrothed."

I didn't miss his hesitation. "But you don't think they were actually betrothed."

"No."

I took this in. "She is a very nice girl."

"Oh, no doubt, at least from what I have seen. We cannot hold her to the standard of our beliefs."

A warmth went through me when he said those words. Not just because he withheld judgment of Adreana, but because he and I did have the gospel in common, and it was such a good place to start. I felt closer to him, felt a connection, and he might have too because he fell silent.

We walked on for some time, gradually ascending a large hill. It was green and grassy and as we got higher, the view of the gorgeous blue sea became better. The sunlight glinted through the trees, and I knew as it climbed in the sky it would become clear and fully illuminating.

"You okay?" Lib asked.

I wiped my brow and squinted into the sun. "A bit of a headache," I admitted. I turned to give him a bright smile, but I was afraid it only turned out to be a weak one.

He held out his water skin to me. "Drink more."

I shook my head and held up my own before I took a long swallow.

"I'll take you back if you want," he offered.

"So obliging for a man who couldn't stand me at first sight," I said as I replaced my water at my belt.

"I thought you were Ethanim's girl. I thought he brought you here, I don't know, to meet me and show you off."

He was half right. Ethanim *had* brought me here to meet his friend.

"If you had thought that, you would have feigned excitement. You would have grinned at me and congratulated him."

He frowned. "I suppose you are right. But I know he likes

you. I have seen him watch you."

"It's like you said." My breaths were becoming shallow. "Perhaps our journey did foster feelings neither of us were prepared for."

"Do you return them?"

"There is nothing to return." I tried to smile but it turned into a wheeze instead. "You have seen his fickle affection is turned already to Adreana."

He huffed. "Then if he did not bring you here to meet me, tell me why he brought you."

"Another time perhaps," I said. "It is somewhat complicated, and it is sure to embarrass me." My eyes drooped. My long night with Adreana was catching up to me. "And I'm kind of tired. Maybe you could just do the talking for now."

I could see he was perplexed that I wouldn't tell him, but he said, "I'll take you back." He touched my elbow.

"No, Lib," was all I said. I would feel crummy alone on the ship. At least here I could feel crummy and be with Lib.

We were walking up a well-worn trail. Lib pointed out the peak from which we would see the narrow pass. These weren't like the majestic mountains I could see from my home—from the West Road near Orihah—but as we climbed higher, I became more and more out of breath. Lib stopped altogether when I coughed.

But I just kept going, one foot in front of the other. "Tell me about your mother."

He sighed and followed me. "She died a long time ago."

"I know that much."

"Then you know how she died."

I did. "In childbirth."

I was looking up at him, so I noticed when he bit his lip. "Mm-hmm."

She died giving birth to him, and I knew, because his father had told me, that Lib had not dealt well with the knowledge.

"So it's just been you and your father."

"Mm-hmm."

I could tell the air was still cool, but it felt so hot. I wiped my brow again, but my head felt cold, and my hand felt clammy.

"He's really smart," I pressed on.

"He is."

"And he raised you alone."

"He did. What are you leading at, Miriam? He's a good man. I respect him, and I love him, and I'm not sure what more you want me to say."

You blame him.

But I didn't say that.

"I need to sit for a minute," I said instead.

The slight irritation on his face turned again to worry. He glanced around the trail. "Here." He led me to a soft patch of earth under the trees. "You look really pale," he said as he went to his heels in front of me.

I closed my eyes. There was pride and then there was foolishness. I should let him take me back.

"I feel pale, Lib. How much farther is it?"

"Only a few more minutes. Just up that rise." He gestured to the trail above us.

"I would like to see the pass," I breathed. "We are already here. Just need to…to catch my breath."

"You're sick."

"I think I might be. At first I thought it was just fatigue. I didn't sleep much last night."

"Why not?"

"Adreana was homesick."

He nodded slowly. "Did she keep you up?"

I shrugged. And then I coughed again.

Lib gathered some twigs into a small pile. He reached into his satchel and came up with a flint. Quickly and efficiently, he coaxed a small fire from the kindling.

"What are you doing that for?" I asked. I was cold now, but he couldn't know that. The fire couldn't be for me, and a fire that size wouldn't help anyway.

He reached for some larger pieces of wood, which were abundant here in the hills. Suddenly, he had a little clay cup he must have pulled from his satchel. He tipped out whatever was inside of it onto a rock, some kind of leather pouch, and filled it with water from his water skin. The fire was so small it was already dying down, and he set the small vessel in the center of the warm coals.

"It's willow bark," he said, opening the pouch. "I can tell by looking at you that you have a fever. Are you chilled?"

"No." I was burning up now. "Please can I see the narrow neck of land before we descend the hill?"

He pinched some of the willow between his fingers, and dropped it into the warm water. "If the willow works."

59

Willow tree bark would cool a fever and could help with aches and pains.

"Do you always carry willow bark?" I asked, wrapping my arms around myself.

"Since the war."

"I'm glad. I don't feel very well."

"We'll get you fixed up," he said with a really sweet smile, but there was worry in his eyes, a deep worry that made me wonder if I should be feeling it too.

When he judged the willow tea to be steeped sufficiently, he found a cloth in his satchel and, wrapping it around the small clay cup, he picked it out of the coals and blew on the liquid inside. Then he passed me the tea.

"Drink slow. You'll have to strain the bark with your teeth."

I smiled. As I sipped the tea and we waited for it to have an effect, we talked about the magic that Hagoth called lift, and Lib told me of an idea he had to use it to keep a man aloft in the air.

"That's absurd!" I laughed.

He gestured beyond my shoulder, and I turned to see an eagle circling majestically above us.

"Lift," he said.

I passed him back the cup. "Is it the same?"

"It has to be."

"Magic," I said.

"No." He shook his head slowly. "Miracle."

"But if you could figure it out, it would not be a miracle."

"True. A miracle is something God does that we do not understand. He is limited to the natural laws just as we are, but

He knows how to use them all and we do not."

"But you would try to learn it for yourself."

His eyes got bright as he talked. "Of course! I would learn all things for myself. The more I learn, the more I see God's hand in the world around us. He has infinite knowledge and He wants to share it with us. He wants us to learn to use it for ourselves. A miracle is a mystery that we think can't happen and yet it does."

"Like faith. Like forgiveness. Like love."

He hesitated for just a moment. "Sure. I hadn't thought of it in those terms, but sure."

We fell quiet again, and I knew Lib was reassessing what he knew, applying it not just to the physical world, but to the spiritual things as well. After a moment, he reached up and put a large hand on my head.

"You're still warm, but your pallor looks better."

"I feel a little better. Race you to the top?"

He laughed and helped me to my feet, but he did not race me to the top.

The morning light had burned away into the clear light of day, and the view from the top of the hill was stunning. Lib pointed out the narrow neck of land to the north, but he needn't have. A thin path of land cut through the dark blue waters that stretched out as far as I could see.

"And then are ye in this strait and narrow path," I quoted softly. When Lib stared down at me, I felt renewed heat in my cheeks.

"Don't be embarrassed," he said. "Never be embarrassed for

knowing the words of the scriptures." Then, in a movement that felt as natural as the waves of the sea that crashed to shore far below us, in a pull that felt almost magnetic, with a coming together that was as old as time, Lib took my hand.

For a long time we basked in the view, and then Lib said, "I'll take you back now," and I said, "Okay."

We walked swiftly down the hill. I felt better and nearly convinced myself it was just a harmless cold when the medicine Lib had given me must have worn off. I felt faint very suddenly.

"Oh," I breathed out.

I meant to lean against a tree at the side of the path, but Lib was there before I could make my feet move toward it, and when my legs went out from under me, he must have caught me up. He must have carried me down the remainder of the hill and all the way back to the coastline because when I woke in a dim room, he was there on a low stool next to my pallet.

"Drink," he said when he saw I was awake, and he helped me to lift my head.

"Lib, what is wrong with me?"

He set the cup down and dipped a cloth in a bowl of water, wrung it out with his big hands and placed it on my forehead before answering.

"Not sure. Hagoth has gone to the docks to inquire as to what came in on the ship from Thessalonica."

"But you already know," I said. I closed my eyes because it hurt to open them.

"I have a suspicion," he clarified. "Hagoth has gone to confirm it."

I sensed very clearly that he didn't want to tell me what he suspected. I was smart enough to know it was bad, whatever it was.

"Where are we?" I asked instead of pressing him about the illness. I forced my eyes open and looked around. We were inside a small room that was dim, but I didn't think we were on board the ship. And then it occurred to me. "Is this Hagoth's hut?"

Lib straightened a little. "He brought you here?"

I must have drifted off again because the slight irritation in his voice turned quickly to concern.

"Miriam?"

"Hmm? Oh. He pointed it out to me. That day. That day he took me sailing."

Lib cleared his throat. "Well, yes. Hagoth owns a hut on the beach. We are inside it."

"I don't love Hagoth," I said. I knew it was a silly thing to say. Lib must have thought I was delirious. Maybe I was delirious.

Lib reached for the cloth on my head. He slowly stroked it over my cheeks and my neck. For a long time he tried to cool my fever with the cloth. I laid still and let him

"Is it consumption?" I asked. I was surprised that I was nearly breathless.

"Possibly. I thought so. That's what the little boy—the one you held while he coughed—that's what he had. I was sure you would catch it when I saw how close you held the child."

He seemed to trail off.

"But you think it's something else."

"Yes."

Another long silence passed, and I heard him dip the cloth in the bowl of water again.

"You can't nurse me," I breathed out. "You have to build your ship."

"Nah. They don't need me. There's an entire crew."

"I don't love Hagoth," I said again. For some reason I thought it was important that he understand.

"You mentioned that." I heard amusement in his voice.

"I don't," I reiterated.

"I believe you."

"Okay." I sighed. "I don't."

"Shh."

"I don't love him," I whispered.

Chuckling, he swept some damp hair from my forehead.

The next time I came to consciousness, Adreana was sitting near me. I groaned and she looked up. When she saw that my eyes were open, she took a cup from the table and pressed it to my lips. I realized she was holding my head up, too, because I was too weak to do it myself. She eased my head back down, murmuring softly in the language I did not understand, but even my feverish mind understood the compassion in her touch.

I didn't fall back to sleep immediately, so after a time she went to her trunk in the corner and withdrew a scroll. She brought it to the bedside and read to me by lantern light. I loved the lilt and fall of her language. We couldn't speak to each other, but we didn't have to sit in silence.

I let my eyes roam over the small room while she read. Why was her trunk here? Lib had said we were at Hagoth's hut, but as hard as I looked I couldn't find anything that bespoke of his ownership. Had he moved his possessions? Or was it as he said and there wasn't much here to guard?

I coughed suddenly, and I couldn't stop. It turned violent before the spasm ended. Adreana quickly set the scroll aside and reached over to wipe my lips as naturally as if she had done it a hundred times, and I wondered how many times she had done it. I wondered how long I had been sleeping.

I fell back into a fitful sleep, and each time I stirred, Adreana was there offering me water, cooling my skin, humming softly. I was miserable, and I was afraid. I ached everywhere. I was dizzy, even lying down. My breaths were shallow even though I was lying still. I knew I was very sick, and the only thing I could do for myself was pray.

At last, the sun rose. I could see the soft light around the mat at the door.

"Where is Ethanim?" I asked. "Lib?"

Adreana's eyes were tired, but she smiled at me. Then after a yawn, she stood to stretch her legs and walked toward the door, calling out to someone. In a moment, Lib came through the door.

His eyes went straight to mine, but he was speaking to Adreana. She replied, and worry creased his eyes.

"What…" My throat was dry and very sore. I tried to swallow. "Is it morning?"

He smiled. "Yes, it's morning. Do you feel you could eat?"

I shook my head.

"A little tea then?"

"Maybe."

He nodded and spoke again to Adreana who slipped out the mat at the door. I saw Ethanim and Hagoth were sitting at a fire on the beach.

"Was Adreana here all night?"

"For seven nights."

"Seven!"

"You're very sick, Miriam, and it's going to get worse before it gets better."

I licked my lips and closed my eyes.

"It's the Fever, Miriam."

"I know," I whispered.

"Well," He cleared his throat. "The good news is—"

I put my hand on his. "There is no good news."

"The Fever has a duration. You should come through just fine."

"Some don't."

"You will."

Tears welled up and slipped from my eyes.

"You will," he reassured me again softly, and after he brushed my tears away, he gently tucked my hair behind my ear.

"You are a busy man. Ethanim should take me home so you can work."

"Nonsense. You can't travel." I noticed he didn't deny what I said, though. Just stated an obvious fact. "And besides, Adreana is shouldering most of the work."

I scoffed lightly. "I'm a burden."

"No!" He seemed surprised at my words. "That's not what I meant at all. I think Adreana is glad to be of use. She feels like the burden and is harboring more than a little guilt."

"You are so expert on her feelings?" I said. My words were harsh and I knew it was the pain and frustration talking, but I also knew it was that first jealousy I had felt for her. She had spent a week with Lib while I had done nothing but sleep in delirium.

The understanding on Lib's face made more tears well up in my eyes. "Hush," he said. "You're speaking nonsense." He bent and placed a kiss on my head, much like my father had done when I was small. "Here is Adreana with your tea."

It was bitter, much worse than the willow, and I knew it was medicinal. I drank it all, and then I was exhausted and fell back to sleep with the sounds of Lib and Adreana's foreign conversation swirling around in my mind and the feel of Lib's warm hand on my arm.

CHAPTER 6

I lost track of time, but I knew many days passed. Adreana spent every night with me, seeing to my needs. Another woman was there during the days, maybe more than one. I couldn't tell and usually felt too miserable to care. But sometimes Lib or Ethanim or Hagoth came into the hut and saw to my care themselves, at least to the things a man could see to.

I liked to be awake for these times, but I was rarely more than aware, and the people that came and went were like ghosts.

One day, I thought I heard Noah's voice.

"And how long has she been like this?" he was saying.

"Nearly three weeks." *Ethanim.*

There was silence for a time—or perhaps I fell back into the delirium, but I thought I heard them breathing, and my skin prickled with the weight of their eyes on me.

"I shouldn't have asked you to bring her. This journey was ridiculous from the first moment." *Noah.*

I tried to open my eyes, but they were too heavy.

"She said it was the Spirit's guidance." *Ethanim.* His defense of my actions touched my heart deeply. He had proved a very good friend. Not just to Noah, and not just to Lib, but also to me.

"She told you why she wanted to come?"

Noah's voice sounded surprised—as if I wouldn't have honesty between myself and the man who protected me and fed me from the forest.

"Of course," Ethanim replied, just as I would have if I could have pulled myself out of the thick fog that filled my mind.

"Does Lib know? Has she been so foolish as to make such a claim to him? We advised her strongly against it. What he must think of her, brazen and presumptuous!"

There was silence again, but this time I knew I did not drift away because it took only a moment for the Spirit of God to flood the room, and Ethanim said, "I do not think she has told him anything. Be still, Noah, and listen to your heart."

I heard Noah heave a deep sigh, and I imagined he had his arms crossed over his chest as he often did.

Ethanim continued. "Your young sister is not brazen. Bold, perhaps, and I admire her bravery. If Lib suspects her reasons for being here it is because he is observant, not because she has been improper in her pursuit of him."

"Alright," Noah said reluctantly.

But Ethanim went on. "Miriam has earned nothing but friendship and respect here, and if you intend to demean her character as she lies on that sickbed—"

"I don't. I didn't know, that's all."

There was a rustling, as if perhaps one of them had reached up to run a hand through his hair or rub his neck or adjust his satchel.

Noah gave a low groan. "I can't believe it. You like her!"

Why did he have to make that sound like an accusation, like it was the worst thing that could happen to a boy?

If Ethanim replied to that, it wasn't out loud. "Come on. I'll take you to the ship so you can settle in."

I sensed the light when they swept back the mat at the door.

"I can't stay long," Noah said.

"How are Sarah and the baby? A son, you said?"

"Yes. Corianton." There was pride in his voice and something else, like strain or fatigue.

The light vanished. They were gone, and I was alone.

In all, it was two fortnights from the day I fainted on the hill until I was well again, and. Noah said I should go home with him.

"You met him. You said that was all you wanted. You've burdened them enough with this illness, and I fear you've overstayed your welcome."

I wanted to argue, but he was only putting voice to the things I had already thought myself.

I was sitting up on the low pallet in Hagoth's hut on the beach. I ran my hands over my face, rubbing gently at my eyes. Slowly, I stood, still somewhat weak and dizzy from lying down for so long, and I turned to my brother.

"Walk me out to the shore?"

He gave me an irritated look but followed me outside. We

walked slowly, and I tried to breathe deeply as I looked around at the beauty of the beach. I did not need to wonder why Hagoth had chosen this place for his home on land. It was shaded by the shabby beach trees and colored by the scrubby, green grass that rustled in the sea breezes.

The sun was low in the west sky. I watched it fall and felt the sea breeze lift my hair and swirl it around my face. I fought the urge to tuck it back behind my ears, and I said, "I will go home with you."

I sensed Noah give a deep sigh, but he kept his thoughts to himself.

The pinks and oranges of the setting sun mingled with the gray of heavy dark clouds on the horizon.

"It looks like a storm," I said.

Noah grunted. "We'll have to wait it out before we can leave."

"I know you're anxious to get back to Sarah and the baby."

He sighed.

"You're not looking forward to returning?"

He certainly wasn't being pleasant about staying here.

"Father has been giving me more responsibility as to the running of the farm. Jed, too. Systematically, as if it were part of a plan."

I frowned. "What kind of plan?"

He rubbed a hand over his face. "I'm not sure."

"Has business been suffering?"

"No. It seems to be more profitable than ever. Father is known far and wide to be fair and honest in his dealings. His birds are healthy and plump. He has more business than he can handle sometimes."

"Father doesn't do things half-way," I said.

Noah actually smiled and shook his head. "He definitely doesn't."

"Perhaps that is why he is delegating his responsibilities."

We turned and walked in the direction of Hagoth's big ship.

"Ethanim said I can return to my room on the ship now."

Noah squinted at it in the distance. "That would probably be for the best. Then everyone else can return, too. It won't be such an inconvenience."

"What do you mean?"

He glanced at me. "They take turns sleeping outside your door. Don't tell me you didn't know that."

I did know that. I remembered seeing the glow of their fire and their dark silhouettes in the night.

"It's been several weeks since I have needed constant care."

He gave me a look that was almost scolding. "Did you think they would let you sleep out there alone?"

"I guess I did."

When we weren't far from the ship, he said, "Go on up. It will start to rain soon."

But I could see he didn't intend to follow me as he turned away.

"Noah?"

He turned back, a blond brow raised.

"I haven't finished what I came here to do." I didn't know if I was asking him to let me stay or just informing him of the undeniable fact that if he took me away now I would fail God.

He glanced out toward the shore, and when I followed the direction of his gaze, I saw two men standing knee deep in the waves. I could make out the blond of Lib's hair in the twilight.

"I wish you'd just let me tell him."

My heart started to pound.

"That is the honest way. I wish you'd just let me make him a formal offer on behalf of Father. That is the way that shows respect—for both of you."

I put a hand to my throat. "You know I don't want that." I had made a step by coming here. I wanted Lib to make a step as well. I wanted him to decide for himself, not be coerced by whatever my father was prepared to offer him.

"Miriam." Noah folded his arms, and I bristled, preparing myself for another one of his lectures. But his voice was gentle when he said, "I know you think I am against you in this, that I am acting with my head and not paying heed to the feelings of my heart, or yours, but you're wrong."

"I don't think—"

"I do nothing but by the Spirit of God, sister, and I know it is time for me to take you home."

"But I'm not—"

"If you won't accept Father's hand in it, then you've done all you can. You intended to come here and meet Lib, and so you have. I do not think it was ever your intention to bring a husband home."

I frowned and crossed my own arms. "I suppose not."

A low roll of thunder came in from the west.

Noah nodded toward the ship. I offered him a weak smile and went up into the ship where I would be sheltered from the coming storm.

My things were just as I had left them the morning I had gone into the hills with Lib. I lowered myself to my bedroll and let my eyes fall closed. That day seemed so long ago. I didn't remember much from the past month I had spent with the fever, but I remembered that morning with Lib.

I had still been reveling in the day we had spent at the docks together, and I felt wonder that he would take me exploring again, because by then he had an idea why I had come, even though it made no sense to him, and even though I had not been brave enough to put it into words for him.

And then I had begun to feel faint.

Lib had offered to take me back to the ship when he had seen I was ill, and then he had administered medicine when I had stubbornly refused his offer.

He had shown me the narrow path between the seas.

He had held my hand.

He had carried me down the mountain.

It was dark when Adreana came into the room with a lantern. Her smile was sweet when she saw me, and she held a small vessel filled with fruits and soft cheeses which she passed to me.

I ate while she prepared for bed, and then, without a word between us, she blew out the light.

I woke early. Adreana was still and quiet in her bedroll when I slipped out into the morning. A thick mist covered the deck. It was infused with light, and I thought perhaps dawn had come and gone and no one had seen it.

Mist often rolled off the waters in the morning, but this mist was different. I could scarce see a cubit beyond the length of my arm, but though I had yet to experience fog this dense, Hagoth and the crew told many stories about sailing through mists such as this.

"Good morning, Miriam." Hagoth's words seemed muted in the quiet morning.

"You're up early," I said.

He glanced around, though there was nothing to see. "It's not so early. Though no work can be done until this mist rolls out."

"It seems eerily thick," I said.

"Aye, it does."

"What causes it?"

He shrugged. "I just enjoy the beauties of nature. I don't claim to understand them."

I thought of Lib, how he wanted to use lift to fly in the air like a bird, how he had designed his ship with numbers and calculations.

"You should ask your scientist," he said, leaning on the rail and seeming to search through the fog for a glimpse of the sea.

I sighed. I wished Lib wasn't between us so our friendship might have been open, but it wasn't to be.

"When the weather clears, I'm going to go home."

He didn't seem surprised. He kept his eyes trained on the gray nothing before us. "Have you something to get back for?"

"Noah says it is time I left."

"You are welcome to stay as long as you wish, Miriam."

I huffed and leaned on the rail next to him. "Tell that to Noah."

"I have."

"Sometimes, Noah seems to hear only what he wishes to hear. He has a young wife and new son he needs to get back to, but…" I threw a look over my shoulder and lowered my voice. "He doesn't seem to want to."

Hagoth looked down at me, his brow raised.

"And yet he is adamant that we leave."

"He came here alone. He can leave alone."

By the tone of his voice, I didn't think the invitation to stay as long as one wished extended to my brother.

I traced a finger over the unfinished wood of the thick rail. "I think I am perhaps an excuse he used to leave home, and returning without me would place him in an uncomfortable situation."

"What do you mean? What kind of situation?"

"I'm not sure. Something to do with my father, maybe, or Sarah. The baby? I don't know."

He was silent for long moments, and the world was quiet around us. Only the soft sloughing sounds as water lapped at the hull broke the stillness. The tide was in, but it was moving out, which told me dawn had indeed come and gone.

"And you're caught in the middle of something you don't understand."

"Yes!" But I hadn't been able to put it into words.

"And your duty is to your family."

I wrinkled my nose. "I suppose."

"Are all of your family members as self-serving as your brother?"

I glanced over my shoulder again. "He's not. Noah's not." I sighed and leaned my elbows on the rail. "I wish you could have met him when he wasn't so burdened. He's never been particularly thoughtful, but he's generally good-natured. Ethanim and Lib have been lifelong friends with him and seem to have tolerated him well enough."

Hagoth smiled. "Do you always find the good in others?"

"What is the point in looking for the bad?"

"And do you see any good in me?"

"Oh, aye," I said.

I heard a muffled footstep behind us, and we both looked over our shoulders toward the sound.

Lib appeared out of the mist, a frown on his face, his eyes darting between us. He wasted no words.

"I was wondering if Miriam would like to help with the pitch."

Was he talking to me or to Hagoth?

Hagoth swiveled toward me. "How about it, Miriam?"

"What is the pitch for?" I asked Lib.

"You don't know what pitch is?"

I bristled at the critical note in his voice. "Of course I know what pitch is, but I thought this boat was built to be watertight."

"The pitch is just another layer of protection. It prevents the breakdown of the wood."

"Ah."

He opened his hand, almost as if he meant to extend it out to me but didn't quite manage it, or maybe he thought better of it.

"Of course I will work for my breakfast," I said, offering them both a smile.

Hagoth turned to fully face Lib. He folded his arms tight against his chest and leaned back against the rail.

Lib started away.

"Aren't you coming?" I asked Hagoth.

"No." His answer was immediate and subdued. "Lib will take you."

I couldn't read the expression in his eyes.

"I'll see you later, then."

"Aye," he said and turned back to the gray mist.

"Will it be strenuous," I asked Lib when we were making our way carefully down to the ground on the long plank.

"It doesn't need to be. We would save it until the end, but it's one of the only things we can do in this weather." He paused. "Have you eaten?"

"No."

"Wait here then," he said and shot back up the plank.

The plank was not so very narrow, but I was aware that I was suspended over the ground with no real idea how high up I was. I decided to carefully continue down while I waited for Lib. Soon he was back with a hand on my elbow.

"Easy now," he said low into my ear.

When we alighted, he steered me toward the stern at the

south end of the building yard. He stepped confidently through the mist that seemed even thicker down at ground level. Presently we found supplies that he had obviously already placed there in the damp sand.

I picked up a stick and stirred the contents of one of the buckets. "This is very thin," I said.

"It's not made to fill cracks, more as a coating for the outside. A very old mariner's recipe. We'll brush it all along the hull like this." He demonstrated with a wide brush. Turning back to me, he said, "If you feel faint or something like that, just tell me. Or just stop."

"Alright," I said, brushing the pitch from the stick with a brush.

Lib watched me for a moment. "We have plenty of pitch," he said.

"Still no reason to be wasteful," I replied as I dipped the brush and made a long stroke along the timbers. "That color is fine," I said as the wood was stained a rich brown.

"Here. Eat first." He held out several wrapped parcels. "Your hands will get dirty."

I set my brush down and took the parcels. Lib guided me a few yards away where I could sit on a portion of the framework. I folded back the linen and found corn cakes and fruit.

I hadn't taken more than a few bites when Lib said, "Noah told me you're going home."

"He thinks it best."

"And Ethanim told me why you came."

The corn turned to sand in my mouth.

"Oh." I tried to swallow. "Are you mad?"

He took a breath. "Not mad."

"Angry then?"

He laughed. "No, not angry."

I set down the remainder of the food and took up my brush again. Settling on a position near Lib, I began to put pitch to the great, curved beams, though I suspected it had not been his intention to bring me here to do work.

"I was building up my courage to tell you," I said. "I just…I just got sick before I could."

"I understand why you didn't." He wasn't looking at me, and I couldn't look at him, but we stood next to each other and passed our brushes over the wood.

"After I got better, well, it didn't seem important anymore."

He huffed. "I think I'll take that as an insult."

My eyes shot to him. "Don't." I coughed. "I only meant—" I coughed again and had to put my brush down.

"Are you okay?"

I nodded. "The air is so humid. It's thick. Hard to breathe."

"Maybe it would be better if you went home, then. The air is drier in Orihah."

I licked my lips. "Shall I take that as an insult?"

His head turned toward me, and his eyes were weary as if perhaps he had not slept well.

"No."

"Alright," I said quietly and picked my brush back up. It was his plain speaking, something I had often admired in him. It was Lib stating a fact. The air *was* drier in Orihah.

He watched me work for several long moments. I could feel his eyes on me.

I dipped my brush in the bucket again, and again put it to the beams, but before I could brush it smoothly across, Lib stopped my hand with his. I stilled and looked up into his eyes.

"I don't know what to think of it all. It's huge and sudden, and Noah is mad, and Hagoth is acting weird." He took the brush from my hand and repeated, "I don't know what to think."

In that moment, with the mist floating around us obscuring everything, I knew exactly what he meant.

"I don't either," I said.

CHAPTER 7

It was another week before Noah and I left, and even then, I didn't feel strong. My lungs were weak, my muscles had atrophied, my heart hurt, and my faith had dwindled.

The night before our departure, we made a great and beautiful bonfire on the beach. All the men were there. Noah talked and laughed with the others, and even played their old game of ball with them, but when he sat near me, his demeanor changed.

"Are you mad at me?" I finally asked him.

"No."

"Have I embarrassed you in front of your friends?"

"No," he said again, but I heard his hesitation.

"Then what is the matter? You didn't have to come fetch me home."

"We shouldn't have let you come in the first place."

He was in quite the mood.

"I would have come alone. You and Father both know it.

And I don't need your permission."

"You need the guidance—"

"No I don't."

"—of your kinsmen. You've done quite enough throwing yourself at my friends."

I gasped. "I have done no such thing!"

We had let our voices raise over the din, but we both realized at the same moment that the camp had gone quiet. Nobody was even pretending not to listen to us.

I felt my face flame. Childishly, I balled my fist and hit Noah in the arm—there was no way I could ever hurt him—and I stormed away before I could burst into tears.

Why was he being so pigheaded about it? I had agreed to go home, hadn't I? He had gotten to see his friends, hadn't he? I knew he had had a good time with them.

I didn't know where to go. I figured my room aboard ship was as good as anywhere, so I started for it.

"Miriam!"

I glared at him over my shoulder. The ship was not far enough away. I turned on my heel and walked out toward the beach hut I had left only a week ago.

I stood in the doorway letting my eyes adjust to the darkness inside. My heart was pounding. How could he humiliate me like that? What was wrong with him? What had I done that was so inappropriate? I had only tried to follow the guidance of the Spirit. I hadn't even wanted to wed Lib when I had come here, and I had wanted to even less after I had met him. Throwing myself at him?

The terrible fever, my weakness, Ethanim giving his whole attention to Adreana, my brother breaking the trust I had in him. I was far from home. I was no closer to marrying Lib than I had been when he was a complete stranger to me. It really was too much. Overwhelmed and discouraged, I broke down into sobs.

I did not cry long before I felt firm hands at my shoulders bearing me up, bidding me to turn into the strong chest at my back. I did not even resist, and perhaps that was what Noah had meant.

He did not say anything, only held me firmly until my body stopped shaking with the ebb and flow of my sobs. When I felt more in control, I raised my eyes to his, feeling the teardrops still in my lashes. He hesitated for a moment, as if asking permission. Then he bent and kissed my lips tenderly, and I was so alone and so hurt and so attracted to him that I let the kiss happen.

And perhaps that was what Noah had meant.

"I don't like your brother," he said and then turned to leave.

I knew he meant for me to take the hut and the pallet for the night.

"You have given me too much already," I said to his back. "My brother is right—I have taken advantage."

He stopped, but only turned his head so I could see his profile. "I do not have much in this world, Miriam, but all I have is yours. You have only to take it."

I watched as Hagoth walked away through the sand and the beach grass. Starlight filtered down on him through the trees.

And when he was gone, my eyes fell on Lib, who watched us from the beach. But his eyes did not follow Hagoth as he left. They stayed fixed on me. In just a moment, when the sound of Hagoth's steps faded into the sound of the breeze through the tall grasses, we were alone.

We watched each other, silent and unmoving. I knew he had heard everything Noah had said. And then he had watched me let Hagoth kiss me—not stepping back or pushing him away or even turning my face aside. I couldn't face him or the questions in his eyes that were so clear I could see them even in the moonlight. I dropped my gaze, turned and went inside, letting the mat fall closed behind me. I lay down and covered myself with a blanket, a new one I noticed, and used a corner of it to dry my face.

Noah was right. I needed guidance, but he certainly wasn't qualified to give it.

I squeezed my eyes shut and willed myself to sleep.

When I awoke, it was still night. I listened for any sound that might have awakened me and thought perhaps it had been the pounding of my heart, for it was pounding as I lit upon a course of action.

I may have had to suffer an escort's presence on my journey to the sea, but I could certainly travel home on my own. I did not need Noah. I did not need Ethanim. I did not need anyone.

I rose and looked around for anything that might be useful on my journey. Hagoth said I had only but to take what I wanted, though I did not pretend—even to myself—not to realize he had meant his heart. My eyes fell on a bow and quiver leaning in the corner. They were old and well-used, but I took them and a knife that was stuck in a block near the door. I had almost passed through the door when I stopped. I took the knife and with one swift motion, I cut off a lock of my yellow hair and tied it tight with a strip of fabric I tore from the bottom of my sarong. I quickly folded the blanket Hagoth had placed over me and left the lock of hair on top of it.

Goodbye, I thought.

I tread lightly on the ship so I would not wake anyone, but I thought Adreana must have been already awake because she sat up when I entered the room we shared. She watched me as I gathered my few belongings and put them into my travel pack. She didn't say anything to me as she watched, and I didn't say anything either, but as I hefted my pack onto my back, she leaned over and caught my hand in hers.

There was much I wanted to say to her, and I saw in her face that there were things she wanted to say too.

"Thank you," was all I whispered.

"Safe journey," she replied haltingly.

I squeezed her hand and left quickly.

I shouldn't have, but I stopped for a moment at the rail that rimmed the deck. I looked out into the midnight blue of the sky and the black of the water. White crests broke as the small waves hit the shore.

I wondered if God was disappointed in me, in my failure to see this through, to make it happen, to help his son. I wondered if He was disappointed in what I was about to do.

I was.

I heard a scuff behind me and tensed. I wondered if Hagoth employed a guard aboard ship at nights. Why didn't I know that? Had I ever seen one before?

I listened hard, but I didn't hear it again. The only sounds were the soft sloughing of the waves and a dull clunk against the hull where the tide touched the ship. The prickles on my neck went away, and I relaxed.

The breeze blew my hair free and I let it whip for a time around my face. I thought of my failure here and let a tear drop. Then I pulled myself together and wiped the tears quickly away. I sniffed, tucked my hair behind my ear, and reached into my satchel.

It was dumb, but I withdrew a piece of writing charcoal and placed it on the rail. He wouldn't know it was from me, couldn't know it was his father's. I took a step backward. Unless... I stepped forward and picked up the charcoal and drew him a mathematical complication that would tell him goodbye—or at least tell him which way I had gone. I smiled to myself as I completed the last angle and placed the charcoal next to the figures.

Then I sighed, and giving one last look to the dark sea, I turned and left.

I traveled through a deep gorge Ethanim and I had seen from the Sea Road above on our way to the coast. By the time I emerged at the top, the sun was rising on the city of Ammonihah. I expected Noah to catch up with me at any moment and scold me for leaving without him. I didn't see him even though I kept glancing over my shoulder.

But I did see many other friendly travelers which I greeted as I passed them.

I was beginning to think I would be camping the night alone when I caught a glimpse of a man I thought was Noah, but he was coming toward me from the direction of home.

It was Noah. He was so relieved to see me—and I had to admit that with the twilight falling I was relieved as well—that I didn't see his scowl until after he had caught me up into a quick embrace and let me go.

"Why did you leave?" His voice was entreating, almost tender, in direct contradiction to the hard look on his face.

"I was mad at you," I said simply.

"So it was childishness."

"Is there any other way to act with one's older brother?"

"I wouldn't know. I don't have one."

"You can take my word on it then."

Seeming not to hear me, Noah glanced toward the sinking sun. "Come on. We have to make camp, and not here."

He led me deep into the forest.

"How did you get ahead of me?" I asked as I started a small fire so we could cook the grouse he had tied to his pack.

"I took the coast road. I didn't find you, so I ran ahead. But when I still didn't find you, I ran back."

"Didn't Lib tell you I took the path through the gorge?"

"Lib told me to take the coast road." A half a grin stole over his face. "And I'm thinking he's had a good laugh by now."

I was confused for a moment because I was sure Lib would have interpreted my message correctly, but I smiled too when I realized Lib had sent Noah on a wild goose chase on purpose. And I silently thanked him for giving me this day without my brother's lectures.

Growing up on our father's bird farm had made Noah quick in cleaning the grouse. He put it on a spit over the fire and then wiped his hands. He tossed me a cloth bag he pulled from his travel pack. When I opened it I found dried dates. I took several, cinched the bag closed, and tossed it back.

"I guess he thought more of you than I assumed he would," Noah said.

I knew he meant it to be, but it was hardly a compliment—even less an apology.

After a long silence he cleared his throat, and I thought he might take it back or laugh it off, but he said, "Miriam, I'm sorry."

I stopped chewing and looked over at him.

"For the way I acted back there." He gestured to the north. "I guess I have a hard time thinking of you as a grown girl."

"Your friends don't."

He visibly grit his teeth, and I laughed.

"I've been a grown girl for a while now." I was not very much younger than Sarah, his own wife.

"I know." He paused and then said again, "I'm sorry. Forgive me?"

I swallowed down the last date. I knew Noah to be free with his forgiveness, but he was definitely not free with his feelings. This was unusual.

"Of course I forgive you. I only wish I had more time. I

wasted so much of it being ill."

"Ill! You nearly died!" he burst out.

I studied him curiously. Had it really been as bad as that?

"Were you afraid for me?" I said even as I realized he had been—very much. Had that been at the root of all his lectures?

He was sitting on his heels, but he stood then. "Let the fire die down when the bird is done." And he walked into the woods without a backward glance.

My eyes followed him as he disappeared into the brush, and then they turned back to the fire. I would let the fire die down, but I would not let the embers go out.

CHAPTER 8

"David," I called out as I walked up the path toward his home.

He had been walking around the side of the house but stopped when he heard my voice. A large smile spread over his face, and seeing it, I couldn't help but smile back.

"How was your journey?" he asked.

"First, food." I held up the covered dish of stew I had brought with me for our meal.

When we were seated in his yard, each with a plate of the stew, he asked again. "How was your journey?"

The question was very loaded. I knew he cared about my trip, but what he really wanted to hear about was his son.

"He is well," I said and then scooped some of the meat from the plate into my mouth.

"Yes. Good. Good. But your journey."

"His ship is magnificent. I slept aboard. It smells of pine and oak and cedar and they almost have the masts erected."

He chuckled. "Miriam, how was your journey?"

I swallowed. "I got sick, David."

"I heard."

"Eat," I said, motioning for him to do so.

His eyes turned to the dish. "Ethanim came by."

But of course he had come by, and of course he had told David all there was to tell about Lib.

So, while he ate, I told him all there was to tell about my journey to the sea. I told him of the long trek with Ethanim, of meeting Hagoth, and of the girl Adreana. I described the beauty and vastness of the sea and how it felt to sail on the water. I told him of the markets and the docks and the sailors. And then I told him of the Fever.

He listened and asked his questions which I eagerly answered until he said, "And what did my son say about a marriage?"

I looked toward the children who were playing down the lane. "We…I got sick before we could speak of it." Then I twisted my lips and admitted, "Bringing it up myself seemed much too forward. Too presumptuous. Lib is very proper, and—"

David's laugh cut me off. "He wasn't always so very proper, you know, raised without a mother as he was, only me to look after him." His laughter died as he spoke of his wife.

I sighed.

"You are disappointed."

I nodded. If only I had been able to spend more time. If only Noah hadn't come to bring me home.

94

"Was Lib unkind to you?"

"No."

"Was he unwelcoming?"

"David, no, of course not." *Only at first.* "He took me to see the village and the boats and to view the isthmus that leads to the north. I wish..." I glanced at him. "I wish I had more time. I feel as if I failed."

He put his dish down, his food finished, and turned to me, a clear protest on his lips.

I put my hand up. I didn't want him to say meaningless words to make me feel better. "I feel as if I have failed you."

He was quiet. I could feel him regarding me, and it made my skin hot. He hadn't asked me to go to Ammonihah, to meet his son, but we both knew he had approved of the idea. And we had both had expectations for the outcome.

"Miriam, would you like to work some sums?"

I burst into a smile, nearly laughing. "Yes."

So he brought out the writing implements, the paper and charcoal sticks, and he gave me some problems to work out. Problems I *could* work out. Problems I knew how to solve, and I solved them swiftly while he cleared away the dishes we had used. When I had worked through most of them, I became aware that he was staring at me again.

I stopped writing and looked up at him, this kind and friendly man who so easily made friends and was yet so lonely. His dark hair fell in straight locks around his ears much the same as Lib's did. He had aged quite handsomely and did not look his nearly forty years.

He looked down at my hands, the paper, my calculations, and he smiled.

"You did what you felt was right, Miriam. The Spirit can ask no more of you than that."

"I suppose."

"You have been obedient. You will be blessed."

I offered him a smile, for in my heart I knew he was right.

He grinned in return, and I did not wonder that his son was so handsome. "Try this," he said and passed me another paper.

I saw immediately that it was not like the ones I had just completed. Indeed, it was not like anything I had ever done before. I leaned forward, tucked my hair behind my ear as I studied the problem, and then I started with what I knew. David got up and started a fire as the evening was coming on. I worked the problem as far as I could, but it wasn't complete. I tried a few things, but finally looked up when I could not solve the problem. It took a moment for my gaze to adjust as I searched the yard for him.

"David—"

"Ah," he said, as if he had expected, anticipated—planned—my question. "You have done all that you know how to do?"

"Yes."

"And what do you normally do when you come to the end of your knowledge?"

"I ask you," I said on a laugh.

His expression became more serious. "Why?"

He was not talking of difficult equations, but of difficult questions.

I looked down. "Because you know the answer. You know how to solve it."

David put his hand on my shoulder. "Thank you for the meal."

"I missed being able to bring meals," I said, though the whole truth was that I had been so busy and so caught up in the journey and meeting Lib, I hadn't missed it as much as I might have.

"David," a voice interrupted us.

We both turned and David took his hand from my shoulder. Self-consciously?

"Shad."

He stood and walked forward to clasp arms with the young man who stood at the edge of the yard where it met the lane. "What brings you around this fine evening?"

We all three knew. This was not the first time he had come for me here.

"I've come for Miriam. I have her father's permission to walk her home."

Permission that had been granted long ago.

David turned to look at me, and I stood, straightened my skirt, and went to them.

"Until next time," I said to David.

He nodded to us both, but as we started to walk away, David called after us. When I turned back, he came forth and pressed a paper into my hand.

"Take this and work on it. See if you can come up with a solution on your own."

I looked at my sandals as we walked away.

"What is it?" Shad asked.

"Just a math problem."

"May I see?"

I passed it to him. All he would see, where I saw counsel and guidance, were numbers and computations.

But he studied it for a long time before folding it over and giving it back.

Shad was the son of Liam and Naomi, who owned and worked a barley farm a half morning's walk to the south. He was the youngest of four brothers, all of whom had fought in the Nephite armies. Shad wanted to join with the army of Moronihah, but there was always a circumstance that kept him home. He was handsome and kind, and I considered him a good friend. He had begun to court me formally several months before I had left Orihah with Ethanim, informally long before that, and it appeared he intended to continue.

After that beautiful day alone on the hill when the idea had first come into my mind to seek out Lib, after prayer and contemplation, I had confided to my parents, to Noah and Jed, my two oldest brothers, and to Ethanim. I had told them what I felt I felt I must do concerning Lib and my marriage and future, but of course I had told Shad nothing of it. I hadn't known how. If I had been faithful enough, I would have.

But I must. To remain silent was to lie, and to let him continue this courtship was misleading.

But he was a dear, he was my friend, and I did not wish to hurt or disappoint him in any way. And if I was being honest, to tell him I would not consent to a betrothal would be a disappointment to myself as well.

Making the grand gesture of going on a long journey to find Lib showed an amount of faith I did not feel when it was time to simply tell Shad the truth—that he could no longer expect this courtship to go anywhere. What if I had misread the Spirit? What if I was wrong and my actions caused pain to someone who didn't deserve to be hurt?

As we came into the most populated parts of Orihah, I suspected Shad was not taking me home. We began to pass streets that were filled with houses and people, and I saw my sister sitting on a fence, laughing with a boy.

Shad saw her, too. "What does she see in that guy?" he asked as we passed by.

"I don't know," I said as Sasha sent me a look that was almost smug and then turned back to Giddoni, a boy who was young and reckless to a point that bordered on cruel. But he was handsome, I had to give her that. "She doesn't have the strong circle of friends that we have," I said.

He grunted.

"We've been blessed in that, I think."

He was quiet a moment before he said, "Why does David give you the problems?"

I shrugged. "It is how we bond."

"Do you have a need to bond with him?"

"No, I…"

"You were sitting rather close to him." A note of something I had never heard in it had crept into his voice.

"Shad?" I laughed when I realized what he thought and shook my head. "Not bonding like that. Like friends, that's all."

"Like us?"

"No. I am different kind of friends with different people. Aren't you?"

He looked at me with a glint in his eye. "I suppose."

"Now, where are we going? Will we be out late?"

"Not too late."

He didn't answer my question, but it didn't take more than a few minutes more to realize he was taking me to his uncle's in the center of town.

Jeremiah was his father's brother. He owned a timber mill where he employed many of the young men from the area. Deborah, his wife, was a friendly woman who was an excellent cook and seemed to have a knack for finding people who needed help and bringing them into the safe haven of her home. Their home was large and well-crafted, and when we got together with friends, we frequently did it there as two of his cousins were among our closest friends.

"What is going on tonight?" I asked. I hadn't heard of any gatherings, not when I had gone to the church meeting, not whispered among the girls of the town.

"A welcome party," Shad said.

He wouldn't look at me, and I could see he was trying to hide a smile.

"Who are we welcoming?" I asked slowly.

He shrugged. "It's really more of a welcome home party."

"What?"

He laughed. "Come on. We're already late."

Shad and I were part of a large circle of friends and they were all there when we arrived in the courtyard. Deborah was beaming and hugged me tight. Aniah, her daughter, was next and the grinning faces became a blur as Shad and I moved through the crowd.

"Who did this?" I asked him when we had a few moments alone.

He shrugged again.

"Was it you?"

He laughed. "I wish I had thought of it, but no. Aniah asked me to bring you, but I don't know whose idea it was."

We ate and laughed with friends. The boys played ball and wrestled at the edge of the yard. When twilight fell many of my friends said goodbye and started for home before full dark hit. Those who lived close by stayed a bit longer.

"Aniah says you were sick," Esther said when the yard fell quiet.

I nodded. "The Fever."

"But you're better?"

"Yes."

"Who cared for you? Were you visiting family there?"

I glanced at Shad. I could see he was interested in the answer. It was true I had been rather vague about the details of my journey and my reason for going.

I tucked my hair back. "I was with friends. They arranged for women of the village to see to my care."

Esther giggled. "But all your friends are here! Who could

you know in Ammonihah?"

Aniah smoothed Esther's hair back. "Friends of her family."

"Oh!" Esther said as if that made perfect sense. "Then what is the sea like?"

Esther, Aniah, Shad, and his cousin, Jared, all leaned in to hear my answer.

"So beautiful. The sea is a deep blue, beyond the blue of the sky, and the water makes the most relaxing sound as it laps against the shore. On stormy days, there are white crests on the waves and the sky and the sea blend together so you can't distinguish one from the other."

"Waves?" Aniah asked.

"It is the way the water moves."

She nodded, but I knew she could not understand it until she saw it for herself.

"Did you swim in the waters?" Esther asked.

I shook my head. "I went out in a sailboat. When the sails catch the wind, it's almost like you're flying over the water." I looked around into their curious eyes. "I experienced much there, wondrous sights, new foods and smells..." Hardship, loyalty, first love. "But I'm so glad to be home. It's like being in the arms of a loved one. I missed you all very much."

They all seemed pleased with this pronouncement. Shad and Jared got to their feet as Jared's brother came into the courtyard from the street.

Enos was older than us by at least seven or eight years. He was Noah's age, or perhaps even a bit older. He looked like Jared. He had a kind face and had always seemed quite friendly. He was well-liked in town as he was helpful and treated everyone with respect. When he came through the gate, his eyes went right to Esther.

She stood, too, and waited for him to come to her.

"I didn't know you'd be here," he said to her, glancing around at the rest of us and offering us a slight nod in greeting.

She gestured to me. "We had a party to welcome Miriam home."

"Ah." He glanced at me but looked back to Esther. "Are you ready to go home? I could walk you."

She bit her lip and nodded. She gathered her things and gave me a tight hug. "Welcome home!" she said into my ear.

Enos raised a hand to us and disappeared into the street with Esther.

I looked back to the others.

"That's new," I said.

"Not so new," Aniah said. "They had a betrothal ceremony a few weeks ago."

I smiled. "You will finally have a sister," I said to her.

"Alright," Shad said to Aniah. "Give her a hug. I've got to get her home."

"I'll go with you," Jared said. "It will be full dark before you get her there."

He didn't wait for a response from Shad before he went inside. After I had hugged Aniah goodbye, he returned with a lantern, and his parents followed him through the door.

"Thank you for the welcome home," I said to them. Deborah hugged me and Jeremiah laid a hand on my shoulder. They were generous people, with both their worldly goods and their affection, and it was not hard to see where Enos, Jared, and Aniah came by their own generous spirits.

I walked home between Shad and Jared, comfortable in their companionship and sure of my safety. They were both strong and capable. Neither of them had been to the battles their older brothers had, but they both wished they had.

The lantern was bright and we made our way easily to the farm. The birds were settled for the night, roosting, and evening was temperate and peaceful.

The boys, cousins and best friends, talked with ease about the mill, the party, our mutual acquaintances and friends, but I sensed Shad was annoyed at having the extra company. As I had something weighty to get off my chest, I was a little annoyed as well. But Jared was good, funny and friendly, one of my favorite people, so I let them talk on and thought of the sea and the descriptions I could not give my friends.

"We went on a journey as well," Jared said.

"Oh?" I said, coming out of my thoughts.

But he didn't reply. I looked from one to the other as they exchanged a glance over my head.

"I'll tell you about it another time," Shad reluctantly said after a drawn out moment, and after that, they fell into silence.

I bid them goodbye at the gate. When they walked away together, I was glad Jared had come so Shad would not have to walk back alone through the darkness. I assumed he would stay at Jared's for the night since his home was quite a distance in the opposite direction, and for a moment, I wished I had a friend that close. My closest friend was probably Shad.

And when I thought of what I had to do to him, had to say to him, I felt my heart squeeze in my chest.

"Oh, Miriam." Shad turned and walked backward for a few steps. "That equation David gave you?"

"Yes?"

"You need to change your variable."

CHAPTER 9

That night as I lay on my pallet, long after the breaths of my sisters had gone slow and deep, I wanted to feel what I had felt on the grassy knoll, the prompting that had taken me to Ammonihah.

But I felt nothing

I couldn't sleep. I turned over many times. Even with the deep breaths of so many around me, it was too quiet.

I missed the sound of the sea. The water that lapped at the hull. The waves that crashed on the shore. The cries of the sea birds and the bawdy laughing of the workmen.

At long last, I got up and crept outside.

I pulled my wrap around me and strolled slowly to the middle of the yard. The birds were roosting and quiet. At the edge of my consciousness, I heard a baby cry. It would be Noah's little son across the clearing.

I scuffed my bare foot through the grass and missed the sand in my toes.

I looked up into the vastness of the sky. Shining just where it was supposed to be, I found the moon. White. Luminescent. Faithful. It was the same moon that shone on Ammonihah, on the sea, and on Lib.

I could love him.

God had known what He was doing when he sent me there.

But how would it work? And could Lib love me in return?

"Can't sleep?"

I turned to see Noah coming toward me, bouncing the baby in his arms.

I shook my head and sighed. "No. Pass him to me." I held out my hands to accept the fussy little bundle. "Is Sarah sleeping?"

He stretched and rubbed his palms into his eyes wearily. "She has been up with him half the night."

"You're a good father—to take him for a while, I mean."

He crossed his arms tight across his chest. "I don't know what I'm doing," he said quietly.

I smiled. "You're doing fine."

He just sighed deeply.

"You are."

"He cries all the time."

"Why don't you ask Leah if there is anything to do for it?"

"That's a half a day's journey."

"And your wife's sanity is not worth a half a day's journey?"

He sighed again.

"Ask Keturah then. She knows everything her mother knows."

Noah snorted softly. "She knows how to stab a knife into a man's heart."

I laughed the comment away. "Gabriel seems all right."

A yawn. Noah tilted his head way back, stretching more than looking at the sky as I had been. "Maybe I'll suggest that to Sarah." He was quiet for a few moments, willing to let me calm his son.

"You're not comfortable speaking of it to Keturah yourself?"

"No." His eyes were closed. "Even you were surprised I was the one up with the baby."

He had a point. Noah was good at many things, but child care was out of his scope of experiences and definitely not in his skill set.

Corianton was settling down and with a few more bounces he fell into sleep.

"You're good with him." He watched us for a moment. "It's time you had your own children."

"I know," I said and kissed the baby's head.

Another long silence. "Still dead set on Lib?"

"Yes, but Noah, you know I did not just pull the idea out of the blue." I was weary of explaining.

"I know," he said.

"What do you have against him?"

"Nothing," he said in surprise.

"Is there some terrible thing about him I should know?"

"Of course not."

"Then it is me. You think I am not good enough for your friend."

"Miriam."

His voice held a note of warning, but I cradled the baby more firmly to my chest and lowered my voice which had begun to get loud. "Is it Keturah? Because I do not see how that is insurmountable. So he developed some feelings for her. It happens every day. It's not that big of a deal."

"It was more than feelings. You know that was why he went to Ammonihah—to get away from her."

"And so he has. Do you have so little faith in your friend to get over it? To right himself? Or do you have so little faith in my ability to help him?"

He looked at me curiously. "You would do that? You would tie yourself to someone who—"

"Who had a crush on a pretty girl when he was a stripling youth? It was a long time ago."

He nodded slowly, conceding.

"I am capable and kind, and I accept that he has this limitation. It is not unconquerable."

"You're right."

"You were friends when you were boys. You should acquaint yourself with him again before you judge him based on a mistake of his youth."

"You're right," he said again.

"And I know you liked Keturah, too, and yet you have managed to get over it."

His brows rose.

"Oh, please. I heard you boys talking." I hid a small smile as I nuzzled Corianton's soft hair again. "Once or twice."

"I get your point." He paused. "Did Lib ask you why you were there?"

I studied my brother for a moment in the stillness of the night, the moonlight illuminating us. "Why do you even care? You have your young family, the running of this farm."

"You are my sister."

I frowned. "I guess I didn't think boys cared about their sisters."

"Why wouldn't they?"

I shrugged and stepped to him to pass his son back.

"I'll make him cry," he said, but reluctantly took the baby in his big hands—hands that were skilled at many things and yet so awkward with the sleeping bundle I laid in them.

"Don't wake Sarah in the morning. I'll come over and do her morning chores."

He swallowed hard and nodded. "Thanks."

I watched him go. I had been wondering why he seemed so stressed and irritable lately, and I was afraid it was that adorable baby. I wondered if his relationship with Sarah was suffering. I wondered if Father was right to give so much of the running of the farm to him. And I wondered what I could do to help, but I was afraid it was something he had to work out on his own.

I said a prayer for him in my heart, and I determined not to be upset at the way he had been treating me—insulting me in front of Lib and the others, making me come home before I was ready, not having any faith in my abilities or intelligence. He was reacting to something else.

I managed a few hours of restless sleep, but just before the break of dawn, I walked across the large clearing to Noah's house. It was dark and quiet, and the fire was cold so I stacked some kindling and got it going again. I had the morning meal ready before Noah pulled open the door and came out. He sat beside me and rubbed his eyes.

"Did you sleep?" I asked him.

"Yeah. I don't know what you did to Corianton, but he slept through the night after you calmed him."

"I'm glad."

"How do you do it?"

I frowned. "There is no trick to it."

He sighed deeply. "There is." He lowered his voice. "And Sarah doesn't know it."

"Don't forget, I have had many little sisters to practice on. She will learn."

He looked at me for a long moment, and there was a soul deep weariness in his eyes. "I'm starting to think she doesn't want to," he whispered.

Placing my hand on his arm, I said, "I am sure she is just over tired."

He just continued to give me that weary look.

"Have you talked to Mother?"

He shook his head.

"There is no shame in asking for help. That is what a family is for."

"It is admitting defeat."

I searched his eyes. I believed he really meant that.

But this was not a war. It was child. "Noah, bring me the

baby and go back inside and get some sleep."

"The birds—"

"Will be handled. Bring me the baby and see to your wife. She needs your strength, and you haven't got it to give."

It was not hard to convince him. I took the baby to my father's house during the morning where there many hands to help and loving arms to hold Corianton, and in the late morning, I strapped him to my chest and started the long walk out to Gideon and Keturah's.

I found Keturah preparing the evening meal and packing for a journey.

"We're going to my village for Lamech's betrothal," she said with a smile. "And who do we have here?"

"Corianton."

"Noah's?"

I nodded. "Mm-hmm. I'm afraid they are having some trouble with him. Noah and Sarah are both exhausted."

A sympathetic frown crossed her face. "What is the problem?"

"A great deal of crying, or so Noah says."

"He is two months old or so?"

"Yes."

"Is he awake?"

I peered inside the sling to see that he indeed did have his eyes open. Cooing to him, I unwrapped the sling and passed the baby to Keturah.

"Noah was reluctant to ask your opinion on the matter."

"He sees me as a warrior. They all do." She gave me a wry

smile. "And that is my own doing. Now, let me see this beautiful boy." Her face took on an animation and she smiled broadly at Corianton as she held him before her.

Corianton eyed her and started to cry.

But his cries did not seem to bother Keturah as she prodded his belly and swiped her finger in his mouth over his gums. I felt a flood of relief and knew I had brought the baby to the right person. If something was wrong with the baby, if he was sick or afflicted in some way, Keturah would be able to tell me.

"I think he will have his father's curly blond locks," she said as she massaged his tummy. "Ah, I think this is your problem."

She proceeded to show me how to hold him over my arm. When I did it, Corianton's cries turned to fussing, then to whimpers, and finally disappeared completely.

She gave a little nod and got up. "I'll be right back."

She went into her home and when she came back, she placed a jar full of herb paste into my satchel.

"In the coming weeks they can rub this on his gums."

"Thank you."

"And," she leaned forward conspiratorially, "I will come to see Sarah since she will not come to see me."

"I would be very grateful."

She waved it off. "Noah is my friend. He was once a very good friend. He saved my life more than once—many times in fact. I will see to his wife's care. Perhaps it is as you said and only a lack of sleep. Perhaps it is something more."

I nodded. I did not know much about their time together in Helaman's army, but I knew, at least with the boys, that the bonds they had formed went deeper than mere friendship.

I looked at this woman who had spent so much time with Noah and his friends—lived among them, worked with them, fought beside them. I could see why the men loved her.

I could see why Lib loved her.

"What is it?" she asked, noticing the way I looked at her.

I took a deep breath. "I went to Ammonihah—to meet Lib."

I didn't know what I expected, but it was not the look of fondness on Keturah's face when she heard his name. For some reason—like the fact that she had married Gid—I had thought that Lib's feelings were not returned.

"And how is Lib?"

"He was well."

"A long journey," she remarked.

"It was."

"We noticed your absence at church."

"I worshiped with the members of the Church there—when I was not sick."

She nodded, and a baby started to fuss from the inside of her home. Keturah offered me a quick smile and went inside to retrieve her own son.

Gabriel favored his father—with wood brown hair and dark eyes. His fussing had stopped and he seemed content to be in his mother's arms.

"What do you think of Lib?" I blurted out my ulterior reason for making the trip to see Keturah.

"I think a great deal of him," she said as she sat beside me again.

"Yes, but—"

She leaned toward me.

"He was your captain."

"He was the leader of my unit, yes."

"And you were close."

"Miriam, by necessity." She looked around as if someone would overhear. "When I first joined with the militia, Lib and Ethanim took it upon themselves to be, well," she bit her lip, "to be my personal guards you could call it."

"If it was so very dangerous—"

"It wasn't. Most of the time it wasn't. Only the battles were. We spent a great deal of time fortifying the cities and providing for the people. In this, in the day to day, either Lib or Ethanim accompanied me everywhere."

"Everywhere?"

She gave me a meaningful look, her eyes widening and her head dipping to catch my eye. "Everywhere. Which annoyed me to no end."

I giggled.

"Eventually, the other men started taking a turn, but for a while, Lib's sole focus was on me. He was my friend when everyone else wanted to ostracize me."

"That was kind of him."

"I think he was ordered to do it, but I don't know who issued the command. I sensed, at first, that he resented the assignment, but he was very faithful in doing it. It embarrassed him, I think, to be seen with me."

"Why would it embarrass him?"

"Many of the boys felt I had overstepped my bounds. Many believed I should not be in the militia. It was insulting to them, as if implied their efforts were not enough. I understood that."

It was not a popular thing to encourage her unconventional actions. I could understand that too.

"I could best nearly any man on the training ground—I didn't think I needed a full time guard. So Lib had to fight me because I didn't want to be followed around, and to tell you the truth, I think he got in more than one fight with the other boys about it."

"Helaman's stripling warriors?" Because not one of them had died in battle, they were already a legend—a standard for righteousness. "Fighting?"

She shrugged. "They were still just boys. You know Noah. He is not perfect, is he?"

I laughed. "Goodness, no."

"So you see it was not easy for him to keep a watch over me, but he did it with exactness and diligence. I made it difficult at times, but I admired him for it too."

"And when did he fall in love with you?"

She looked down at her son, and she spoke quietly. "With almost constant companionship? It didn't take long."

"And you? Did you love him?"

"Of course, but the way I loved them all. As brothers and friends. I knew of his feelings and for a time, I accommodated them. I didn't want to hurt him."

I nodded.

"But my brother told me to keep my actions consistent with

117

my feelings. He said if I confused Lib or led him on, I would lose his respect, and that, above all things, was something I did not want to lose."

I wondered how a girl could spend so much time with Lib and not develop feelings for him, but Corianton became fussy again and I did not get the chance to ask. It would not have been appropriate to ask anyway.

"I could give him a little goat's milk," Keturah offered, a question in her voice.

I nodded. "We have had him all day at my mother's house and mother has been giving him goat's milk. He takes to it fine. I confess it didn't occur to me he would need to be fed again so soon when I ventured out here."

"Every few hours when they are this small," she said, and she went indoors and returned with a vessel that looked like a very thin water skin. Corianton was in full blown cries before we got the milk into his mouth. And for all his cries and her own son beginning to fuss as well, it did not seem to rattle her. She was very good with children, and though I knew she would know a remedy for Corianton's fussiness, her calm demeanor still surprised me, especially in light that the baby's cries had been making his own mother—and me—just a little crazy.

Corianton did not take much milk before he drifted to sleep. I nearly nestled him inside the sling in preparation to leave, but Keturah woke him up and offered him the milk again. She did this twice more until the milk was gone.

"I will instruct Sarah to do the same thing. I will make it a point to see her before we leave Orihah."

"But you are very busy." I motioned to the travel packs and supplies. "I can relay your suggestions."

She shook her head. "This will only take a few more minutes, and I am expecting Gideon home soon. He can do it. He is particular about how his pack is organized anyway." She placed a loving hand on Corianton's fine curly hair. "My advice will make a difference," she said confidently. "It is important that I go. We will stop on our way."

I finally wrapped up Noah's son close to my chest, hugged Keturah, and thanked her. As I began to walk down the long lane back to Orihah, she called out.

"You'll take good care of him, won't you?"

My hand went to the baby snuggled at my chest.

She shook her head, and I understood that she did not mean Corianton. She meant Lib.

I looked at the ground and smiled. She laughed and took Gabriel back indoors.

I took a breath and turned toward the other house in the clearing.

"Hello?" I called when I walked into the yard and Naomi came out. When she saw me, her smile was sweet and welcoming, but it did not seem to reach her eyes. Was that pity in her eyes? Regret?

"I'm looking for Shad," I said, as if she wouldn't know. What other reason could I have for going there? I assumed he would be hunting or maybe at the mill with his uncle and kinsmen. I could leave a message with his mother, an invitation to come see me, and be on my way.

But Naomi pointed to the east. "He's working on Lamech's house today. Just walk on out."

I steeled my courage and turned east. It wasn't far to Lamech's new house, but it took me a few minutes to walk there. It was set back against the hill that rose to the West Road. Corianton was sleeping and still, and I hoped he would remain so long enough for me to say what needed to be said.

He was in the yard when I arrived, setting stonework around an outdoor stove. He looked up when he heard me, and I saw the same look in his eyes I had seen in Naomi's.

"I took Corianton to see Keturah," I said by way of an explanation of my presence. Many from Orihah and surrounding villages came to Keturah for healing, and the explanation didn't surprise him.

But Shad was nervous. He was usually very polite with me, never nervous. We were friends and we had been for a long time, but I had seldom come to his home, and never without being invited. It was too different, and he knew something was wrong.

I closed my eyes for a moment and said a silent prayer. What was I going to say to this boy who had every reason to believe I would accept an offer of marriage from him?

"Miriam, I have to withdraw my courtship," he blurted suddenly.

My eyes flew open. "Shad? But…why?"

"I'm sorry. It's just, I'm going to Zarahemla, and I can't take a wife with me."

I slowly lowered myself to sit on the edge of his stonework.

"I think you have a story to tell, and I see that you feel

terrible, but tell me why."

Shad sat beside me and took a deep breath.

"You remember when I was summoned to the estate of Helaman?"

"That was months ago." I had been extremely curious about the reason he had been summoned, but he had never told me and I had never pressured him to.

"Do you know Darius, Keturah's brother?"

"I've met him."

"He works for the prophet, Helaman." He paused. "In a way. And they have asked me to join them. I have thought on it a great deal, and while you were gone, I went to Helaman and accepted."

"And you feel this is the right thing for you?"

"I do," he said solemnly. "I know I have been courting you for some time, and you have every reason to expect that we will marry, but I don't know what this job will require. It will take a time commitment of several years, maybe longer, and I can't ask you to wait that long. It's, well it's kind of a special assignment for the army, and you know I've been dying to fight Lamanites."

I could let it go at this. I did not have to tell him about Lib. But he seemed so apologetic. He would find out about Lib. Soon. I could not just let it go at this.

I shifted to face him and tucked my hair behind my ear. "I couldn't marry you if you asked," I said. "That trip I took to the sea—it was to meet a boy."

His eyes narrowed. "What do you mean?"

"I didn't know how to tell you."

He stiffened. "Tell me what, Miriam?"

I took a breath. "After that night we went to the river together—do you remember?"

"I remember it." His words were soft. There was only one night I could mean.

"After that night, I prayed about what you said. I just asked it outright. I felt very distinctly that I should go to the sea to meet Lib."

"David's son?"

"Yes."

"You prayed about me and got an answer about someone else?"

I nodded and looked down at my hands. I wished I didn't have to tell him what I had done.

"Is that why you spend so much time with David?"

"No. I had no such notions when I began taking meals to David."

"And what did you intend?"

"I only intended to do as I was prompted. I did it, and it is done."

"So you are courting Lib now?" I couldn't mistake the hurt in his voice.

"No. Maybe."

"Miriam, I don't understand."

I sighed. "Neither do I. But I am beginning to understand that we have both been led in separate directions."

He rubbed his eyes and pinched the bridge of his nose.

"I wish I had told you before I left," I told him gently. "I didn't know how to. I didn't have enough faith in it."

"You were going to keep me as a backup," he accused.

I shook my head, but thought it better not to say any more. When I heard him chuckle, I looked up at him.

Sheepishly, he said, "I think I've been doing the same thing. If we were both willing to commit to each other, we would have done it by now." He leaned down and kissed my forehead. "We should have admitted it long ago. I love you, but marriage isn't really what I want right now."

I knew he had just been waiting for the right opportunity to fight in the army—the right captain and unit, the right place and time—a time when his brothers had returned home to protect his parents.

He tucked my hair behind my ear and smiled sadly. "Be happy, Miriam." Then he leaned down and whispered, "Keep me as your backup."

I felt his movements as he got up rather than watched him. I felt humbled and relieved, disappointed and eager for the future all at the same time.

"Come. I'll walk you up to the main house."

I let him take my hand to help me up, but he didn't hold it.

"Does my father know of your plans?"

"I told him. I know he wanted to have you settled before he leaves, but he was not angry. I suppose he means for your Lib to offer marriage."

"He doesn't."

At his curious look, I clarified, "My family feels that I have made a fool of myself, that I have been too forward with Lib."

Shad rubbed a hand over the back of his neck. "A guy would have to be crazy not to take the hint."

"Well, I am not exactly young or beautiful. I have three younger sisters who are old enough to marry."

"Only you could understate in one moment and exaggerate in the next."

We reached the house. Naomi was nowhere to be seen. We were both sad, but I could sense Shad's excitement for the future too. I offered him a smile.

"I wish you the best of luck in Zarahemla."

"And I wish you well at the sea."

"But I have no plans to go back."

He stared down at me. "You will," he said, and then he cleared his throat. "Thank you, Miriam, for your friendship. I have enjoyed our courtship a lot. I only wish..." He shook his head, took a deep breath. "I only wish you the best." He placed another light kiss on my forehead.

I nodded and swallowed hard. Then I watched my friend turn back toward his brother's house and walk away.

CHAPTER 10

The weather was mild and Corianton nestled against me as
I made my way toward Orihah. His weight was minimal, and he
didn't wake. I thought about all the things Keturah had told
me—filed away the things to tell Noah and his wife, and savored
the things she had confided about Lib. Before I had met him,
those things would have been little more than bits of
information, but now that I had met him—and liked him—they
swirled around and came to rest near my heart, nestling as
warmly as the baby.

I was thinking about Lib so completely that it nearly didn't
surprise me when he stepped into view—coming toward me on
the lane. But when I realized how unlikely it was for him to be
in Orihah—walking this path that led only to Keturah's home—
I stopped still in my tracks.

"Miriam, what is wrong?" he asked with what looked to be
genuine concern shadowing his face.

"You're here."

He grinned. "That's wrong?"

I glanced back toward Keturah's home. She was there alone. What did he think he was doing?

Lib was not stupid.

"Miriam," he said as he quickly closed the distance between us. "I went to the farm. Noah said you had come here."

I eyed him. I wanted very much for that to be true.

He watched me, clearly hoping I would believe it, wondering why I doubted it. He glanced over my shoulder and realization barely filled his eyes before he impulsively bent and kissed me.

Taken completely by surprise, I made a small noise in the back of my throat, something that might have sounded like a squeak if his lips hadn't been so effectively covering my own. He only put a hand into my hair and moved closer, but when he brushed up against the bundle at my chest, he broke the kiss and looked down.

Breathless, he looked back up at me, a question in his eyes.

"Noah's son," I said and pulled some of the fabric away so he could see.

"He's not yours," he said on a rush.

I laughed. "Of course not. You saw me not two weeks ago. He couldn't possibly be mine."

"I know. I just panicked for a moment."

Panicked? What had he thought? That I had birthed this child of my own body and then sought him out in Ammonihah? Had I given him the wrong impression of myself by seeking him out, just as Noah said I would?

I backed away and eyed the path around him. "I can see what you think of me." I wanted to sound indignant, but I knew I only sounded hurt.

He caught me by both arms. "No, Miriam. I thought you might have, oh I don't know…" He squeezed my arms tighter, then he deliberately loosened his grip and smoothed over them as if he thought he had hurt me. "I thought you might have gotten married."

I frowned. "In the time since I saw you?"

He stepped back and raked both hands through his hair, then let them fall to his sides. "It was irrational." He scoffed a little. "Believe it or not, I can be irrational at times."

I just watched him standing so handsomely, now so awkwardly before me. Why was he here? And how could I get him to kiss me again?

"I just saw you and then the child, and I knew it wasn't mine and—" He clamped his mouth shut and turned red up to his ears.

And I was afraid I blushed just as deeply.

"I'm sorry." The words were a rush and he took another step back. "I just meant…"

But I stepped to him and took his hand in mine.

"I made a mess of this," he said.

I shook my head. "I have never been so pleasantly surprised."

He might have blushed deeper, but the mortified look faded from his face and he smiled.

"Hagoth wouldn't talk to me after you left."

Steady and devoted Hagoth. He stood as my friend.

"Is that why you came?" *Guilt?*

He shook his head. "No." Slowly, he bent his head toward me, pausing a whisper's breath away from my lips, waiting for me to protest.

But I didn't.

Lib kissed me with a tenderness and finesse his previous kiss had lacked. I did not think he could kiss me so sweetly without emotion behind it, and on the quiet path in the beautiful woods, with the baby still between us, I let Lib kiss me. I sighed when he stopped, and I opened my eyes to look into his.

A throat cleared behind us. "I see I am interrupting."

We turned to see Gid standing in the middle of the lane, arms folded, treating us to a rare grin.

"And very impolitely," Lib all but growled.

Gid burst into a hearty laugh. "There is hope for you yet," he said as he came toward us. He clapped Lib firmly on the shoulder and then moved on toward his home. "Welcome back," he called, and before he turned completely away, he dipped his chin to me in a nod. "Miriam."

"Did he just wink at you?"

I looked up at Lib. I had not thought of it before, but the look on his face told me he was still dealing with a good deal of jealousy.

"I believe he did."

He looked back at me. "Miriam, may I walk you home?"

What a silly question. "Have you Noah's permission?" I joked.

"I do."

His green eyes said he was serious.

And his formality! Biting back a smile, I nodded, and we began to walk. The silence was not uncomfortable, but filled with questions I wanted to ask. We exchanged little more than observations on the weather and the countryside until he noticed me holding some of Corianton's weight in my hands.

"Do you want me to carry him for a while?"

"Oh! No, Lib, he is not heavy. In fact I enjoy carrying him. He is starting to wiggle, that's all."

His eyes warmed and he reached out to the knot at my shoulder. "All secure then?"

I nodded.

And Corianton started to cry.

It could have been very disconcerting as all along the lane Corianton's howls became worse and worse until it sounded as if he could barely get air. But I unwrapped the pathetic little babe from the sling and positioned him over my arm just as Keturah had shown me.

It was the same as before. The cries subsided into soft whimpers and he gradually drifted off into a fitful sleep.

"He will be hungry again," I said apologetically.

"We should hurry then."

"Probably, but…" I winced. "He is much more awkward to carry this way."

"I can take him."

I looked up at Lib, wondering if he meant it.

"Show me how," he said as he drew me to a stop and reached out for the child.

So I positioned Corianton over his arm just as Keturah had positioned him over mine.

"You've got him?"

"I am capable of holding a small child."

"I know."

"Then why do you look so worried?"

He was joking—or he enjoyed carrying the child for me. Either way, he was smiling.

I shook my head and tucked my hair back into place before I rubbed the ache from my arm. "It is a relief. Thank you."

"I missed that by the way."

"Missed what?"

He gestured to my ear. "The way you tuck your hair back."

"It's been little more than a fortnight," I said, not knowing what else to say, and we turned onto the lane that led west toward my father's home.

Mother came from the house as we approached and when she saw us, she looked like a startled deer.

"Lib!" she exclaimed and the disbelieving look she openly sent me was utterly embarrassing.

Lib at least pretended not to notice it and greeted my mother with kindness and formality, and when the girls gathered around her skirts, he only seemed slightly uncomfortable with them.

"Noah is with his father and Jed, all out working with the birds." She gestured with her hands toward the farm with a motion that reminded me of the flutter of wings. She clearly thought he was here to see Noah, and she probably thought I had found him in town and made a nuisance of myself by tagging along.

"I would like to speak with Jeremiah." He paused and took in the sight of all the girls still crowded around Mother, staring at him, their curiosity bordering on rude. "About Miriam. I think I will wander out and find them."

Mother licked her lips and threw another glance at me—less obvious this time.

"I'll return in an hour," he said to me. He reached out to transfer Corianton to my waiting arms. "Will you be here?"

I licked my lips, suddenly aware of repeating Mother's nervous habit. "I had planned to provide a warm meal to your father tonight."

His eyes narrowed. "I will take you there." He left but turned back for a few steps and called, "Assuming Noah gives his permission."

The moment his back was turned, Mother grasped me by both arms, much the same way Lib had done in the forest near Keturah's. "What can he mean by talking to your father? Have you gone so far as to harass him?"

I gasped. *Harass him?* "Mother! No!"

"He will rebuke your father for sure." She shook her head and shooed the girls away, bidding them back to their chores. "You've proved yourself a hoyden and brought shame upon your father."

It was not the first time she had insinuated this, but always before it had been under her breath.

I pressed my lips together and thought of the kiss in the

woods. I thought of the patches of red that had dusted Lib's cheekbones, his fair skin so unable to hide his embarrassment. His fumbling words. Gid's lighthearted relief. Gid recognized it, even if Mother didn't.

"I don't think that is what he wishes to speak to Father about," I said, but Mother was already bustling off, irritated, rattled, and calling orders.

I looked down at Corianton, peaceful for once. "I guess you'll be wanting your milk," I said and hurried to fetch it for him.

By the time I returned Corianton to his mother, Keturah was there visiting with her. I could see she had brought additional herbs with her and they were talking earnestly.

"I have brought your son," I called and they both turned. I was pleased to see Sarah's smile and eagerness to take her baby.

"Thank you," she said as I passed the baby to her. She sent a surreptitious glance toward Keturah, and I knew that her thanks wasn't merely for seeing to Corianton for the day.

"I hope you are more rested," I said.

"I am. And Keturah has already given me much to think on."

I bid them both goodbye and returned to my father's home to dish up a meal for David and Lib, twice what I normally took. I couldn't contain a smile as I waited for Lib to come for me.

He walked into the yard with Father and Jed. He and Father clasped arms and then Father, a man of generally few words, nodded for me to accompany Lib before ducking into the house.

"Was that Gid headed out to Noah's?" I asked when we were on our way.

"It was. He said Keturah had business here."

Her name stood between us like a person.

After a moment, Lib lifted the dish from my hands. "I liked the geometric problem you left for me." By his tone, I didn't think he was going to discuss the reason he had sought out my father.

"I wanted to say goodbye, but I wanted to leave Noah more. It was ungracious of me to leave without bidding a proper farewell."

"I thought it was fitting."

"Not just to you, but to Ethanim. I owed him that. And to Adreana and Hagoth."

Another name that stood between us like a person.

"I'm embarrassed when I think of it."

"They thought no worse of you for it."

"It is not so much what they think of me, but what I think of myself. Noah was right. Mother was right. I'm an impulsive hoyden."

He put a hand on my arm. "I do not believe that is what you think of yourself."

I studied the path before me.

"I certainly don't," he added quietly.

CHAPTER 11

"David!" I called at the same moment Lib called, "Father!"

Lib gave me a strange look, and I returned it with a little shrug.

David looked up from a scroll and when he saw me he smiled. It took him a moment to realize Lib was standing next to me.

"Lib." He stared at his son and then glanced at me.

I raised my brows and smiled.

"Lib?" David said again, not as though he didn't recognize his son, but as though he didn't believe his eyes.

Lib took a moment to pass me the dish of food, and then he stepped to his father and embraced him.

"When did you arrive home?"

"This afternoon. I had to see to some business." He put his hands on his hips and backed up.

David hesitated. I could see he wanted to ask why we had arrived together.

But Lib anticipated the question. "Miriam and I ran into each other on the road."

The truth.

It was quiet for a moment, and I thought they might like some privacy. "I will serve this up," I said and took the food into David's home. I knew where the dishes were—I had served food there many times. I found the dishes and filled three of them.

But I couldn't carry three of them. I took the two I had filled full for the men and slipped through the doorway.

David and Lib were still standing, and Lib was giving a general account of the construction of the ship.

As I passed him his food, I said, "David, you should go see it. It is a sight to behold, despite Lib's incorrect calculations."

"I do not make incorrect calculations."

"Except on the main mast."

Lib tried to stare me down, but in the end he hid a grin and admitted, "Just that once." Then he turned to David. "Miriam found the error on the drawings."

David turned his whole body to look at me. Instead of remarking on it, he said, "Eat."

So, smiling, I ducked into the hut to get my own food.

As we ate and talked, I caught Lib looking between his father and me. He wore a puzzled frown. It was probably very disconcerting for him to see that his father and I had an established relationship.

"How long will you stay?" David asked.

"I don't know," Lib replied. He took a deep breath and continued. "They don't need me for the finishing work. Hagoth said I should come home and prepare to sail."

I smirked into my food. I doubted that was exactly what Hagoth had said.

David was quiet for a moment, chewing on his meal. Chewing on the information was more like it.

"So you've decided to sail away."

"I have."

Silence again.

"It will be a great adventure," I said.

"I'm glad you think so." Lib caught my eye for the barest of moments and then looked back to his food.

"This pheasant is good, Miriam," said David. "Did you make it?"

A change of subject. "Thank you, and you know I did."

Then to my embarrassment, he turned to Lib and prompted, "Isn't this pheasant good?"

Lib glanced up at his father ready to make a reply, but then I saw him distinctly take note of my embarrassment. He stared for a moment and then back down to his food his attention went. "Miriam has cooked many good meals for me," he told his dish.

David grinned over at me. "What would we do without her?"

Lib peered up at me, his blond hair falling over one eye. "I am beginning to wonder that myself."

Well, my food was just as interesting as Lib's, and I smiled down into it.

"It has been a long time since we had a woman around here," David said.

I thought the previous silence had been awkward, but this one was awful. It stuck in my throat. It must have stuck in Lib's, too, because he had to clear his throat several times before speaking.

"It is time we changed that, Father."

David's throat worked, and I knew there was more behind the simple comments than I understood. I supposed it had to do with Lib's mother. But it had been so long! Then again, perhaps that was the point.

David turned to me. "Has he talked you into a betrothal then?"

I giggled a little. "Oh, David. You know I need no convincing." The Holy Ghost had already convinced me, and David and I had talked it over many times before I had gone to Ammonihah.

And then I wished the lighthearted words unsaid. I realized what was wrong, what had not been there in Lib's impulsive kiss that afternoon.

The Holy Ghost had convinced him too.

He was only here because he had felt the same thing I had. He hadn't miraculously fallen in love with me—not when I showed up with Ethanim, not while I sailed in Hagoth's boat or lay with the fever in his hut, not while I laughed with the sailors, and not while I pointed out how Lib's calculations were incorrect.

He was acting on faith, not love.

"No!" I said suddenly, interrupting Lib as he opened his mouth to respond. "No, he has not talked me into it."

Lib frowned, clearly confused by the look I was giving him. I felt it on my face—accusing and hurt.

"Miriam, what is it?" David asked, slowly setting his dish aside.

I turned my eyes to him, swallowed hard.

"N-nothing." I tucked my hair behind my ear—I couldn't help it. Then I did it again, uselessly. I tried for a smile and felt it fall pathetically flat.

I hadn't loved Lib either when I had gone to Ammonihah. I had barely known him and I had, in fact, disliked him at our first meeting.

That was no longer the case for me.

But for him? Unmoved and fighting his distaste—that was the way he now felt about me. He was just being obedient.

I winced and took a sharp breath.

"I need to leave," I said.

"Lib will walk you."

I shook my head.

"Is something wrong?"

I shook my head again. Why wasn't I rational enough to just accept what was? I would. I had to. I took a deep breath and clenched my hands in my skirts. I would.

"I just…need to go," I told them and added an awkward, "Sorry. And welcome home, Lib."

Both men wore identical frowns. It was so endearing I almost smiled as I ran away.

What had just happened back there? My heart was pounding, and my stomach churned with embarrassment.

I needed to be alone with my thoughts, with my feelings, and I needed to talk it through with the only one who would have answers for me.

I thought of all my little sisters at home and knew I couldn't go there. I had a place on the hill, the place I had been kneeling when I first felt the promptings to find Lib.

I let my questions drift up to heaven as my fingers drifted over the tips of the tall grasses I passed. I wanted very much— I *needed*—to feel the conviction I had felt that first day. But I didn't feel it again—not even close.

It was one thing for me to have thought I would marry a boy I didn't love, to have accepted it as God's will and hoped for a change of heart. But it was another thing entirely to accept that the boy did not love me. I had accepted it for myself, but I had given little thought to how it would affect Lib. He had been just a stranger to me before, a boy I had seen in the town. But now? Now he was *Lib*, and I knew his strength of character, his ambitions, his regrets.

It was not fair to him. He should marry someone he loved, not someone he felt obligated to because of his sense of—what? Obedience? Righteousness? Faithfulness?

Those weren't bad things to start a marriage with. They weren't.

But I could have had those things with Shad, someone who was my friend and who I loved and who loved me—in a way.

I heard a twig snap behind me. I knew a moment's fear until I realized no one who intended me harm would have let me hear his footfall.

"How did you find me?" I asked without turning.

"I want you to go to a wedding with me."

I turned to face him.

"My captain is getting married in Antionum. I want you to come."

I was flattered by his invitation, but at that moment, I didn't care about his friend's wedding.

"You intend to take me to wife," I said plainly. It was his plan. It was why he had come here. I had seen signs of it all day.

He sat beside me. "I do."

A flood of emotions welled in my throat, and I closed my eyes to try to separate them, to try to determine the appropriate one, the one I should be feeling. Relief. Validation. Heartbreak. Rightness. They were all jumbled together, compounded and making each other worse.

Slowly, I shook my head.

"How do you think I felt when Ethanim finally told me why you had come?" he asked quietly.

"Insulted."

He smiled a little. "Not exactly. Is that how you feel?"

"Yes. And betrayed."

"By who? By Ethanim?"

"No. Betrayed by God."

"God speaks His wishes to your heart and you feel betrayed?"

"I didn't know you wouldn't want it. I thought the Lord would prepare you somehow. I thought...I thought it would all fall into place. I feel that He asked me to start something with you against your will."

"But you did—you did start something, and you can see my will has brought me here to you." He paused. "You were scared to come to the sea."

I nodded. "Of course I was," I said softly.

"And yet you came."

I looked away. "I was naïve."

I felt his fingers on my cheek. He gently urged me to look at him, and slowly, I lifted my eyes to his.

"To trust in God is not to be naïve. To trust in God is to show your true strength." He looked at me a long time. I watched his eyes travel over my face before he abruptly said, "So, He has brought us together—unconventionally to be sure—and it is our responsibility to do the rest."

"Responsibility," I said dryly.

Lib quirked a brow, and a smile crept into his eyes. "Privilege?" Then he laughed a little. "I'm sorry, Miriam. I am not very good with the pretty words."

His laugh was wonderful, deep and rich sounding and genuine. I tilted my head. "Do you wish to say pretty things, Lib?"

"I want to say things that would put you at ease, yes."

I licked my lips, something he didn't fail to notice, which made me even more ill at ease. "You must first determine what my concerns are if you intend to say pretty things to ease them."

He leaned back on his hands. "I think you are afraid of inconveniencing me."

Oh! That was it exactly.

"I can see I am close." He squinted into the falling sun. "You are afraid we won't love each other."

I swallowed past the lump in my throat.

"And you are most afraid that I will not love you."

I dropped my gaze. I was so self-centered.

Lib sat up, but his voice dropped low. "When I think of you, Miriam, you will first and always be the girl who had enough faith to make a three day journey on the strength of a prompting from the Holy Spirit. If I don't love you now it is because there is a fault in me, not in you."

That was kind of pretty.

"I guessed your concerns because I share them. Don't you think I want to be loved as well? Don't you think I want to kiss my wife and know she is not thinking of the feel of Hagoth's lips?" He took a breath, but I could see he was not done. "You have beauty, Miriam, and your face glows with the Spirit. You are intelligent and quick and you fascinate me. That is why I could not help but follow you here. Your obedience and integrity humble me. They humble me, but this is my question. When does obedience stop being just obedience?"

I understood what he was saying. He wanted to know we could fall in love, too.

"When we add our faith to it."

It surprised me when he wouldn't meet my eyes.

"So what would you say to ease my concerns?" I asked.

"Being married will not inconvenience me," he answered. "You and I have much to build love on, and when I marry, Miriam, I intend to love my wife with my whole heart."

143

I reached up to tuck my hair behind my ear, but Lib caught my hand in his and completed the action with his own fingers. Then he pulled my hand down and placed it over his chest.

"My whole heart," he emphasized. "And to that end, I would like you to go to a wedding with me."

I searched his face. It was fair and angled very much like his father's. He was smiling, and he meant what he said. I bit my lip. "Okay," I finally said. "Assuming you can gain Father's permission, I will go with you to this wedding."

"He has already given it."

"Oh!"

He smiled at my surprise. "Your father likes me. He has always liked me. Can you be ready in a week's time?"

"Of course. Shall I pack the same provisions I took to Ammonihah?"

"Yes. The distance will be about the same. We will travel with friends."

"With your friends?" I asked dubiously. I knew some of his friends, but I didn't know them well and wondered if I would have anyone to talk to if he spent all his time with his friends. Clearly he didn't want to be alone with me.

"Yes." He leaned back on his hands again, more at ease. "Your friends too, I think. Ethanim and Adreana will travel with us, and I believe you know Beth and Esther."

"I do." I was relieved to know Esther would be there. She was a particular friend of mine. Beth was her older sister, but she was kind and I had been in her company many times.

"Beth is married to a friend of mine, Zachariah, and they tell me Esther has just become betrothed to Enos, Gid's cousin."

"I heard about that." And I had tried not to be jealous.

"Ah."

I looked down into my lap, wondering if he needed to know about Shad. I decided he did.

"I think Enos will be a fine husband for Esther, but I feel I should tell you I am much better acquainted with his cousin, Shad. He…he and I…up until yesterday, Shad was courting me."

Lib took a breath. "Your father told me."

"Oh."

"But thank you for your honesty. What happened yesterday?"

I frowned.

"What happened to cause the end of the courtship?"

"Oh," I said again lamely. "He, uh, said he was going to Zarahemla and couldn't take a wife."

"But you wanted to go."

I shook my head, but I didn't think he believed me. "I told him about Ammonihah and about you, and we agreed that the Lord was leading us in different directions."

He thought about it for a moment. "Responsibility," he said.

I shook my head. "Privilege. Did you tell your father? You know…" *About us.* "Did you tell him why you came?"

"No. But he knows. He is a smart man."

"Yes, to be sure, but sometimes he does fail to see what is right in front of him. You must know this."

His brows rose, and a half smile touched his lips. "You do know him well."

"He is my friend."

"How long have you been taking him meals?"

I started to respond, but he cut in. "And why?"

"I saw your father alone week after week at the sermons, and I asked Mother what could be done."

The sun shone on his golden hair and he squinted into its rays. "Your mother told you to befriend an unmarried older man? I'm sorry, but I don't believe that."

"She told me that if I saw a need I should see to it, and I should not let my left hand know what my right hand doeth."

"I can understand that," he said after a moment. "But why *my* father?"

"I didn't single him out because he's your father, if that's what you mean."

He searched my eyes for a moment, and though I was afraid of what he would find in them, I let him.

Befriending David was a process that had taken years. The prompting to find Lib was very recent, and in my mind, one had not caused the other.

I had not singled out David because of Lib, but in my heart, in the deepest, most secret, most tender part of my heart, I knew I had singled out Lib. Long ago. Without knowing it. He had always been different from the others. Separate. Alone. Better. I had always been aware of him.

It was the reason I couldn't love Shad the way he wanted, the way he deserved.

It was the reason I had been eager to learn to solve equations. It was the reason I had gone to the sea, the reason I had gone to that grassy hill in the first place.

Months ago, when the rains were coming to an end and the air was clean and cool but the sun was warm, I had gone to the river with my friends. With Shad and Jared, Esther and Aniah, and many more from the town. And when the sun had gone down, the boys had made a fire and we huddled together for warmth so we could stay longer.

I watched Shad in the flickering light, and he watched me. He sat on his heels, tending the fire. The ground was so wet he could barely keep it going. He stoked it, blew air into it, fed it the driest wood we could find, but eventually, we had to admit defeat and everyone started back toward town.

I huddled in a blanket with Aniah, and we followed the others, but Shad fell back from his friends and came alongside me.

"Miriam."

Aniah giggled, slipped out of the blanket and ran to catch up with Esther.

"It's not so late. Let's stay," Shad said.

I looked up at the stars and it was tempting.

He took my silence for agreement, and I guessed it was.

"Come on," he said and led me back toward the fire, now little more than smoking coals.

I looked at it and laughed. "It might not be too late, but it is too cold."

He was confident. He was gentle. He was everything he should have been.

"I won't let you get cold," he murmured into my ear and

wrapped his arms around me. He drew me close to his warm chest, and I let him.

Shad found a shelter in some thick brush and we shared the warmth of the blanket. I knew he would kiss me, and he did. But I was self-conscious, and I obviously didn't do it right.

He pulled back and searched in my eyes.

"Why don't you kiss me back?" he whispered.

I had. I thought I had.

I looked at his lips, felt his warm arms around me, his hands on my back. His eyes were dark and full of concern. He was indisputably the most handsome boy in Orihah. He was my closest friend. He loved me.

And I couldn't muster a kiss that would please him.

"I don't know." My voice felt strangled.

He pulled in a slow breath. He was gentle, patient with me.

"Do me a favor," he murmured, "and find out."

"Miriam," Lib said. "Are you all right? You've gone pale."

I shook off the memory of Shad and focused on Lib. What if I couldn't please him either?

"Not yet," I said. "But I will be."

He nodded. "It can take years to fully recover from the effects of the Fever."

I smiled weakly, thankful for the excuse, but my heart twisted.

CHAPTER 12

I was ready when Lib came to get me before dawn. I sat in the glow of our cook fire drinking warm tea with my mother who was for once sitting still.

"You're sure Esther will be traveling with you?"

"Yes. I talked to her yesterday. She is very excited."

"Settling into her betrothal, I assume."

I wasn't really sure about that. "I suppose. She didn't say much on that."

"Well," Mother said when I could see she had noticed Lib come into view on the path lit by twilight. "Be a good girl."

I rolled my eyes, and Mother smiled, seeming pleased. I picked up my pack, ready to go out to meet Lib on the road.

Mother touched my elbow. "Let him come to you."

I already felt bad that he had come all this way before dawn. My father's bird farm was not on the way out of Orihah.

"Let him come politely greet your mother, Miriam."

She was right. It should be proper, even before dawn. I ran

the risk of offending Lib if I did not heed our customs. He would want to greet my parents. I set my pack down and waited for Lib to come all the way to us. He gave me a smile and then greeted my mother.

"Good morning, May," he said.

"Hello, Lib. It is a fine day for a journey."

Lib glanced at the sky. "Aye, it will be." He turned to me. "And we had better be going."

By then Jed had stopped chopping wood and Father had come up from the well. Lib stepped forward to clasp arms with Father, and everything was right except that Lib didn't love me and I didn't know him.

Father held my travel pack up, and I slipped into it then gave him and Mother each a kiss.

"Behave," Mother said into my ear, but she did not sound nearly so reprimanding as she had before.

When we were on the lane, a soft morning breeze rustled the leaves overhead. The ground was soft and crunched beneath our steps. The light was rising slowly in the east.

"I'm sorry you had to come all this way to fetch me so early in the morning."

"It's no trouble," he replied so easily I nearly believed him. "Are you excited to go?"

"Yes, and I can see you are as well."

He shrugged. "I like to travel."

"And see your friends."

"Yes. I haven't seen them in a while."

Lib was charming me. Not on purpose, not by any

deliberate attempt to be funny or sweet or flattering. But he was different, or I was seeing him differently. Something had changed.

He was darker than I remembered him being, maybe made so by the dim light we walked in. On the sea he had seemed so light, as if the light shone from him or he reflected it. But his skin was dark from his days at the sea, and the straight golden hair of his youth appeared darkened into burnished honey.

He was describing Antionum to me, and I was thinking that something was happening inside my heart.

"You know what you want," I observed. "From life, I mean."

He looked down at me. "I am no longer a young man. Do you know what you want from life?"

"To be a wife and a mother."

"Nothing more?"

"More? I do not wish to join the army if that is what you mean," I said, and I was afraid it had sounded snide.

He ignored the tone if he heard it. "Do you not wish to learn all of Father's formulas, for instance?"

"Well, yes, of course. As many as he will share. But you are right—I have no application for them."

"And do you not wish to travel to, say, the land northward?"

I laughed. "But there is nothing there! It is desolate."

We were coming into the town, and it was brighter now that we were out of the trees, though the sun had not risen yet.

"How do you know?"

"That is what they say?"

"Who is they?"

"Lib," I laughed. "I don't know."

"What if it were possible to live in desolation?"

"Is it?"

"Yes." He pointed to the left. "This way."

We passed through the town and walked up a grassy knoll outside of it. Several people were already gathered, but I was surprised to see that we were not the last to arrive.

I knew Corban and Reb, who were talking quietly while they waited. Corban had his arms folded, and Reb was kicking at a clump of dirt.

"Hey," Lib said. He hesitated a moment before he said, "You guys know Miriam," and added awkwardly, "Noah's…little sister."

I was somewhat surprised when they each stepped forward and placed a quick hand on my shoulder. I had known them both my whole life—or rather known of them—though I had never been introduced to them, and certainly never introduced in this way. They were welcoming and not surprised to see me.

"Noah's not coming?" Reb asked as Lib lifted my travel pack so I could slip out of it while we waited on the others.

"No," I said. "The baby. The farm. My father is turning over more of the farm to him all the time."

Ethanim and Adreana arrived next. Ethanim had come out to the bird farm a few mornings after my arrival to assure himself that I had made it safely home, but I had not seen Adreana since the night I ran away over three weeks ago now. I went directly to her and we embraced like old friends, and somehow it felt like we were. I thought of the nights she had spent nursing me back to health and wished I knew the words in her language to express my gratitude.

"Miriam!" Ethanim gave me a broad grin as he motioned to Lib with the slightest tilt of his head. I could tell he thought our plan had worked, and I looked at Lib and wondered why I thought it hadn't.

Then Esther arrived with her sister and their men.

The sun was just peeking over the hills, and Enos said, "Let's begin our journey with a prayer." Enos offered it up and we hefted our travel packs and began our journey toward Antionum

I had suspected, if not feared, that Lib would be comfortable with his friends and abandon me for them. I was discouraged to see I had been right when he stayed near me for a time but gradually drifted over to Corban and Zach.

I sighed.

"What is the matter?" asked Esther.

Esther was a good friend, one I knew I could confide in. When I looked over at her beside me, I noticed her sister, Beth, beside her. Looking to my other side, I noticed that Adreana, too, walked near us. It seemed the boys had split off and pulled ahead—perhaps because their legs were longer, or perhaps because they wished to talk amongst themselves.

I shouldn't begrudge Lib his reunion with his friends— surely they had much to talk about, from his friends' recent journey to the Land of Nephi to his own construction of the massive ship—but I suppressed another sigh and confided, "I had hoped to come to know Lib better on this journey."

All the girls looked up toward him just as a burst of laughter came from the boys.

"There will be plenty of time for that," Esther replied. "I would like to know Enos better too."

I looked over again and noticed she worried her bottom lip.

"Of course you are right, Esther. I am just impatient."

"Enos says Lib is courting you." Her voice held curiosity, and I could sense curiosity from Beth as well.

"I believe he asked my father for permission, yes."

Esther all but squealed and clapped her hands together. "But what of Shad?"

"Shad has been courting you for some time, has he not?" put in Beth, who was never nosy.

"He withdrew his courtship," I told them, and to avoid the next question, I went ahead and told them the reason why.

"But what does he plan to do in Zarahemla for which he cannot have a wife?" Beth puzzled.

"Is he going with Jared?" Esther asked.

"He did not say. Is Jared going too?"

Esther lowered her voice. "Enos says it is to be some kind of spy mission. They are to infiltrate enemy forces." She bit her lip. "But I don't think I was supposed to tell you that."

"Esther," Beth reprimanded softly. "You should not ever betray your husband's trust in you. When he tells you something in confidence, you should keep it between you."

Esther leaned across me and spoke to Adreana. "Beth has been married to her Zach for years. She knows everything about being married."

Adreana nodded as if she understood.

"How did you come to know Ethanim?" Beth asked her.

I was about to tell them she did not understand our language when Adreana said, "I came here on a large ship across the great deep. My father and uncle died, their bodies flung into the sea. I am alone, and Ethanim brings me to his home."

The girls showed appropriate dismay at her tragic tale, but I was shocked.

"Adreana, you speak so well!"

She smiled. "I began to learn on the ship. The sailors teach me. And Ethanim teaches me much."

There was another loud laugh from the boys.

"We will have a splendid time together," Esther said. "And I have a feeling we will be seeing much more of those boys than we want to. Do not worry about that, Miriam."

"I won't. You are right." And giving one last longing look at the tall, blond boy ahead of me, I turned to the girls and had a lovely morning in their company.

I did get my time alone with Lib. I thought perhaps he made it a point to walk with me. That first afternoon he brought me a cleaned grouse to cook. He prepared it, laid it on a stone near our fire and buried the entrails.

"Do you know what to do with this?" he asked.

I looked at him and rolled my eyes. Of course I knew how to cook a bird.

"Oh. Right," he said.

"There is not much to it."

Lib took a deep breath.

"Did you have a nice day with your friends?" I asked into the awkwardness and then nearly winced as I tried to curb my jealousy. "It has been a while since you've seen them."

"Aye, it has." He scratched the side of his nose.

"Still as you remember them?" I glanced up at him and saw his eyes narrow as he thought. He always did that, and his eyes crinkled at the corners.

"Yes and no," he said. "They have all moved past what we used to be."

"Striplings?" A word that had come to stand for more than just a youthful boy, but for one of the righteous members of Helaman's army.

"A unit. One mind. One goal."

"Ah," I said. "And now they have new goals—wives, children, providing them food and shelter." I thought of Noah and Sarah and the baby and the stress they were all under, and thought that the distance between Lib and his married friends went perhaps much further than he thought.

I turned the bird on our simple spit and licked the heat off my fingers.

Lib watched me as I rooted around in my bag of provisions for something to eat with the grouse. "Corn or potatoes?" I asked him.

"You've potatoes in there?"

"Sure." I shrugged.

"How will you prepare them?"

Did it matter? I withdrew two that I had washed clean of dirt before packing them into the bag. "I only planned to cook them in the coals. I've herbs. Nothing fancy."

Lib nodded. "Do the potatoes then."

As I worked, placing them carefully in the coals and then withdrawing the herbs, Lib scanned the camp of friends. There were several small cook fires. Beth and Esther had their own, and the rest of the boys milled around another.

"Miriam?"

Lib and I both looked up at the sound of Esther's voice. She shot a smile to Lib but held a dish out to me.

"We cooked more food than we can eat. Carrots and beans."

I stood to take the food from her. "We can make use of this," I told her. "Thanks."

She glanced at Lib again, smiled, and moved back to the opposite end of camp.

We ate the carrots while we waited for the potatoes to cook deep in the coals. I smiled into mine. "I think she likes you," I said.

"I think she likes everyone." He gave me a look that made me laugh.

"She'll settle down, and I think Enos likes the challenge."

We both looked over to where Enos had his arm half around her back and she was giggling. Then we looked at each other and shared a smile.

I thought the boys kept a guard at night, but the girls all slept soundly in their tents, either not wanted or not required to watch for predators in the darkness. Lib was conversing with his friends at the far end of camp when I went to sleep, but when I woke before dawn, he was sleeping at the entrance to my tent.

I watched him for a while, wondering what I had gotten myself into, wondering what he was thinking about it all, but I fell back to sleep and when I woke again, only his bedroll was there. So I rolled mine, and then I rolled his and set them both at the entrance of the tent.

The light was rose colored as I walked slowly around the camp. People were awake, but to my surprise, nobody was breaking camp. Everyone was going about their morning business leisurely. The men smiled and teased and laughed. Reb, who I knew only a little bit, told the funniest jokes. It felt good to laugh because despite knowing everyone, I didn't know them well, and a smile was something we all had in common.

When finally we were on our way again, I was pleased that Lib stayed by my side. Ethanim and Adreana had taken off to the west, toward home, and when they were gone, I felt really alone.

"How come Ethanim turned around? Isn't he coming?"

His lips tightened. "Decided not to. She is tired of travel."

"You think he caters to her whims," I said.

"No. Well, yes. He's never been like this before."

"It is not a weakness," I told him softly.

"What is not a weakness?"

"Caring for someone. Wanting to make them happy. To love is not a flaw."

"I know that," he said, maybe a little annoyed.

Do you? I wondered.

"It's just that it's temporary," he said, and I thought his comment surprised us both. "Love," he said and stumbled endearingly over the word. "It's temporary."

He walked a few more steps with me then said, "I am going to go...talk to Enos."

I was not without company for long. Esther and Beth came to walk beside me. Esther gave me a commiserating smile, and Beth smoothed her hand down my hair.

"Temporary," she scoffed.

I was embarrassed that they had heard Lib, but then Esther snorted back a laugh and suddenly we were all giggling. And even though Lib resisted looking back over his shoulder, I knew he was very aware of our giggles because the tips of his ears were red.

CHAPTER 13

I watched Lib walking alone a great distance ahead of everyone else. He was thinking, clearing his head. Brooding.

I felt very small and very young. The only one here who was my age was Esther, and I knew how they all saw her.

I had not given enough thought to everything that would be required of me. It was much more than just going to the sea to find Lib, to get to know him, to love even. It was out of my scope of experience. It was beyond my abilities.

I thought of the complicated mathematical problem David had given me. Carefully, I took it from my satchel, opened it, and began to ponder the process. I got no further than I had the first time or the many times I had looked at it since. Even Shad's suggestion about the variable hadn't helped.

David had not offered his expertise even when I had asked for it.

At the risk of looking ridiculous and pathetic, I ran to catch up with Lib.

He looked down at me. He didn't smile. Without a word I pushed the paper at him.

"I can't figure it out," I said and took a deep breath. "I need your help."

He looked at the paper and then slowly reached out to take it. "You could have no possible application for this," he said in the distracted way he had when his mind was puzzling over something.

Not one you can see, I thought. But as I watched him solve the problem, I knew the reason David had given it to me.

"I would very much like to solve it," I told him. "I have been working on it for quite some time."

"Did you ask my father?"

"He wouldn't help me."

He pulled his eyes from the paper to look at me.

I reached out to touch the paper with my finger. "But he has taught you to solve this." I knew it even as I said it.

"He taught me this long ago. Perhaps you are not ready for the solution."

"Then why would he give me the problem?"

He surprised me with a laugh and his great smile. "He is not all knowing, Miriam."

"I am beginning to think he is much more knowing than either of us realize."

He looked at me for a moment and then told me the answer and passed the paper back.

"Thank you," I sighed, not quite able to hide my disappointment.

Lib's straightened. "You're welcome." His tone was sarcastic, something I had not heard much in him.

I touched his arm. "I meant…I guess what I wanted were the tools to solve it myself."

"Oh."

"I don't need the solution so much as I need the opportunity to find it. I didn't ask you for the right thing."

"Oh."

I looked at my sandals and smoothed my hair behind my ear, even though it was already securely tucked back. "And I think I wanted to spend the time together and learn to trust your instruction."

"Oh," he said again. He reached for the paper, but I brushed his hand away.

I slipped the paper carefully back into my satchel. "I'm sorry. I shouldn't have presumed upon your time. It was selfish of me."

I turned to scan for Beth and Esther so I could walk with them, but Lib grasped my arm before I could leave him.

"I didn't know, Miriam," he said. "I didn't know that."

I softened immediately, the hurt draining out of my heart. He was just as confused as I was.

We had choices to make. God had brought us together, and we had to choose to either accept it or reject it. And then we had to choose to accept or reject each other.

At mid-morning we met up with two more travelers. I recognized Darius, Keturah's youngest brother. A dark-haired girl accompanied him. Darius introduced her as Ava. It was clear they had an affection for each other, and it was even clearer that Lib had some kind of prior acquaintance with her.

He greeted her, and I watched his head dip as he listened to her speak. He smiled. She laughed. Her dark, exotic beauty gave me the same feeling Adreana's had, and I did not like the turmoil in my heart or the thoughts in my head.

I knew I had to pray. It was the only way to make jealous thoughts go away. When we stopped for a meal, I told Esther I was going into the woods and set off through the trees until I had found a private place. I just looked around for a moment, taking in the beauty of the world around me and trying to see the bigger picture.

Lord, how can I do this thing?

I closed my eyes and dropped gently to my knees. I folded my hands and waited for the answer. Though I had been stubborn in thinking I was smart enough to develop a relationship with Lib on my own, I knew God would answer my questions.

Unlike David, who had cagily intended for me to seek the answers from Lib.

My mind caught on that thought. Was I to ask Lib for help with the relationship? Even as I thought it, I knew it was right. God had trust in him to lead us down the right path. I did not know Lib very well, but I knew that God did.

I heard someone coming through the trees, quickly and not bothering to be quiet. I jumped to my feet, but not before Lib caught sight of me.

"Miriam!"

"What is it?"

"We need to get on our way."

"Alright," I said, following him immediately. "But I thought we would rest a while."

"We've sighted Lamanites. Enos wants to get into the city as soon as possible—to warn them and to seek protection."

I laughed. "Can a few Lamanites threaten a city?"

"There are more than a few, and it is not the only city that needs to hear the warning call."

"You're serious," I said.

He gave me a grim look and took me by the elbow. I liked that he touched me, but like that? So much for developing a workable relationship. I doubted there would be time for it now.

"How did you know where to find me?"

"I will always know where to find you, Miriam."

The men were breaking camp when we came through the trees. I went to where Esther and Beth were distributing warm corn cakes from a cook fire that was already going cold. Beth passed me an extra share, and I knew it was meant for Lib. I turned to find him at my back, and I passed him one.

Though the rest of our journey was rushed, there didn't seem to be any threat. I hadn't seen what the others had—a Lamanite army, they said, west of the city—but I had no reason to doubt their word, so I treated it as if I did have personal knowledge of the dangers in the wilderness.

The city of Antionum was different from the other cities I had been to. There were many houses and we traveled for a long time through the streets before we finally came to a stop at

Seth's, the man Lib and his friends all called Captain.

I liked him immediately upon meeting him. I wished he had looked at me longer when he greeted me so I could look into his face. Despite the chilling tattoos that surrounded his eyes, his eyes behind them were warm and welcoming. Everyone liked him, and it was not hard to see why they had thought nothing of traveling for days to see him happy at his wedding.

His bride, Noel, was warm and genuine. She had the very distinctive look of the Zoramite people, though it was more in her clothing than in her facial features or characteristics. She and Seth made a lovely pair, and although I had felt twinges of jealousy at recent weddings I had attended, it was not hard to wish these two well.

A great many people attended the wedding celebration, though not many were of Seth's family. Only his immediate family had made the journey from Melek.

"Do you know Seth's brother?" I asked Lib.

"He doesn't have a brother."

I gestured to the man near Seth. He was tall, definitely Zoramite, lean-muscled, with rich colored skin and dark, proud eyes.

"Only friends. Eli's family disowned him when he joined the Church of God. Seth's family took him in."

"As close as brothers then. In all the ways that matter."

Lib shrugged, that way he had with the tilt of his head. "I wouldn't know." When I raised a brow, he clarified, "I haven't any brothers."

"You have Ethanim."

He nodded slowly.

He wasn't going to reply, so I took a deep breath, looked around, and changed the subject. "This is a very lovely celebration."

"Aye."

I giggled. "You remind me of Hagoth when you say that."

He was quiet for a moment, watching the crowd as I was. "About Hagoth," he said, but he didn't look at me. "When you were sick, you told me you didn't love him."

"I remember."

"I wondered if you did."

"I don't remember much," I offered. "Don't want to."

"It was very grave. We were all very worried about you."

"You slept on the beach near the hut."

He raised a brow.

"I saw you. All of you."

"We did. It was easier to care for you from the beach."

"But...Adreana...I thought..."

"She did not do all the work. There was lifting and—"

"Oh." I knew what caring for an unconscious invalid involved, and though I knew Adreana and the other women had done the parts a man shouldn't, we were both embarrassed. I had a hazy recollection of being lifted gently into hard arms while the linens of the bed were replaced with clean ones, and I knew Adreana had not been the one to lift me.

"Though she would have done it all if she could have managed it." He paused. "So." He cleared his throat. "Were you lying? When you said you did not love Hagoth?"

"No, I was not lying," I said indignantly. "Being affected with the Fever is not an excuse to tell falsehoods."

"But that night on the beach, the night before you left…"

I heard the question in his voice. He wanted to know about the kiss. I was just annoyed enough at being called a liar not to tell him anything, but I didn't want it between us, and I knew being stubborn and acting offended would stay between us.

"Hagoth kissed me. You saw it." I sighed. "And I was feeling very alone and hurt, so I let him."

"And why did you let me?"

That wasn't the question I expected him to ask.

"Nevermind," he said quickly when I hesitated too long.

Oh, it was so embarrassing and confusing. It wasn't supposed to be like this, was it? My parents were not embarrassed with each other. And though Noah and Sarah's relationship was somewhat strained at present, they were not embarrassed around each other. Even Jed and Ashti, bright-eyed and hope-filled awaiting their marriage, were not embarrassed to show their feelings to each other.

"Why do you think I let you?"

I thought he might come off with a glib "obedience" or "duty" or "responsibility," but he sighed and said, "I surprised you." Then he snorted. "Scared you is more like it." He was so self-deprecating that I laughed, and the subject easily changed to something else.

We were walking back through the city after the ceremony, nearly back to Seth's, before Lib said, "Miriam, you never answered my question."

I knew which question he referred to. "No, I did not," I agreed.

"That smile looks ominously sly."

Actually, it was nervous—not sly at all. But I feigned a bravado I did not feel. "You must solve for many other variables before you can solve for that particular one."

His laugh was not nervous. It was hearty and pleased.

"I think I see."

We were standing near my tent and Lib glanced over my shoulder to the road beyond. "Goodnight. Esther will be along in a few moments."

I followed the direction of his glance and saw Enos escorting Esther toward us.

"Thank you for your company today."

He gave me a strange look, glanced over my shoulder again, but laid a quick hand on my shoulder and turned to go.

We did not stay as many days as planned after the wedding celebration. We did not even stay one full day. The men felt it necessary to warn the nearby cities of the large Lamanite presence, as the Zoramite army in Antionum—for purposes of their own—apparently did not plan to do so. It was politics, and I did not understand it. What I did understand was that we were not staying.

We were on the road before midmorning, and Lib was actually walking by my side—silently, but still, he was there.

And why shouldn't he be? He had invited me on this trip, and the reason he gave was that he wanted to get to know me better. I kept telling myself that. But I also kept telling myself that he was doing it out of duty.

And what was so wrong with a man who was receptive to the promptings of the Holy Spirit? What was so wrong with a man who was obedient unto them?

But I was as quiet as he was—lost in my burdensome thoughts. So when he spoke into the silence, he instantly had my attention.

"I envy Seth."

"You envy him his new wife?"

He squinted into the distance and then pulled out his water skin. He offered it to me, but I shook my head. I didn't need a drink yet. I could wait.

"I envy his faith."

"But you have faith in God. Do not tell me you don't. I will not believe you for a second."

"No, his faith in himself. His self-confidence, I guess."

I thought about this, about what he really meant by it, about why he had said it to me.

"I have been envious at weddings lately, too. Such as when I heard of Esther's betrothal to Enos."

"You? That surprises me?"

I glanced at him, then down to the ground before us. "It is a new and unwelcome feeling."

"Jealously is a destructive emotion."

"I'm beginning to realize that first hand."

"It eats you up."

"Indeed. How did you get over it?"

He shot me a glance. "What do you mean?"

"I mean Gideon," I said gently.

He sucked in air. "Well…"

"Have you gotten over it?"

"I tell myself I have."

"But when you saw him that day, on the lane to the barley fields—it came back, didn't it?"

A shrug. "Not in the way you think, probably. Miriam, must we constantly rehash this? It is many years in my past. You are the one with the much more recent relationship."

"I told you, Hagoth is just a friend."

"I didn't mean Hagoth."

"Shad? But that wasn't…I mean, it didn't go…"

"But you wanted it to."

"No. I mean yes. There was a time I did, yes."

"But not now?"

"Of course not."

"Miriam."

"Oh, all right!" I was starting to see what his father meant when he said Lib could be exasperating. "Sometimes, even now, I think how easy it would be with Shad. We are friends, and we love each other, in our way. And I think if I do not marry for love, at least I might marry with friendship."

"You think I won't love you."

I gave him what I intended to be a withering look.

"You seem quite expert on what I am feeling. But here's the thing—you do not even know what is in your own heart. You can have no idea what is in mine."

His words were gentle but I winced because he was right.

CHAPTER 14

When the men split up to go warn the nearby cities of the Lamanite army inside the southern border, Lib offered to take city of Jershon, just beyond the mountain pass.

"I'll head north from there. I need to return to the ship anyway."

I didn't dare look at him. My face would clearly show how betrayed I felt. I thought he planned to stay in Orihah, to court me a little—even though I knew he preferred that beautiful ship to me and the boring domestic life I represented.

I was surprised when he asked, "Miriam, do you want to come with me?" He was checking over our gear. "Or would you prefer to continue on with the other women?"

Could he really not know? "I would like to go with you."

He gave a slight nod, no other indication that he heard me, got up and walked over to Enos and the others.

He was taking me with him. Would he take me back to the little village on the sea?

Did he want me to go with him, or was inviting me just what he felt he should do?

Did I even want to go to the sea with him?

I looked for the answer in my heart. I thought back to my prayer in the woods, to the moments I had begun to feel that I should go to the sea and find Lib. How determined I had been! I would have done it without Father's permission. I really would have. I would have traveled without Ethanim's escort and protection. I thought of running through the gorge—away from the village and from Noah. Impetuous as it had been, it had been my decision to leave.

I knelt and checked to make sure the bindings on the packs were secured, to finish what Lib had started, and when Lib returned I stood and said, "Give me your water skin. I will fill it."

By the time I returned, most of the boys were gone. Lib stood in the same place, waiting patiently with his pack on, mine in his hand, and a very strange look on his face. He took the water skin and thanked me quietly.

I looked around. "I'm sorry," I said. "I didn't realize everyone was moving out so soon."

"Don't be. Jershon is close, and I fear it may be a hopeless cause anyway."

"What do you mean, hopeless?"

He lifted my pack for me to slip into. Then he ran his big hand through his hair and sighed. "The way it looked, an attack is imminent."

"How can you know that?"

"How can you know how to cook a bird or soothe a fussy baby?" he returned.

Experience, he meant.

"Is that an insult?"

His eyes shot to mine, and I felt very foolish for letting the impertinent question slip out.

"Why would I want to insult you?"

I blushed fiercely.

"And what would be insulting about that? I admire the way you were with Corianton."

He was dead serious, and I was such a little fool.

"I think I am the one who has insulted you," I said quietly.

"You have," he said bluntly. "If you think I value women so little that an honest description of your domestic skill is an attempt to demean you! And to what end? I want to marry you, not alienate and belittle you!"

"I'm—"

"Don't say you're sorry. Is it perhaps you, Miriam, who holds womanhood in such low esteem?"

Did he expect an answer?

"Answer me."

He didn't raise his voice, but the low growl of it was much more menacing.

I cleared my throat. "I can see I have touched on a nerve. Of course I don't regret my womanhood. I cherish it, as I can see you do. It was an impetuous thing to say. That's all. I may know when a bird is cooked, and you may know when an army means to attack, but I fear neither of us knows much about how to form a partnership with each other—as neither of us has done it before."

"Then what do you call what you had with Shad."

Clear, biting jealousy.

We were tromping through a thick patch of forest, and Lib's long legs were making it hard for me to keep up.

"Lib, slow down," I panted.

He glanced at me and then made a deliberate effort to slow down, but his posture and huge sigh let me know he was exasperated with me.

I laughed a little, and when he looked at me with a questioning brow, I said, "This is what it is like to have a little sister."

He almost smiled. "Guess I didn't miss out on much." It was another moment before he said, "I don't think of you like a sister, Miriam."

He had drawn to a stop, and I stopped, too, and turned to him.

He reached over and nudged my hand with one long finger, lifting it toward him before slipping his around it and holding it. "Miriam. I can be oblivious of some things, but I am not blind or unfeeling. I know you see me as more than a distasteful duty."

I could feel my face getting hot. I knew my pale skin showed every bit of it.

He shook his head. "Don't be embarrassed." His words were gentle and I knew he meant them. "It is good. It is natural. It is desirable and expected that we should be attracted to each other. Don't be embarrassed for it."

I offered him a small smile.

"I keep telling you I am on board with this whole idea. I think you are having trouble believing me." He took a step closer to me. "Don't let my inadequacies and your insecurities ruin what we already have." He bent and brushed a tender kiss over my lips. "It is there," he whispered against them. "Between us already." Another soft kiss. "Admit it." I felt his hands at my waist and then his arms encircle my back as he pulled me close to him. "Accept it," he said. "Put your trust in me. I am worthy of it."

I had long awaited a confirmation of that first prompting on the hill. I had wanted the fire in my heart to return, to reassure me I had made the right choice, taken the right action, but I had never again felt anything more than a peace so gentle I could easily deny it.

But there in the long beautiful moments we held each other and kissed in the trees, I felt the sudden and unmistakable spirit of God come over me. It fell over both of us, confirming we had chosen the right thing. It applauded our obedience and rewarded us with the beginnings of love. It was so heavy in my chest and throat and behind my eyes that when Lib stopped kissing me and rested his forehead on mine, tears were sliding slowly down my cheeks.

"I will not hurt you," Lib murmured.

I had thought I would be the one to be strong for him.

"Trusting me will not mean you are helpless or incapable."

He had backed up a bit, but his hands were still at my waist.

I took a breath. Another.

Lib looked down and tried to hide a smile.

"Okay," I said. "I will trust you." But could just saying it make it so? I thought I already trusted him. But the truth was I hadn't given much thought to the need for trust.

"Do you trust me?" I asked as we made to leave.

"I am working on it," he said after a slight pause. "But the fault is my own, not yours."

He had said something like that before—that the fault was his own.

"You take much guilt upon yourself," I pointed out.

He moved a limb out of the way. "That is where it belongs."

We were looking over Jershon in a matter of hours. The main city was tucked neatly up against the northern side of the mountains we had just traversed. Many outlying villages and farms were clustered outside the city walls. The buildings housed people who would have to find shelter inside the city should the Lamanites invade here.

I glanced over my shoulder at the pass, envisioned an army spilling through it, and knew that even if Jershon was not an intended target, the army would most likely march through the valley.

Lib caught the direction of my gaze. He took my hand and gave it a warm squeeze.

"It won't take long to deliver the message. Then we will be gone."

"But what about the people here?"

"They can leave if they want to."

If they got the word in time, and if they had the means to

travel. But where would they go?

"It is mostly men of the army here, and their families." He looked at me. "They are trained for battle."

"Have their wives been trained for battle? And their young ones?" I asked. It sounded bitter, but Lib and I both knew it was fear.

"They have been instructed to retreat to the inside of the city walls. The gates will be closed and they will be safe. Their fields might be trampled when they return, but they will be safe."

"Will the men go out to fight?"

"Possibly. It depends on a lot of things. From the looks of it, they have sufficient men to defend this city."

"But do they have sufficient men to safeguard the inner holdings?"

Lib shook his head. "No. Not against the army we saw."

Despite the trepidation I felt, the walk down the mountainside was otherwise pleasant and quite pretty. The air was a little too warm, but there was a breeze that lifted the hair off my neck and ruffled Lib's.

We passed farms and homes where Lib just raised a friendly hand in greeting to their occupants.

"How can you smile at them when you know what will happen?"

He gave me an odd look and a quick shake of the head.

When we approached the gate, I could see there was a military guard much like the one I had seen in Melek and Ammonihah, perhaps a little larger.

To my surprise, Lib walked through without a word to anyone.

I followed him through and when we were alone in the city, I said, "I thought we were here to warn the people."

He gave me another odd look. "We are not here to cause mass panic. We will take the news to the appropriate official, and these people will be warned through the proper channels when preparations have been made for their safety." He paused for a few steps. "Besides, they wouldn't even believe us—strangers yelling through the streets."

Oh. "I understand."

"It's nice that you didn't know that. I went to war so you wouldn't have to. So you wouldn't have to know things like that, I mean."

I knew he was speaking in general terms, but his comment caused me to blush.

"What was it? I mean, what really made you decide to go?"

"Join Helaman's army?"

"Mm-hmm."

He frowned. "There wasn't another choice."

"Your friends pressured you?"

"Not exactly."

"You didn't want them to think you were scared?"

"No. Not exactly."

I bit my lip, and he laughed.

"A messenger came from Melek to announce that boys were preparing to go. He asked us to consider going too."

"I remember." He had come to our church meeting.

"Do you?"

I nodded.

"He gave all the reasons and specifics, but it didn't take more than the first word for me to know I was going."

"I think I understand. It is why I went to the sea. In one moment, I had never thought of going to the sea, and in the next moment, I was going there and nobody could stop me."

Lib smiled. He didn't laugh or grin. He just smiled at me, and it made the sunlight more like sunlight, and then the breeze kicked up and ruffled his hair again.

"That was it exactly," he said.

I could see we were entering the busy part of the city. The large buildings reached into the sky.

"Did you have trouble leaving your father?"

He took a breath. "Of course. He doesn't have anyone else."

"You worried that he would miss you."

"Of course."

"Did you not worry that you might miss him?"

"Miriam."

"Don't reprimand me like I am a little child for asking a perfectly understandable question."

He stopped and put his hands on his hips. He stared at me for a moment, clearly trying to think of a way to deflect my question without answering it. It would be so simple. A yes or a no. Suddenly he looked beyond my shoulder and then glanced about us. "Wait here," he said.

He touched my arm as he left. A deliberate placation. But when he moved past me, I turned and followed him up the steps of the grand building behind us, what was clearly a building of government.

He ducked inside the building, but I didn't follow him any further. He would find who he needed to find. I turned slowly and surveyed the city from this vantage point.

It wasn't a market day, but there were plenty of people in the plaza. Children. Mothers. Men of business. Friends. They were walking together. Laughing. Living.

I stayed there, quiet and alone until Lib came back.

"Miriam."

How long had I been melting inside when he said my name?

I turned to him and offered him a sad smile.

"We'll stay here tonight and be on our way in the morning."

"Here?"

"Don't be so alarmed. We will be safe enough here."

We began to descend the steps.

"Tomorrow we will continue north and catch the road west."

I wanted to ask him if it was safe to travel, but he clearly thought it was. Or else he wanted me to believe it to be.

As we walked among the people, he kept his voice low. "The governor already knows of the army. The spies here have reported its presence for many months now. It takes a long time to amass an army like that, and it takes a long time to move it. A few more days here..."

"Won't make much of a difference," I finished for him.

"Probably not. They could be sitting on the border for a year or longer."

"Perhaps they wait for our men to come out and engage them in battle."

"Perhaps. Or their presence might be nothing more than a psychological tactic."

"What do you mean?"

"They might only want to scare our leaders into doing what they wish."

"Like what?"

"I don't know. Handing over the ancient relics or yielding their power to Lamanite rule."

"They wouldn't do that!"

"Of course not. Here we are. The governor said this is the best inn."

I eyed the building over its low courtyard wall as we approached it. "Have you enough money for an inn?"

Lib didn't reply for a moment. He was searching in his satchel for something, but suddenly he bent to my ear and said, "I can take care of you, Miriam."

"Alright," I said quickly, wishing I hadn't said anything about the money.

The inn consisted of a courtyard, two large sleeping areas into which men and women were separated from each other, and a smallish grand hall where everyone was fed twice a day.

I met Lib in the hall as he had instructed me when it was time for the evening meal. His hair was damp from a bath in the well water and his face was shaven. I wanted to reach up and touch his face, but I was aware of all the people around us. I glanced around at them and grabbed fistfuls of my skirts.

While I waited for Lib to retrieve our food from the proprietress, I took a vellum and charcoal stick from my satchel and set about preparing a mathematical complication on it.

It was a game of sorts that David and I played, and when Lib got back and seemed to see nothing out of the ordinary when I slid the vellum across the table toward him, I knew David had played the games with him as well.

He looked it over after he passed me a dish of wild rice.

"At least give me a challenge," he said, maybe a little smugly.

I snatched my vellum back and wrote another problem.

He only snorted when he looked at it and then scooped some food into his mouth.

Annoyed, sort of, I took the vellum back and wrote the impossible problem David had last given me.

"Perhaps you would tell me how to solve this," I ventured.

He glanced at the problem and stilled, and when he looked up at me there was tenderness in his face.

He held out his hand for the charcoal, which I placed in it, and he proceeded to patiently explain every step including a new theorem I did not yet know.

"Well, it is no wonder I couldn't solve this. I do not know what your father was thinking when he gave it to me."

"You're better with geometry," Lib said, taking his food up again.

He could have been saying I was bad at what he had just taught me, but he wasn't. I was coming to know that Lib always meant just what he said.

CHAPTER 15

We didn't stay in the city long, just overnight. Lib said there was little to fear, but when morning came, he was as ready as I was to put Jershon behind us.

We climbed up through the hills and for several hours before Lib stopped for a break.

"You're wheezing," he said as he scanned the terrain below us.

Even as I took a breath to deny it, my lungs felt tight. Ever since I had been ill with the Fever, breathing had not come as easily for me as it once had. I hated admitting it, but I tired more easily, too.

"Now that we are out of that valley, we can slow down some."

"I thought you said it was safe."

"It is. Probably." He stopped scanning and looked at me. "But I don't like the idea of you being there."

"I'm not so fond of the idea of you in battle either."

He didn't seem to know what to say to that.

"Here," I said and passed him my water skin. "You've not taken enough."

"Yes I have."

I held the container out until he took it. But he only held it absently in his hand as he said, "It's another few hours to Zarahemla, then we will catch the road north."

"Drink first," I said.

"You sound like my father," he said, but he lifted the skin to his lips and drank.

"A compliment, I think."

He nearly smiled as he retied the skin and passed it back.

"Have you caught your breath?"

I nodded. "Yes." But when I took a deep breath to test it, I winced at the sting in my lungs and my breath audibly caught.

"That fever," I said, irritated but also worried.

"I know," he replied quietly. "We'll take it slower now. And it's downhill."

We started down the slope, and I said, "I hope you do not have to carry me down the entire mountain again."

Lib didn't say anything. When I glanced over at him, he was rubbing his elbow. Then he rubbed the back of his neck and the side of his nose before he grasped the straps of his pack, obviously to keep from fidgeting, and I wondered what had transpired on that trip down the mountain. Had it embarrassed him to hold me so close? Or had my faint scared him nigh unto death?

We bypassed Zarahemla on the south, and when I

expressed interest in seeing the capital city, he paused for a moment but only shook his head. "I don't feel good about stopping."

I wondered why I didn't have the feeling for myself, but he had asked me to trust him, and I would. So by late afternoon, Zarahemla was in the distance behind us. I hadn't been there since I was a child, and passing so close without stopping was a disappointment. But we stopped to make camp early, and I knew it was for me. I was struggling to get deep enough breaths, so I was grateful when we stopped, and I didn't complain about passing Zarahemla.

"Do you get like this a lot?" We had been traveling in quiet for so long that Lib's voice was very stark.

"My breathing, you mean?"

"Yes."

He set down his own gear and stepped to me to assist me with mine. His hands lingered on my shoulders.

I shook my head. "Only on too much exertion." I paused. "It gets better though."

"This journey was too much. Too soon."

"I'm fine." I knew the fast hike through the mountains had been too much. Trying to keep up with him was too much. But I turned and smiled. "Just this last little bit. I just need to rest. I'll feel better after some sleep."

He nodded slowly. "I'm going to find water. There's a spring in that direction, but it's a bit of a walk from the road."

We were already quite a distance off the road, tucked into the trees. We might have camped closer to the water. He had made camp here in consideration of me and my weakness, and he was making the walk for water in consideration of me also.

"Can you start a fire while I'm gone?"

"Sure." I gathered some kindling to get it started, and Lib walked away. I was blowing on the embers when Lib dropped an armful of dry wood near me. Then he was gone again.

When the fire was going, I sat back on my heels and watched it for a moment. I fed it just one more branch, one Lib had broken. I only needed this fire for cooking. The evening air would cool when darkness fell, but it wouldn't be cold enough to warrant the fire until just before dawn.

I stood and crossed the camp to retrieve a shallow bowl from my pack. I could mix up some flour for a flat bread while I waited. But then it occurred to me that Lib had the water skins, and I had no liquid to mix into the flour. I turned abruptly to put the bowl back, but my foot caught on a stone. I teetered, nearly fell into the fire, but somehow managed to land on the rocks I had placed around it.

I took a moment to catch my breath. The hem of my skirt was lying in the coals. My hands were embedded with sharp pebbles. My ankle hurt, and my arm was assuredly broken.

My hand lay dangerously close to the flames, but when I tried to move it, I sucked in a sharp breath of air. Gradually, I moved my unbroken arm and rescued my hand from the fire.

I was sitting up but tears were streaming down my face when at last Lib walked into view. As he drew closer, he seemed to sense something was wrong and broke into a jog through the trees.

It only took him a moment to assess what was wrong. My tear-streaked face, my damaged sarong, my elevated foot, and my arm lying limply in my lap.

"What happened?" he asked rather grimly as he took a knee beside me. His voice was so soft it was nearly a murmur, but I couldn't detect any tenderness in it. He swiftly ran his hands over me, checking for more breaks. When he assured himself there were none, he put his attention to my arm, prodding it gently with his fingers.

Glancing up at me then back at my arm, he said, "It appears to be a clean break. I can set this." He looked up at me again, silently asking for permission.

I felt fat tears fall anew, but I turned my head and nodded.

He was quick. His hands were cold from the stream, and with one sure movement, it was done. I tried not to cry out, but I couldn't help it.

"Don't move it," he instructed. I turned to look at him and his fingers came up to brush away my tears. His eyes had softened, and I realized he did feel tenderness toward me. He was good at pushing it aside when necessary. It must have been very hard for him to set my arm, hurting me as he'd had to. He kissed my temple, and got to his feet. He moved off into the trees again, and I knew he was looking for a good splint.

While he was tramping through the forest around us I thought about the warmth I had seen in his green eyes. It made me feel like crying even more.

He came back with an armful of supplies, but before he even set them down, he reached out and whisked the hem of my sarong from the coals. It had caught on fire, and I had not even noticed. He quickly tapped out the flame and set about administering to me. First he set some water to heat that I could see was for willow tea. Then he cut the branches into splints for my arm and sanded down the edges on a rough stone I had used to ring the fire.

"I don't think willow will be very effective," I said as I watched him work.

He held up another plant I was not familiar with. "This will help."

I did not ask him where he had learned about the plant. I already knew, and it nearly turned my disappointment into depression.

"It seems you are always taking care of me," I said.

"It is my duty and privilege," he replied.

I looked down at my arm. He was very proficient at making the splint.

"It saddens me that you have so much knowledge of healing."

He quirked a brow, only half listening, his full attention on what he was doing.

"That you have had so much experience with it, I mean."

"I know," he said quietly.

When my arm was set, Lib took up the dish I had meant for mixing flat bread. He placed the strange plant inside it and, taking a flame from the cook fire with a small twig, he set the plant aflame.

Holding the bowl before me with one hand and smoothing

my hair with the other, he said, "Lean forward and breathe in the smoke. That's how it works best."

The plant burned itself out in the bowl. I began to feel sleepy, and Lib made up my bedroll.

I watched him make a simple meal.

"I don't like you seeing me hurt," I said.

"I don't like seeing you hurt either." He paused. "I shouldn't have left you here alone."

"You couldn't have prevented it. I was clumsy."

"You were overtired and short of breath. I knew that. It made you dizzy. I should have been here."

I watched him carefully for the next minutes. He worked efficiently. He was competent with the food and the preparations, but the meal was very simple. I watched his face, his eyes, his attention to what he was doing.

"You had to go. We needed the water, and despite this injury, I am not incapable of preparing a cook fire and a meal."

He shot me a look.

"At least I wasn't," I amended. "But you don't have to take care of me."

He shot me another look, but didn't say anything.

"And you are not to blame for what happened."

"I thought you were sleepy."

"Lib."

"Miriam."

I fell into a restless sleep with a smile on my lips but an ache in my heart.

In the morning, Lib made no move to break camp. He

leaned back on a large stone near the fire with his legs stretched out before him. When I stirred, he looked over at me.

"How are you feeling?"

"Surprisingly good."

"I administered some more medicine while you slept."

I guessed that meant he had burned the plant near me.

"Were you up all night?"

"No."

"Where are we?"

"We're half a day west of Zarahemla."

"When will we turn north?"

"A few hours after we get going."

"And when will we get going?"

"You're full of questions today."

"I can travel," I insisted.

He gave me a long look, his lips nearly curving into a smile. He glanced at my ankle, but there had been no swelling and it was fine.

"I can."

"With your injury, I think we should just head for home. But is it so hard to believe I might not want to return you to your parents right away?"

I frowned. Return home? "Well, no, I guess not."

"Besides, I don't want to be on the road right now. Too many travelers."

"Wouldn't it be safer if we were in a larger group?"

He shook his head. "I saw some people near the spring. Not the kind of people I want to travel with."

"Oh."

"We'll wait a day for them to go on."

"A day!"

"Your parents don't expect you home for another sennight at least."

"No, but…"

"You said you trusted me." Was that a smile? A little gleam of amusement in his eyes? "These are very unsavory people we're talking about."

I sighed and then yawned. "Of course I trust you."

"Besides, you need the rest. We went entirely too fast through the hills."

So I slept, and when the night came, I was no longer tired. I lay awake staring at the starlit sky through the canopy of trees above us, my arm throbbing. There were so many bright stars. It was impossible to look at them and not think of God. I thought of what He wanted for me, of what I wanted for myself. Were they the same thing? Had a made a mistake in going to the sea? Could I be happy with Lib? Could I care for him like I could have cared for Shad? Could I care for him more?

I turned my head to look at him across the cold fire pit. He slept on his stomach and his slow, deep breaths told me he was sleeping soundly. I already did care for him. I knew it, and maybe it was just that I had been friends with Shad for so long, but I felt a twinge of disloyalty.

I looked up again when the breeze rustled the leaves overhead, but the leaves were not moving—not enough to cause the sound I had heard.

After a moment of straining to hear in the darkness, I heard the rustle again, and it was accompanied by low murmuring.

Silently, I reached out for Lib's arm. The only indication that he had awaken was the sudden cessation of his breathing. I squeezed his arm so he would know what had wakened him. The rustling came again in that moment, closer than before and very clearly not the breeze.

I hadn't known if it would be worse to lie there in the darkness wondering what was out there and hoping it did not come upon us or to get up and risk our own sounds of movement carrying on the still air. But Lib answered that when he got silently to his feet. I could barely see his silhouette above me, but he found my hand and pulled me to my feet. Leaving the bedrolls and our supplies, taking only ourselves, we stole away into the night away from our camp.

But we didn't go far. We couldn't have been more than ten steps away, but we were upright and alert. Lib eased my back up against a thick tree and he stood before me, completely covering me with his own body. He didn't say anything. Didn't offer any instructions. There was no need. In a moment I felt him drape something over my head, and I knew he was hiding my blond hair from any glint of the sparse moonlight. Then we were both still, listening as the steps came closer and closer to our camp.

Whoever was walking through the forest in the dead of night did not find our camp. The racket they made eventually drifted away to our west and finally faded away into the stillness of the forest.

"They've gone to the spring," Lib said into my ear.

I assumed most people who traveled this road would know of the water sources. "Just be careful," I breathed.

"Hmm?" I felt his question come from within his chest beneath where my cheek lay.

"You want to follow."

He hesitated.

"I will stay right here."

"I just want to see who they are," he admitted.

I didn't know what he could discern in this darkness, but I suspected he had been through many dark nights alone.

"Go quickly, then."

I felt him ease away from me. "You'll be okay for a few minutes?"

"Don't insult me."

He gave a single nod and moved to leave. "I'll give the call of the margay when I come back into camp."

"I know," I whispered, but he was already gone.

It was more than a few minutes wait. I had known it would be, and so had he. I slid my back down the tree until I was sitting on the forest floor and was still and silent as the night. Watching Lib disappear into the darkness should have unnerved me, but I was calm. I trusted in his ability to be silent, unseen, and safe as he put himself between me and potential danger, and I loved him all the more for it. It was the kind of man he was, the kind of boy he had been. Hadn't he done as much for his father?

The margay called and soon Lib stole back into camp. He straightened my bedroll and said softly, "Come back to bed. All is well."

"No one dangerous?"

"Not to us."

I wondered what he meant by that.

"Two men. Following the people I saw earlier near the spring."

I yawned. "More unsavory characters?"

"Lie down. You need more rest."

I did as he bid me, and I was just drifting off to sleep when I sensed him get up. When I dared to open my eyes, he was gone. Again, I might have been unnerved, alone in the night as I knew myself to be, but I wasn't—not unnerved, and not alone. Sleep overtook me, and I sensed dawn through my eyelids when I heard the shrill margay again.

My arm ached, but I sat up and tried to put my hair to rights while I waited to see Lib. When I didn't see him right away, I finally knelt and blew on the coals to get the fire going. I breathed in the smoke and began to cough.

The margay sounded again. I looked up. Lib was leading two people into our camp. One was a girl who, despite dark circles under her eyes and hollow cheeks, was quite beautiful. The other was Shad.

CHAPTER 16

I looked between Shad and Lib and back to the girl. Shad was not surprised to see me. Probably Lib had told him we were traveling together, but I was surprised to see him. What was he doing here an hour west of Zarahemla?

I broke into a grin. "Shad!" I rose, and he came to me. We embraced, and then he stepped back and paused.

"Who is your pretty companion?" I prompted.

He looked to the girl who was standing near Lib, arms folded, maybe trying to keep warm in the cool morning air, maybe just uncomfortable.

"I'm Olivia," she said before he could introduce her.

Her candor surprised me. Something about her, perhaps the look in her eyes, seemed wounded. I would not increase her wounds by acting jealous that she was with one of my dearest friends. The way Shad looked at her, I might have been jealous, but I looked at Lib, who was silently assessing the situation, and I couldn't be.

"I take it you have been traveling all night," I said, stepping closer to Olivia. "Sit here and rest. I will prepare some food."

Lib gave me a pleased nod. He bent to retrieve my empty water skin and, without a word, loped off through the trees in the direction of the spring.

"I should go with him," Shad said. "We're out of water too."

Was it apology in his tone?

"Of course you should," I told him. "Go on."

He glanced at Olivia but returned his gaze to me. I knew him well. We had spent our whole lives together. I had seen every expression on his face at one time or another, and in this one I saw a question. An exhortation.

Did he think I would be mean to this girl?

I waved him away and then turned to Olivia.

"I'm Miriam," I told her.

She smiled, a tired but genuine smile. "Yes. They told me."

I wondered what exactly they had told her. I wondered, too, what Shad thought when Lib told him we were traveling together.

I sighed. "You look tired."

Another weary smile. "We've been traveling since yesterday morning. We meant to camp, but no sooner had we gathered tinder for a fire than Shad caught sight of pursuers."

"Are you in some kind of trouble?"

Her only reply to that was to stare at me.

I met her stare for a moment. Finally, I gestured to my bedroll. "You need sleep more than you need food, I think. Be at rest. Neither Shad nor Lib will let any harm come to you." Of that I was very sure.

She lay down and curled onto her side, her gratefulness evident on her face. "Do you know Shad well, then?" she asked.

I bit my lip and tucked my hair back behind my ear. "Yes." How much did she need to know? "Shad has been courting me for several years now."

She nearly sat up. "Oh."

I reached over and placed a hand on her arm. "He withdrew his courtship."

She relaxed back down. "Ah. When he said he meant to take me to his mother's, I thought it meant he was unattached."

"As far as I know, he is. Except…"

"Except what?"

"Well, the reason he gave for withdrawing his courtship was that he meant to live in Zarahemla and take a job which required him to be free of attachment."

She yawned and her eyes closed. "How fortunate for me that I am not seeking an attachment. I'm withdrawing from an unwanted courtship myself."

Withdrawing? Was she running away?

"Have you known Shad long?" He hadn't been in the city long, but I was a little ashamed to wonder if this pretty girl had been part of the reason he had gone there.

"No," Olivia murmured, eyes still closed. "I ran away from my father's home, but I had nowhere to go. Shad found me two nights ago and offered his help. He gave me food and clean clothing and offered me shelter at his mother's house."

I watched her as she drifted off to sleep. The poor girl. Her dress did not even have to slip off her shoulder for me to see her arms had large healing bruises on them. I was sure Shad had seen them, too. I felt tears prick at my eyes when I thought of how blessed I had been to have him for a friend, to have known such a boy who would offer assistance to a girl he didn't know.

I couldn't help a sad smile as I let my eyes wander over Olivia's pretty face.

I heard the margay before the boys came back into camp. I had the corn flour prepared and when Lib passed me the water, I quickly mixed up a dough for corn cakes, easily done, even with the brace on one arm.

After a few moments of silence, I realized both men were watching me, but I kept my eyes on my work. "You should sleep, too, Shad. You were out all night."

"As was your Lib," he returned quietly.

The jealousy was not biting, but it was there.

I took several breaths and then looked up. Shad was sitting on his own bedroll and Lib had gone to his heels on the other side of the cook fire.

"Can we all agree that God has led us to the paths we are on?"

Lib looked into the fire, but Shad shrugged and said, "Sure."

"Then we've no need for resentment among us."

They glanced at each other, and they both nodded.

I flipped the hot cakes in the coals. "There is no need for guilt either. Shad, you've not wronged me, and Lib, you've not wronged Shad."

Lib's jaw tightened, but he said, "You're right, Miriam."

I took another breath and looked to Olivia. "I don't know what troubles she has, but we must see to them."

Shad gave me his grin, the one I loved. Then he cleared his throat and spoke. "I could use an extra set of eyes on the back trail." He looked to Lib for a moment and then back to me. "And Livi could use an extra pair of hands to prepare food. When I found her she was nigh unto starving, and she's not much of a cook on an open fire."

I smiled and held up my one good hand.

"How did you break it?" Shad asked, gesturing to my splinted arm.

Twisting my lips, I said, "I tripped over the fire. Lib set it."

He sucked a commiserating breath through his teeth.

I flipped a corn cake up onto a stone and smeared it with cooked beans.

"Looks like you don't need the extra hand though."

I shrugged. I could make corn cakes in my sleep. "Here. Eat your fill and then get some rest." I looked to Lib as I flipped out another cake. "You too."

He moved suddenly toward me. "I can get my own food," he offered.

"Nonsense. I am capable. And besides, you went for the water," I pointed out.

He scoffed, but I didn't realize we were staring into each other's eyes until Shad cleared his throat. Lib broke the gaze to turn to Shad. I looked at the ground and felt my face heat.

"Wake us when you are ready to leave," I heard Shad say.

"How long will she need?" Lib asked.

There was a pause. A heavy sigh. "She slept deeply before we left, but I've no idea how much sleep she's had since she left her home." Shad paused again. "Or before she left, for that matter. I think she's probably had a lot of sleepless nights."

"I think she's running away," I put in.

Lib scoffed rudely.

"Staying at home is not a safe option for her just now," Shad said. "That's all I know."

I thought perhaps Shad knew more about Olivia than he was saying. But that was his business. His and Olivia's.

Lib got to his feet. "Come on, Miriam. I'll walk you into the woods."

I looked around at what had turned into a beautiful morning. The sky beyond the forest cover was brilliant blue. Birds chirped and called. Did I really need a guard?

I stood too. I didn't need a guard as much as Lib needed to be one for me. Service and love, I reminded myself, were so inseparable. And I wanted him to love me.

"Can you manage with just one hand?" he asked.

I knew my face flamed. "I don't need your help," I told him. "But my arm hurts tremendously. Could you find some more of that plant? The one you burn."

"Sure." His voice was both gentle and grateful.

I heard him tramping around through the undergrowth, and when we were on our way back to camp, he held several herbs in his hand.

"I hate that you're hurt," he said.

"Life is not meant to be without pain."

"I wonder you can say that when your arm is throbbing."

I laughed. "Have you ever broken anything?"

He paused. "No."

"Truly? And were you not hurt in the war?"

Another long pause. "No. Not really."

"Then you were lucky."

"It wasn't luck."

"Blessed then."

"Perhaps."

"Of course you were."

He reached out and took ahold of my hand. "It is no good thing, Miriam, when another gets hurt in your stead."

Ever so pleased that he had reached out to me, I smiled down at my sandals, though I sensed something like guilt in his tone.

"But what of the Savior, Lib? What of the Messiah who will come? He is to suffer the pains of all in our stead. Is that not a good thing?"

I studied his profile while he considered.

Finally, he shook his head. "I don't deserve you."

I laughed again. "It has little to do with being deserving. Sometimes the Lord's blessings are not rewards for what we have done, but tools for what is to come."

He laughed a little too. "Are you saying my future will consist of something for which I must have a wife like you?"

I shrugged, somehow uncomfortable with the idea and with the idea that my future might require someone like him—a sailor, an adventurer, an engineer. "And all the knowledge and experience you have thus far gained, I dare say."

He didn't say any more until we were back in camp, slipping quietly around the two sleeping persons there.

"You might as well get some more rest too," Lib suggested. "We've still a long walk ahead of us."

"I might. Now, lay back." I sat on his bedroll and patted my lap, and he hesitantly rested his blond head there. While he drifted into sleep, I smoothed down his hair at his brow and thought about this boy who felt guilt and jealousy, resentment and compassion, and a need to protect and comfort.

But he had no one to comfort him. I didn't think he knew how to let himself be comforted. He had nearly said no just now when I offered him my lap. He might have been more comfortable without it. In a moment I would spread Olivia's bedroll and lie down near her. But Lib needed to know I cared about his comfort—that I cared about him.

I thought he was sleeping when he said, "Miriam, why are you friends with my father?"

Surprised, I blurted, "I already told you, and I am not a liar."

He was silent and still.

I glanced toward Shad and lowered my voice. "I know I didn't tell you why I had come to the sea. I was nervous. My faith was small. But it is not my intention to deceive you at every turn. I hope that is not the kind of girl I have shown myself to be."

He turned onto his side and moved his hand to rest lightly on my leg. "It's not," he said. "It's only, well, before, during the war, Keturah told Zeke she loved him all the time, and then she chose Gid in the end."

My hand stilled in his hair, but I made my fingers move again.

"Zeke?"

"Yeah."

"Did she never tell you she loved you?"

He snorted. "We weren't like that."

"I thought you wanted to be."

I detected a small shrug. "For a time."

"I thought...I'm sorry, I guess I thought she had chosen Gid over you."

"No," he said quietly. "She would never have chosen me."

A huge lump formed in my throat. I wanted him to look at me, but I was also glad he didn't.

"Did she...did she tell Gideon she loved him?"

"Not that I ever heard."

"So her decision surprised you."

He scoffed. "You could say that." He paused, taking the time to roll onto his back again and open his eyes into mine. "I thought she would choose duty over infatuation. That's the kind of girl I thought she was. The kind who would chose duty, loyalty, family."

I looked at him, the face that was becoming beloved to me, and took a deep, silent breath. "But it wasn't infatuation, was it?"

He slowly shook his head.

"She made it look like it was."

His eyes fell closed, and he nodded. "She was duplicitous. And I know..." He shut his eyes tighter. "I know she did no wrong, and I know you are not her, but I see the looks you share with Shad—"

"In the ten minutes he was awake?"

"I see them," he went on as if I hadn't spoken. "Things you share that I've no part in, no knowledge of, looks I cannot read, and I..." He shook his head vigorously, eyes still shut tight, and he didn't say any more.

I prayed every night that I would know how to help Lib. He acted as if he was fine, but I had known from the moment I first looked into his eyes on the ship that there was an ache inside him, and I had learned it was an ache he guarded fiercely.

"You told yourself she would not choose Gid because he was a passing infatuation, that she would honor her family's wishes and choose Zeke instead."

I was guessing, but he didn't say anything to the contrary, just opened his eyes into mine, so I went on.

"You told yourself she would not choose you because she *could* not. Not without dishonoring her family."

Still no reply.

I looked down at him. I tried to keep pity from my eyes. "I do not think she was duplicitous. I think she struggled greatly within her heart, and I think you deceived yourself."

The vulnerability left his eyes. I watched as he put the shields up over it.

I wanted to apologize for speaking the truth, but I would not.

"Now you wish I was a liar," I whispered despite his deepening scowl.

He rolled away from me. "Get some rest, Miriam."

I nearly said I was sorry then, but something told me I would only make things worse. I stared at his back for a moment more, and then did as he suggested.

When I woke, Olivia was still sleeping next to me, but Shad was sitting up near the fire, and Lib was gone.

"Hey," I said quietly. I glanced at the sun. It was early afternoon. "Are you ready to eat again?"

Shad gave his head a slight shake.

"Where's Lib?"

He straightened. "He's scouting around. I think the extra company disturbs him. He doesn't seem to like people much."

I thought we had agreed not to be jealous. I frowned at him. He just raised a brow.

"Shad," I said as I got up to sit near him. When I sat, shoulder to shoulder with him, he turned to look at me.

"Yeah, Miriam?" he asked quietly.

Our faces were close, closer than I had planned, but there was something nice about being near him, something that felt like coming down the road toward home or laughing with good friends. I didn't move away. "Why did you really go to Zarahemla?"

He looked at me for a moment. "I already told you that, and I am not a liar," he said, almost smirking. Then he looked away.

It didn't surprise me that he had heard.

"Shad."

He looked up into the trees, avoiding my eyes.

"Would you have stayed?" I swallowed hard. "If I had asked

you to, would you have stayed in Orihah?"

I watched his face, and I knew. He had wanted me to ask him to stay. He had wanted me to follow him. Beg him. Want him.

He had gone to Zarahemla to get away from me. The girl he loved. The girl who did not ask him to stay.

He looked back down at me. It was all there in his eyes. Longing. Hurt. Readiness to forgive, to take me back, to forget I ever went to the sea.

But I had gone to the sea.

"Shad," I said again, but I didn't know what I meant by saying it. Stop? I'm sorry? I'm *not* sorry?

Before his name was off my lips, his lips were there and he was kissing me so differently than he ever had. Flashes of our previous kisses went through my mind. For a moment I was confused, and then I felt the desperation in this new kiss, and I wasn't confused anymore. "Shad," I said against his lips, and this time I knew what I meant by it. I put my hand on his chest and gently pushed until he moved away—already stung, already knowing what I meant.

"You have been my dearest friend," I started.

He jumped to his feet. "Don't bother, Miriam. It was just a dumb impulse."

It hadn't been an impulse. It had been calculated. But for what? To win my love? To get me back? His posture said he didn't want me back.

"Shad."

"Stop saying my name."

"Sha—" I wanted to laugh. And cry. What was this?

I saw Shad glance at something behind me, and I knew Lib had come silently into camp. He cringed slightly and rubbed the back of his neck, a gesture I had seen many times. He was sorry, but not for what he'd done. He was sorry he'd gotten caught.

I could only imagine the look on Lib's face from the look Shad shared with him.

I heaved a sigh and blew my hair out of my face. Then I tucked my hair behind my ear and wished I could stop doing that. I knew it told things about my feelings that both men would see.

Kneeling quickly next to my pack, I began to rummage through it to plan the midday meal. There were four of us now, and my supplies would deplete faster. I was about to ask Shad what he had for supplies when a limp rabbit dropped near my knee. I stared at it for a moment, and then looked up at Lib with the best smile I could muster.

He started to speak, but went to his heels next to me. "Shad's going to take you back to Orihah." He rubbed the side of his nose. "If I leave from here I can take the north pass." He looked at the rabbit. Cleared his throat. "It will save me an entire day."

My lip started to tremble. He had intended to forego traveling to the sea and take me home instead. "I understand," I said. But I didn't.

I would never understand Lib.

I didn't dare look at Shad, so I took out my knife and made quick work of the poor rabbit.

CHAPTER 17

Lib was gone before Olivia woke up.

Shad stomped around camp, impatient, but not with us. He was impatient with himself. I couldn't tell if he felt guilt over Lib leaving or anger that he had been there at all. No one mentioned Lib or his absence until we had started toward Orihah and Olivia said, "So I guess that other guy is gone."

"Lib," I told her.

"He's gone," Shad affirmed sedately. "He figured since we were heading to the same place, we might as well take Miriam with us."

"Where'd he go?" She didn't sound very interested, but I didn't blame her for trying to make conversation in the midst of our awkward silence and Lib's blatant absence.

"He lives by the sea," I said. "Up north."

"A dangerous road, I've heard."

"A little."

Shad snorted.

Olivia turned to him. "It's not?"

He smoothed a hand over his chest and hooked a thumb into the strap of his satchel. Such a simple thing, an action I had never really taken note of before, though I knew he did it often. I looked away from him—to the ground in front of me, to the trees, to the hills in the distance, the hills that marked home. But still I knew what his face would look like, how his mouth would turn up as he talked, not quite a smile—just a hint that maybe he knew something you did not.

"It can be dangerous," he allowed.

"Have you traveled north then?" Olivia asked him.

No.

"Me? No. All of my brothers have."

"How many brothers do you have?"

Three.

"I have three, and they are all older, stronger, and wiser." He chuckled, but I heard both the admiration and the envy in it. I always had. It had always been there.

"But surely there is not one so handsome as you."

"Then you've met them already." He laughed. "Ugly dogs, all of them."

Were they flirting? Blech.

"Isn't that right, Miriam?"

"Hmm? Oh, um, yes that's right."

Olivia giggled, and our eyes met. She didn't seem to be too keen on men just now, so why was she flirting with Shad? She hadn't said, but I assumed she was betrothed to some man she hated, but a betrothal was an agreement that should be honored.

"You don't sound very sure," Olivia said to me, but her eyes flicked away.

"It's true," I admitted with a roll of mine. "Shad is the most handsome of them by far," I informed her. "And the friendliest. The others are not very personable. Except Jashon, maybe."

Olivia turned laughing eyes to Shad. "Ugly and unfriendly. How very unfortunate."

He grinned. "Only for their wives."

They both laughed, and I nearly did too—Shad could always make me laugh.

We walked until the sun went down, taking care to stay clear of the main road. I didn't know who was following Olivia, but Shad seemed to think they had lost them by doubling back at the stream. If they had eluded the men who were searching for Olivia, it was because Lib had traveled through the night to warn Shad.

I was trying to spread my bedroll with my unbroken hand, and I sat up on my heels with a sudden realization.

Lib had known Shad was traveling ahead of us. He had known! I had begun to tire, so he left me to prepare a meal while he walked on to the stream. And then he had come back, splinted my arm, and said there were unsavory people at the stream.

"Here," came a warm voice near my shoulder. It was nearly too dark to see, but I felt Shad's closeness as he reached around me to finish with the bedroll. I glanced up to see the dim outline of Olivia already snug in hers.

"She's asleep," he said quietly. "Long day. Not used to travel."

Any girl from my town would never have let someone with a broken arm make the meal, as I had, and prepare her own bedroll. Not that I hadn't managed. Any girl from my town could also make a meal with one hand.

"She's like a princess," I whispered when Shad's ear was near my mouth.

"Yeah."

"I hope you don't get your heart set on her."

"That would be hard to do since it's already set."

"I thought it was set on Zarahemla and your secret job."

"It is. You didn't think I meant you, did you?"

I could hear a smile in his voice.

"Of course not. I only meant you would be her servant for life if you marry her."

"Miriam, she's in trouble. I'm taking her home to my mother's care. That's all. Then I'm going back to my work."

"Well, I'm just saying you were flirting mighty hard…"

He sat back on his heels and didn't reply.

"Never tell me that was to make me jealous," I teased.

"Would it?"

"Of course." I turned to him. "I haven't forgotten all we were to each other. Have you?"

He shook his head.

We sat for several minutes in silence. My heart was in my throat. There could be nothing more than friendship between us, and I wasn't going to say there could just to make this awkwardness go away. Finally, I sighed and reached for my bedroll. I was as tired as Olivia and wanted sleep.

"I shouldn't have kissed you." His voice was plaintive and resigned, sweet and familiar.

There were so many things I could say.

Not like that.

The time was wrong.

If only you had kissed me like that a year ago, I could have melted into it.

I could never begrudge you a kiss.

Begrudge? My heart squeezed. Ending it was right.

I made myself crawl into my bedroll and turn away from him. "I'm sorry," I said. "For it all."

I heard him sigh and go to his own bedroll.

In the morning, my arm was aching and I was sad and lonely even though Shad and Olivia kept up a pleasant conversation as we ate a small morning meal and broke camp.

When at last we neared Orihah, tucked back into the forest, safe and familiar and comfortable, I was both relieved and nervous. I couldn't show up at home with Shad, and I doubted very much he would consider letting me walk there alone. I could already see he was veering north so when we came into the settlement, we would come to my home first.

Still, I said, "You don't have to walk me all the way home. It's not really on your way."

He glanced back at me. "You know I do."

"You don't. I know my way from here."

"Lib entrusted you into my care—"

My soft snort cut him off.

After a few moments, he slowed and said, "Let's take a

break." When Olivia gladly leaned against a fallen log and rubbed at a sore foot, Shad turned to me. "Can I talk to you?"

He didn't wait for an answer, and I didn't give one, just followed him a short distance out of Olivia's hearing range.

"I said I was sorry. Lib is the one who walked away," he said as he turned to me.

There was one thing I had to know. I grabbed his wrist. "Did you do it on purpose? Kiss me in front of him?" I looked into his eyes. "Did you know he was there?"

He jerked his head up slightly.

Yes.

"I've known you a long time," he said.

"What's that supposed to mean?"

"I know how you think and act and are."

I dropped his wrist.

He reached up and tucked my hair behind my ear. "You think so logically about so many things that it's hard to set it aside when you need to."

I bit my lip. "It has been many months now that I've been nothing but a confused mess," I said quietly. I looked up at him, feeling almost shy. Definitely unsure. "Perhaps I made the wrong choice."

I was referring to him and to choosing Lib instead, but he ignored it and put his hands on his hips.

"You just watched him walk away." His voice gentled. "You let him walk away. You didn't even say anything. So excuse me if I'm not convinced." His words cut, but his eyes were soft and he touched my hair again.

"Convinced of what?"

He stared at me for a moment and then shook his head. "And I don't see how he could be convinced either."

He nodded toward Olivia and we set off again for Orihah.

But I had gone to Ammonihah in specific search of Lib. He knew that. Was once not enough? Was one act of insane foolishness not enough for him? And how come everyone could see it wasn't but me?

"Will you be alright here?" Shad asked when we could find no one at the main house on the farm.

"I will." I glanced at the sky. "You had better get moving. You've still a bit of a walk yet."

Shad glanced at the sky too, but Olivia didn't bother. She was still looking around the farm with a wrinkled nose.

"They've just gone to town, maybe to my aunt's," I continued, glancing around at the empty house and quiet farm.

He hesitated, nodded, and then took Olivia and went home.

I set my travel pack down and looked around. I had put confidence into my voice when I talked to Shad, but I wasn't sure where my family was. It was time to start the evening meal, and yet no one was around. If my mother planned to be gone at meal time, she always left one of the older girls in charge. Sasha should be here, or Sarah, or even Ashti. I might have taken a rest and put my feet up, but that wasn't my way, so I got some vegetables from the food store and began to prepare them. I stopped when I reached for the second squash, though, and looked around again. Nobody was here. Deciding to fix enough for myself, and only a little extra, I stood to stretch my back.

At last I heard a noise. It was Corianton, I was sure of it. I breathed a sigh of relief as I ate, and when I was done, I walked across the farm to Noah's hut.

"Hello?" I called. I could smell food cooking and hear soft murmurs inside.

In a moment, Sarah came out with Corianton on her hip.

"Well aren't you big?" I grinned at the boy.

"You've scarcely been gone a sennight." Sarah placed a kiss on her baby's head.

"And he's grown a half a cubit while I was gone." I took him from her arms. "He must be eating better."

"He is," she agreed. "Thanks to Keturah. Will you stay to eat?"

"No. I've eaten. But, do you know where my family is?"

"Oh." She cast a glance across the farm. "Your father received a missive from the elders of the church. Just after you left, it must have been. They've asked him to help reestablish the Church of God in places where war has taken so many of its leaders. He means to be gone for quite some time. Your mother and the younger girls are staying in town with Daniel's family."

I nodded. They spent a great deal of time at my uncle's house anyway, and the move would feel natural to the girls.

"To be honest, I suspect he has known about his departure for some time," I said. "I think it's the reason he has been giving more of the responsibility of the farm to Noah and Jed."

"I agree," she said. "Sasha is here." Was that a hesitation in her voice? "She is working the farm with Noah. They should be home soon."

I gave her a grateful smile. "Can I hold Corianton while you finish your preparations?"

"I'd say you were an angel if you did. He won't let us put him down lately. But what has happened to your arm?"

I made a face. "I tripped. It's broken. But I can hold Corianton on my lap."

I played with Noah's son and mostly just sang him funny songs until Noah and Sasha appeared on the path.

Sasha hugged me and we laughed as she began telling me all the things that had happened since I left.

Sasha was the closest sister to me in age, just two years younger than me, and I was closer to her than any of my other siblings. But lately, I had been gone, and Sasha had been spending more time in town. There was that boy, Giddoni, who lived near our uncle, and I knew that was the reason she had been spending so much time there.

I passed Corianton off to his father and helped Sarah serve the simple meal.

"Have you been getting closer to your Giddoni?" I asked Sasha quietly when everyone had settled to eat. I cast a quick glance at Noah and Sarah. "Do you think he is considering a betrothal?"

She wrinkled her nose and shook her head.

I bit my lip. "Well, perhaps he only needs more time."

She gave a one shouldered shrug and took another bite. "Noah's going to talk to him, but I don't think it's what he wants."

Noah was going to talk to him? That was news.

"Well, why not?" I asked, feeling indignant for her. "You are a beautiful, capable, caring, and intelligent girl! He should feel lucky to have your attentions."

"I don't think…" Sasha tucked her hair behind her ear, something that made me feel very tender toward her, and I suppressed a smile. "I don't think he respects me very much, Miriam."

"But, why?"

She put her plate down and turned more fully to me. She started to speak, but then stopped and turned away again. I saw her exchange a look with Noah.

"Why? What is it?" I asked, looking between them.

Sasha sighed deeply and said, "I think I have given him too much of my attention."

I frowned.

"You might as well tell her," Noah said. He paused, raking a hand through is curly hair. "You should tell her," he repeated.

I looked to Sarah, who had her eyes on Corianton, and then back to Sasha.

"I've…" She twisted her lips and said no more, seeming to choke on the rest.

The room got very quiet. After a moment, Noah said, "Sasha is with child."

The words were scary, but I thought I had maybe known it before. I could act shocked, but I wasn't. I could be judgmental and hurtful, but those reactions would not help anyone, least of all Sasha, who needed help the most.

I took Sasha's hand in mine and squeezed, and then I looked

to Noah. "And you plan to talk to Giddoni?" I looked back to my little sister. "You haven't told Mother and Father?"

"You know how Mother is," she said.

I did. I thought of how she had warned me so often that Lib would not respect me if I chased after him to the sea. I wondered if Sasha had received the same warnings. Obviously, neither of us had heeded them. But with Mother, it never seemed like she was as concerned with righteousness, respectability, or even our safety as she was concerned with appearances. Maybe I was judging her harshly because I could not see things from a mother's perspective, but that was the feeling she always gave me when she delivered her lectures. Still, she would have to be told.

"What will you do? Will you marry Giddoni?"

"I do not think he wants to marry me." She put her plate down and ran both hands through her hair, blond like mine, but long and straight.

"And if he cannot be made to?" I looked to Noah.

He sighed and clasped his hands in front of him, his meal finished and his dish set aside. "We're still thinking on that. I've only known for a couple of days."

The rest of the evening was rather gloomy, though everyone did try to be pleasant. When at last it was time for Sasha and me to return to the other house, the moon was low on the horizon but gave enough light to see the path.

"I'll walk you over," Noah said, and neither of us argued, though I was dying to talk to Sasha alone.

"You never said how your trip with Lib was," Sasha prodded

as we made our way across the large fields where Father grew feed for the birds.

I had told them the basic details of the trip, how I had broken my arm, and about the Lamanite army on the southern border. Sarah had wanted details of the wedding, and Noah had seemed interested in everything I could tell him about his friends. I thought he missed them and maybe envied that I had gotten to go while his responsibilities had kept him at home.

"He was really nice to me," I said slowly, wondering exactly how much I wanted to tell her and how much I wanted to say in front of Noah.

"And did he say more about a betrothal?" Sasha asked.

Noah didn't say anything, but I knew he was listening intently.

"He speaks of it as if it is already done."

"What's that supposed to mean?" Noah broke in.

I laughed, tightly because my heart was breaking for Sasha. "Only that he has made up his mind."

Noah harrumphed. "Then it is done. He won't change his mind."

"Not like Shad."

"Sasha! I told you. Shad felt called a different way, and so did I."

"That's not what I heard."

"What did you hear?"

She hesitated a moment. "Nothing."

I might have let it go, but Noah said, "If you know something of importance, you should say it, Sasha."

"Well, I just heard that Shad left because he…he…he wanted more than you would give him."

I gasped. "And what is that supposed to mean?" I demanded.

"Yeah, what is that supposed to mean?" Noah's voice was demanding, too, but he wasn't looking at Sasha.

"You tell me," Sasha said.

"I don't know what you're talking about. I gave him friendship and love."

"Maybe he wanted more than friendship."

It was so hard to bite back the words that wanted to fly from my mouth. They were petty and hurtful. I was never cruel, but Sasha knew how to rile me up. She also knew that I had not been in love with Shad the way he had wanted, and had in fact taken me to task over it more than once.

We were entering the courtyard of the house. Noah and I stopped, but Sasha said a weary goodnight and went inside. After a moment, light came from the far window when she lit a lamp.

Noah and I stood in silence until he said, "She's worried." He rubbed the back of his neck. "And jealous."

"I know," I sighed. "So you don't think Giddoni will marry her?"

He gave me a look and rolled his eyes away. We all knew he wouldn't. He was not exactly an upright individual.

"I don't even want him to marry her. Or, rather, I don't want her to settle for him. I'll raise the baby myself before I let her do that."

I felt the same way.

"She would be better off without him. She has such a low opinion of herself, but she can find someone better." Noah's observation surprised me.

"But not with a baby." I said what we were both thinking.

He paused for a long moment. "I know someone, a couple, who could take the baby. Raise it."

The hesitation in his voice made me frown. It might be for the best, but it made me sick to think of it.

"Friends," he said. "We could still see the baby."

I yawned. It had been such a long day, and there were months still to worry about the baby. "A lot to think about. When will Father be back?"

"Not soon enough to deal with this. I'm going to town to talk to Daniel tomorrow."

I nodded, and I was glad it was his job and not mine. "Goodnight, brother," I said and started for the house.

"Miriam."

I turned back. "Hmm?"

"You should go after Lib."

I pondered that for a moment—Noah's change of heart, and the fact that he knew, he *knew*, Lib was not in Orihah, and probably knew Lib had not brought me here at all.

"I'm tired of travel."

"Do not let him think for one moment that you don't love him. He will be hard enough to convince."

"Who says I love him?"

"If you don't, then you'd better fall fast." Noah's eyes were bright. He didn't want me to hurt his friend.

"He clearly doesn't want me with him. I've been foolish."

"You've been following where the Spirit leads."

I really didn't know if I believed in that anymore. If I had been following the Spirit, wouldn't this all have been easy? Wouldn't Lib be by my side now?

I glanced at the moon and returned for a moment to the deck of the ship, the little beach hut, the high hills overlooking the narrow neck of land.

And then are ye in this strait and narrow path which leads to eternal life.

I wondered if the Spirit would lead me astray, if it would lead me into the dark blue sea on either side of that narrow strip of land.

"Maybe I need more than friendship too," I said toward the sky. Then I turned to Noah. "Goodnight."

CHAPTER 18

The next day I went to visit my mother and sisters, but I didn't stay long. I wanted some time to be alone with my thoughts. If I was honest with myself, what Lib had done, leaving me in the wilderness with Shad and Olivia, had really hurt me.

I should have been angry with Shad, I thought, as I walked to my hill, a place I hadn't been in a while, not since I had been there with Lib. But as I knelt in the thick, humid grass and looked around at this place I hoped would bring me comfort, I knew it wasn't Shad's fault. His action had only shown a weakness between Lib and me that was already there.

I wasn't so sure I had made any right decisions since that first day on the hill.

Crazy. Foolish. That was more like it. Hadn't I always admired Lib? Hadn't I watched him when he would come around with Noah and their other friends? Hadn't I pretended that we were friends more than once? Hadn't that been where the whole crazy idea to go to the sea and find him had come from?

But I had been so sure. On the hill. In my heart.

Why did those sure feelings never come again? I sighed and admitted I had felt a constant peace, but I had expected a repeated burning in my chest like the first time.

I laughed. The only burning I had in my chest was residual pain from the Fever.

And then I closed my eyes against tears as images from my illness, my time in Hagoth's little hut, passed through my mind.

Lib with his big hand on my head. Lib conferring with the woman from town, and then stooping to lift me and hold me against his chest while the woman changed my bed linens. Lib ducking through the doorway and bidding Adreana to go and rest with the others on the beach. Opening my eyes again and again to Lib's still form on a stool beside my cot, the confounded man leaning back against the wall, arms folded, eyes tired but watchful. He had stayed by my side when I was in misery.

Lib was in a kind of misery now.

He would not admit it, but he was lonely. He wanted to deeply connect with someone. He was estranged from his father in a way I could not understand, though I had spent many sleepless nights trying. His best friend had found a girl and was moving forward with his own life, setting their friendship aside. He felt guilt for surviving the war when so many others had perished. He felt betrayed by a girl he had served and loved for years. He no longer trusted his own judgment.

Could I not sit watch while he fought his own kind of illness?

I had been so very selfish.

So. I pushed out a short puff of air. I would sit and wait and watch.

"If an old man can climb this hill, might he keep you company a while?"

I looked down the hill at the sound of David's voice and saw him nearly to the top of the steep incline, steady on the footholds and moving surely. I laughed.

"You are not old, David."

He chuckled and went to his heels beside me, the action reminding me very much of his son. He plucked a long blade of grass and began to worry it between his fingers, an unusual thing for him to do. At least, I had never seen him do it. He was always confident and sure and strong, and this looked like nervousness.

After a moment, he said, "I thought you would come by with Lib."

So, Lib had returned to Orihah without me, and he had seen everyone of importance—Noah, his father, probably Ethanim, maybe Keturah. He had not taken the straighter and shorter path to Ammonihah. I looked down at my hands and wove my fingers together. I thought I knew why David had sought me out here.

"Noah came by this morning while you were visiting at Daniel's."

My heart began to pound, and I caught my breath.

"I saw you come into town. He was nearly on your heels."

I hadn't known that.

He paused and attempted to clear his throat. "He thinks there is something amiss in your relationship with Lib, and I agree."

"I..." What was there to say? "There is."

My words fell into a silence. A hawk called in the air high above us, but other than that, there was nothing to distract me from what he was saying. Would he not allow a betrothal? Was he right to refuse it?

"Miriam, you are very good for him."

"No." I shook my head. "I have no idea how to help him."

He steepled his fingers in front of him and brought them to his lips. Then, suddenly, he sat on the grass next to me. "Consider," he said as he put a hesitant hand on my shoulder. "Consider that he may not need your help, that he is capable of dealing with his own trials."

"I believe he is, David. This is not a new idea you put forth. But if I can be of no help, of what use am I to him?"

He smiled kindly at me. "He needs a wife, Miriam. A mother to his children. Someone he can devote himself to."

"He seems to prefer being on his own." Words I had been trying to admit to myself.

"He doesn't."

"Well then he prefers to not be with me," I muttered. "How can I be anything to him when he," I waved my hand toward the north, "keeps wandering off?"

"I know my son. He needs you to follow."

I looked to the sky and laughed with a touch of bitterness. "He doesn't want me to."

"He does."

I looked down at the gentleness in his voice.

"He doesn't know how to ask it of you."

"I figured that," I muttered again.

"But, Miriam." He held my gaze. "Should he have to ask?"

"Ugh! You are both infuriating. I do not know how to be what he needs, let alone what he wants. I do not know how to help him with this thing he does not need help with!"

"He does not need a savior. He already has one."

I frowned and looked away, and after a moment, he sighed deeply, kissed me on the top of my head, and offered to walk me home.

I gave him a weak smile, shook my head, and waved him away. Perhaps he was only offering companionship, but his protection was not needed. We were close to the wilderness where small bands of Lamanites lived and hunted, and I had seen them there before. But they had never bothered me, and if they did now, David would not be of much use against them. I would have to protect him.

What must it feel like for him, because of his oath to God, to be unable to protect me?

To be unable to protect his son.

To have to give him over to the Redeemer, to trust his most precious gift to the Savior's care.

If David could do it, I could too. Being Lib's wife was entirely different than being his savior. Fixing his meals was entirely different from fixing all his problems.

I decided I might go after him when and if it felt like the

right time, but it was many weeks before I felt like I could leave my family. The girls were still settling in, so I helped there as much as I could. They had felt my absence long enough. And with Father gone, Noah and Jed had almost more work than they could handle on the farm, let alone merchandising the goods, much of which Sasha and I took care of.

No more was said of Sasha's child, and I never saw her making preparations for it. No sewing tiny clothing or weaving tiny blankets. If I brought up the need for these things, she changed the subject. If I persisted, she got up silently and left.

Until one day as she was walking away, I said, "I'm worried about you. It takes months to prepare all the needful things."

She stopped and turned her head. "I am not this baby's mother," she said.

"What do you mean? I can see..." I could clearly see the slight outline of the baby at her midsection. "What is that supposed to mean?"

"I am not keeping it, Miriam. I will not be its mother." She turned again and walked slowly away.

Not keeping it? Was she giving it away? But that was ridiculous. There were many helping hands here on the farm and in our family. Giddoni had not agreed to marry her, but Noah would not disown her as was sometimes done. Neither she nor the baby would want for anything.

As soon as I could, I went to find Noah among the birds. He and Jed were hauling water, and as soon as he saw me he set his bucket down and told Jed he would be back.

"What is it? What's wrong?" he asked as he came over.

"Did you know? Did you know she's going to give away her baby?"

"Of course." He glanced over his shoulder at Jed and let out a breath. "I suggested it."

"Yes, but I didn't know she had decided. You didn't pressure her, did you?"

"Miriam, I think you know me better than that."

"You're right." I folded my arms over my chest and looked down at my sandals.

"It's her choice."

"You're right," I said again.

"And I believe she has made it prayerfully."

"But it is a child of our blood!"

His lips tightened, and he didn't say anything for a time. Finally, he said, "You ought to be more worried about your own children."

I nearly choked on a laugh. "I haven't got any children."

"Exactly."

I grinned, but he returned it with a sober look that made the grin fall from my face.

"Listen. I've already sent a missive to my friend near Melek. In Keturah's village. I'm taking Sasha there in a fortnight, and she will stay until she births the child."

"But that is still months away!"

"It is my hope that Jarom's wife will allow Sasha to stay in their home. I am waiting for word back. Leah is the midwife there. She is a good midwife. Sasha will be well and return when she is unburdened."

"You want her to be away before her condition becomes obvious."

"It's for her own comfort, Miriam. She has to go on living here when this is all over. It's the best option I can see."

"Father would—"

"Father would have already forced a marriage between them."

"No." I shook my head. He would not be so unfeeling and unwise.

"Mother would have made him."

I grimaced. He had a point.

"And you would deceive the next boy who comes to court her?" Because there would be others.

"Of course not." Noah studied me for a moment and glanced over his shoulder again at Jed who had returned to the stream. He crossed him arms. "I have been turning it over in my mind for some time, spoken to Daniel. I wanted to have a firm answer before I discussed it with anyone else." He took a deep breath and looked over my head. "I've approached Jared. He is of marrying age and stands in need of a wife."

"Jared? But he could have anyone of his choosing."

"Then why has he not chosen yet? Do you think Sasha unworthy of him?"

"No, of course I don't. But have you told him all?"

"I have. It must be divulged."

I sighed. "Maybe it's a blessing that Father isn't here."

He looked at his sandals and scratched the back of his head, surprised and maybe a little embarrassed. "Thanks."

"You are fair and good, Brother."

"Let us hope Jared is fair and good too," Noah said.

Jed was back and pouring the final bucket into the shallow pond for the animals. It would have been so much easier to dig a small ditch from the stream, but distorting its natural course was forbidden by the government. This was a good thing for us. Being at this end of the town, we wouldn't have any water if everyone else diverted it. Still, someone had to haul the water.

Noah cleared his throat and went on. "If I could convince Jared to come to Melek with us, I could walk on to Ammonihah with you."

My lips twisted as I tried to prevent a smile. I saw what he was doing. I looked around pointedly. "You can't leave Jed with all this work. You can't even spare Sasha and me."

"I've friends who could help for a time."

I shook my head. "I have reached out to Lib more than once, and it keeps fading into nothing. I won't go." I glanced at Jed, who stood watching us now, wiping the back of his forearm over his sweat-streaked brow.

"The farm is not your concern, Miriam." He reached out and tugged on a lock of my hair. "And you're only using it as an excuse anyway."

"Any work here is for Sarah and Ashti," Jed added as he approached us. Obviously, he had overheard us.

"Are you saying I don't belong at my own home?"

Jed's eyes widened in surprise, and he looked to Noah who rubbed the side of his nose. Was he hiding a smile?

"Of course not!" Jed insisted. "I only meant your duty is to your own husband and his endeavors now."

He had a point, but still I argued. "I haven't got a husband."

"As good as."

I rolled my eyes.

Jed glanced between Noah and me. "Noah says it is as good as done."

"But it is *not* done."

Jed leaned toward me. "So get it done."

I sighed. As clearly as I could, I reminded them, "He left. He doesn't want me."

But I thought of his kisses in the woods, and I couldn't meet either of their eyes.

"I admit, it took me some time to reconcile to the idea of you and Lib. But there are not many men I would rather have for a brother."

"Certainly not Giddoni," Jed said on a laugh.

Noah actually barked out a laugh too, and I tried to stifle a giggle.

Noah removed his headband, rubbed a hand through his hair, and allowed. "Giddoni is young yet, and he has not had the benefit of the gospel as we have."

Jed scoffed. "You're too generous."

"Enough of this," I said. "Let us not talk of Giddoni unless it is helpful."

"He's an immature scoundrel, and I can't speak civilly of him." Jed nodded his head over his shoulder. "So I'm going to go."

I nodded to them both and turned to leave too.

Noah reached out to touch my arm.

When I looked back at him, he said, "At least come to Melek with us."

"Alright. For Sasha."

The fortnight passed quickly, and before I knew it I was packing my travel pack for the trip to Melek. It was a journey of only half a day, but I intended to stay for a time with Sasha, perhaps for the whole time.

"Are you scared?" I asked her as I watched her pack her own things.

She looked up at me and brushed her hair from her face. "No." She looked back down. "It is right and good, and I have a feeling of peace."

I nodded. The only sounds were the rustle of garments and provisions as we slipped them into the bags, the scuffle of our feet on the floor.

At last her bag was full and she laid her hands on the closed flap. She smoothed it down absently. "Noah says Jared is coming with us," she said softly into the silence.

My pack was done too. "Do you know why?" I asked her.

Her only answer was to blush. I went to her and enfolded her into my arms. I held her tightly and she returned the embrace.

Jared had been told all, and he had agreed to accompany Sasha on the trip. He was to make up his mind before Noah returned home.

"It is a very good idea," I said into her hair. "He could make you happy."

I felt the slight shake of her head. "It is a poor prospect for him."

"He wouldn't have agreed to come if he thought so."

"Maybe," she allowed after a moment.

I squeezed her more tightly and then let go. "I'm off to David's," I said.

She laughed, and I could see there were tears in her eyes. "I don't know what that man will eat without you here."

I smiled as I picked up the dish I had prepared. "Perhaps he will wise up and get a wife."

I prepared to go, but Sasha stopped me. "Do you think…" She bit her lip. "Do you think he would take me for a wife?"

I paused, frowned. "David?"

She picked at a thread on her dress. "He is very handsome."

And intelligent and gifted, older and stable, and still in love with a woman who had passed on from this earth. None of the things Sasha would find attractive in a man.

"That is not the only thing to base an affection on," I said.

"I know that!" she said defensively.

"Have you expressed this to Noah?"

She shook her head. "I was hoping you would."

I looked at my sister. Young, alone, with child, very lonely and nothing of the happiness she used to have in her. I thought of how pleased Noah had been with himself for thinking of Jared. I thought of what a nice looking couple Jared and Sasha would make. And I tried to picture her with my friend, David. He was *my* friend, not hers.

"I will try," I told her, and then I left.

CHAPTER 19

Sasha and I were ready and waiting outside near the cold cook fire when Noah came in from the morning's work. Jared was already with him. He greeted us both with a nod and, belatedly, a quick hand on the shoulder. He was uncomfortable, clearly, but with good reason. We all had our reasons for being uncomfortable.

We had an early midday meal and set out toward Melek. Sasha and I walked together a few paces behind the men, but after a time, they fell back and walked with us.

It was strange to think of Jared with Sasha because he had spent many nights talking and laughing with Shad and me and our friends. Sasha wasn't much younger than me, but somehow I had never included her in my friendships, and watching her now, seeing how unsure she was around a fine and good young man, I felt suddenly very guilty for not having included her.

Could I have eased her way down a different path simply by including her in my stronger circle of friends? Friends that included upright boys with strict moral standards? Perhaps, like Lib, she did not need me to be her savior. But something in that thought did not ring true, either. What was a family for if not to lift one another up?

Gradually through the afternoon, Jared engaged Sasha in conversation and they moved a few paces ahead of us for a little more privacy. It afforded Noah and me privacy as well.

"Do you still think that could work?" I asked Noah in a low voice, gesturing ahead of us. The two certainly looked good together, but I couldn't stop thinking about the way Sasha seemed to feel about herself—sad and unworthy—and about how she had timidly asked me about David.

"Of course."

"You think he can come to respect her?"

"He said he could."

I glanced up at Jared. I hadn't known that. Still, I frowned and lowered my voice even more. "But could you? If Sarah had been carrying another man's child at your betrothal? Could you have forgiven her for that?"

"Miriam, of course. I love her. When you live with someone, you offer what you must of forgiveness or life would be too hard. And you hope that they offer the same in return."

We walked in silence for a moment until it was filled with a giggle from Sasha.

"They will fall in love," Noah assured me.

"Sasha has interest in another man."

"Giddoni is beneath her notice."

But what if he were to change? What if he were to make himself

240

into the kind of person a good girl deserved? I thought. But I didn't ask him these things. They were not likely to happen anyway, and certainly not soon enough.

"Not Giddoni," I said, and when he turned to me, I hesitated, but said, "David."

Noah stared at me blankly for a moment, then he burst out, "Lib—" He caught himself and lowered his voice to a harsh whisper. "Lib's father?"

I nodded.

Exasperated, he said, "See? This is why girls need the guidance of men."

I rolled my eyes.

"Silly girls," he amended.

"She is not silly," I said. "At least, not any longer. She is hurting and unsure of her worth."

"But what can she see in him?"

"There is much to be admired in a man like David," I said indignantly.

"For a girl like Sasha?"

I had to hide a small smile because it was nothing I hadn't thought myself.

"I think," I began slowly. "I think she feels that since David has had a child of his own, they would be on more even terms than she and Jared."

Noah frowned and jerked his head to get a curly blond lock of hair out of his eyes.

"I think she feels as if she would be robbing Jared of the pure wife he deserves."

"She can be pure again."

I sighed.

"Well, she can repent if that is her wish."

"I think it is very hard for us to see through her eyes, even if we are men and she is very, very silly."

Noah sighed too and then laughed. "Well, I will keep seeking the direction of the Spirit, and I will keep in mind what you have said. For now," he gestured ahead of us, "we will see where this goes."

We didn't go all the way into Melek, but stopped short of it in a very small village.

"Is this Keturah's village?" I asked, looking around at the small homes that were little more than huts. There was wood here in abundance—in fact, the place was almost overrun with trees. I didn't know why they didn't just build bigger homes.

As we walked down the center lane, Noah counted huts, and after a few, he gestured to one and said, "I think that one there is the Healer's—Ket's mother."

We nodded and walked on. It did not take but a few moments to reach a second lane that intersected the one we were on, and after that, a third. On the third lane, we turned north, and as we traveled, the lane narrowed to a path that meandered through the trees and a few scattered huts set back away from it. Finally, it opened into a small clearing of several larger and newer homes. Noah led us to one and called out as we approached.

"Jarom!"

There was no reply, so Noah approached the door and

knocked on the frame. Presently, a small woman opened the door. She was young, but perhaps not quite so young as me. Her hair was short and dark, but she had rosy cheeks and a pleasant smile that made her countenance light.

Before Noah could introduce himself, the woman's eyes fell on the rest of us, Sasha in particular, and her large, pretty eyes were suddenly bright with tears.

"Noah," she breathed.

Noah smiled at her and offered a brief nod. "Eve. We met at Keturah's wedding celebration, though I don't know if—"

"I remember," she said. "Set your things down and come in." She gestured to a place outside the door that was under an overhang of the roof. She clasped her hands together. "Come in!"

When we had done so, Noah introduced us all. Eve asked us how our journey was, listened when we responded, offered us a drink, and bade us to sit in the large main room of her home.

"I'm glad you caught me here. I spend a great deal of time at my mother-in-law's, and often I go to the tannery with Izz— with Jarom's sister, that is. Sometimes I am just across the way with Cana, tending my nephews."

She was talking fast, and I could see she was nervous.

"Then we are lucky, indeed." I smiled at her. "Where is your husband?"

"Oh! Jarom is at the tannery today." She glanced toward the cooking area. "He won't be home for a while yet."

"Can you give me directions?" Noah asked. "I would like to speak with him."

"Yes, of course." Eve stood and smoothed her dress. "Or I

can send Nahom for him. He is young yet, but he can find the place."

Noah rose. He glanced at Sasha and me. "I can find him. Just directions."

Jared rose too, and Eve began giving directions and led them both outside.

I turned to Sasha to ask what she thought.

"I like her," she said before I could voice my question.

I reached out to squeeze her hand. "I do too," I said. "I think this could work."

I tried to pull my hand back when I heard Eve returning, but Sasha held onto it and said, "And what will work for you, Miriam? I see you are avoiding your Lib."

"He is avoiding me!"

She looked at me for a long moment in the dim room. "Perhaps you are avoiding each other."

"Perhaps," I allowed.

"It's immature, Miriam. That's not like you. As immature as what I have done—seeking comfort in the arms of someone I did not love, and who..." She paused and glanced at Eve as she returned to the room. "And someone I knew did not love me."

Eve sat near Sasha's feet. "Then that Jared is not the...the man?" she asked.

"No," Sasha giggled nervously. "He is a friend, that's all. Noah has offered to let him rescue my reputation of sorts." She made a face. "But he won't do it." She looked down at her small, round belly. "The idea repulses him."

"No, it does not!" I defended.

"He much prefers you," Sasha said softly, but there was accusation in her tone.

"No!" I shook my head. "That is nonsense."

"I can see it when he looks at you."

I was at a loss for words. I hadn't noticed any such thing, but my mind had been very preoccupied with other things on the journey. If what Sasha said was true, then this was a mess.

A sweet, quiet voice interrupted our disagreement. "Then refuse a quick betrothal and stay here with me."

"I am not in a position to refuse such a thing." Sasha would not look at either of us.

I was afraid she was right.

"Nonsense!" Eve said. "There will be other men. Many of them. More than you would wish. You're the prettiest girl in this room." Eve cast me a secret smile. "I can see you are mild tempered, and I see your sweetness in the way you already caress the child."

Sasha's hands stilled where she had been absently caressing her belly.

"Stay here," Eve offered again. "Even after the child is born."

Sasha shook her head. "I don't think I can give it the proper care. I am not strong." Her voice broke. "My heart is hurting."

Eve had tears in her eyes again. "It is not beyond repair. Stay, and I will be Mother to you both."

The idea was silly to me. Eve could offer little more than friendship. But I looked at Sasha, and I looked at Eve again, and I could see that Eve was having an effect on Sasha I had not ever had, not once. Sasha was listening to Eve in a way she had never listened to me or Mother. I thought of our own mother, so harried, so distant and strict, so judgmental, and quite often seemingly unfeeling toward us, and I wondered if perhaps Sasha did not indeed need some mothering.

Why had I not seen this before? Had I become so much like my mother? Did I seem judgmental and unfeeling to those who needed my care the most?

I thought of the deep and aching and strong feelings I had developed toward Lib, and of how he didn't believe I felt any of them.

Could he be hiding similar feelings behind a wall he didn't realize he had built and didn't yet know how to take down?

I decided not to stay with Sasha for the duration. After a few days, she and Eve had bonded in a way Sasha and I never had. It made me sad in a way that I had missed out on an opportunity to be friends with my sister. But I was glad to see a small light return to Sasha's sad and dull eyes.

I thought Jared noticed the light too. Sometimes I could catch him watching her with an interest he hadn't shown on the journey. Sasha hadn't been wrong about that. But sometimes I caught him watching me too. Sasha hadn't been wrong about that, either.

"Have some more to eat," Eve urged Jared once when she noticed him watching me from across the room. She stepped between us, blocking his view of me. I had to smile, thinking she would be a very good mother.

"I already did," Jared laughed as he rubbed his stomach.

There was a shout out in the yard. Jarom and Eve shared a

look as Jarom got up to answer the call. In a moment, he was back and a tall, dark man followed him through the door.

"Darius," was his simple introduction of the man.

"Ket's brother," Noah added for our benefit, though I knew who he was.

"Hello," I said, as he politely placed a hand on my shoulder. "I like Keturah very much."

He smiled in a way that made him look both boyish and older at the same time. "I do, too," he said.

He greeted Sasha in the same way, but he gave Eve a hug. She hugged him back and laughed. Her laugh was frequent and genuine, and I was coming to really appreciate it as I saw how it affected Sasha.

"What's this?" she said and playfully hit his shoulder.

"That's my wife," Jarom teased. "Get your own."

Darius took a deep breath. "I plan to."

Eve had just returned to her seat, but jumped back up and into his arms again, making us all laugh.

"Is it Ava? Congratulations!" she exclaimed.

"It's not official," he rushed to say. "I have one work assignment left to complete, and then I can think about a wife."

"Nonsense!" Eve said. "Other men work and have wives at the same time." I could tell it was a discussion they had had before.

Jarom put an arm around his wife. "Darius has to travel. How would you like it if I was gone all the time?"

Eve affected a pout, but grinned again as if she just couldn't help it.

When it was late, the boys went outside to talk over the fire with some of the other men from the village, and Sasha claimed exhaustion and went to sleep. Eve and I cleared up the dinner dishes, cleaned up for the night, and began preparations for the next morning's meal.

Eve yawned.

"Go on to bed," I told her. "I will take the last of this sweet bread out to the men. It will be stale by morning."

"Alright. I am tired."

I picked up the basket of bread. "Having company for an extended time can be taxing on the emotions," I said. "You are very good to us all." I wanted to say thanks, but it didn't seem like enough.

She just smiled and went into her room.

I took the bread and made my way out toward the fire which was in the middle of the small clearing. I could see several men on their heels in its light and the shadows of others milling in the darkness just beyond it.

I was still in the shadows myself when I heard Darius say, "You must be ready to sail soon. The winter is over and Lib intends to sail as soon as possible."

I stilled, and my heart began to pound.

"There is a settlement in Desolation that needs much in the way of supplies. Then there is a river, a great river, Hagoth desires to explore. Lib has secured an invitation for us to accompany him in his exploration—up to twelve families."

He talked more about the voyage, but the only thing I heard was that Lib was leaving, and the only thing I knew was that he did not intend to take me with him.

That just couldn't be.

When at last I stepped into the light with the basket, Jared eagerly took from it. He took a bite with a grin, but when he noticed my face, he stopped chewing. I took bread to the rest of the men, but he pulled me aside when I was done.

"Is something wrong?" he asked.

Yes, everything.

Noah joined us. "You heard," he said quietly.

I managed a nod, but I knew if I tried to talk I would cry.

"Heard what?" Jared asked.

"Of the families who intend to sail," Noah told him. To me, he said, "I mean to stay in Orihah. I think the government can be fixed, and I've no desire to tromp through Desolation looking for something that doesn't exist. If there was anything in the land northward, we would have found it by now." He took a deep breath. "You will have to make a decision for yourself."

Jared looked between us. "What decision? You want to go, Miriam? I'll take you."

I shook my head.

He glanced at Noah. "I'm not marrying Sasha," he said. "I already decided. I can take you on the journey if you will—"

"No." I shook my head again.

"If you will consent to marry me," he finished.

"She won't," Noah said. "I won't."

"What's this?" Jared turned to Noah. "The elder sister should marry first. But you would offer me the younger, defiled sister?"

I gasped. "She is not defiled!"

Noah quickly put a hand on my arm. "Be calm," he said. "We should not call it anything but what it is. Sasha was careless and impulsive, and she must accept the consequences. All of them. Jared is right. It is proper for me to see first to your marriage."

"So may I offer again?" said Jared.

Noah kept his eyes on me. "Miriam's heart is engaged elsewhere." Then he turned an apologetic smile on Jared. "I'm sorry. Truly, I am. You have my sincere gratitude for taking the time to consider Sasha. If you've made your decision, you can go—with no hard feelings between us. I plan to return soon myself. If you've a mind to wait, we can share the journey."

Jared looked between me and my brother.

I swallowed. "So you don't intend to take me north?"

Noah's brow rose, and he smothered a small smile, but it still showed in the firelight that flickered in his eyes. "I thought you didn't want to go."

I thought there was time. "I don't," I lied.

Noah took the last bread from my basket. "Goodnight, Miriam. Better get some rest."

I nodded, but there was no way I would rest that night, and we both knew it. I imagined Lib on the deck of his ship, looking into the distant north as he sailed away from me. I thought of the smell of the sea, the deep blue of the waters, and the sailors there I had become friends with. I did manage a few hours of sleep in the third watch, but I was ready to go before dawn—my travel gear secured to my pack, my knife strapped to my belt, and food packed into my satchel.

I left the house silently and stole through the yard. Should I go back down the lane towards the village or directly north through the forest toward Melek? I hesitated a moment and decided to take the traveled paths.

"Safe journey."

I peered back into the dark shadows of the house. "Noah?"

But he didn't come forth, only chuckled and said, "I knew you would go."

I hesitated again. Was he trying to stop me from going? Or did he mean to accompany me as he had formerly suggested?

"You can't stop me," I said. I would not let Lib sail without me.

He chuckled again. "This is not the first time you have done this." He came off the wall of the house and into the predawn moonlight. He gestured at the dark sky. "I thought I would save myself the trouble of chasing you through the forest."

So he meant to stop me.

"I've made up my mind, Noah."

"Oh, I've no doubt." He approached me slowly, arms crossed over his chest. He stopped short of the lane and stared at me, his eyes dancing in the moonlight.

Was this amusing him?

I wanted to take a step back for some room but held my ground.

"You were right," another voice came from behind Noah, and I looked past him to where Jarom stood in the doorway. He reached up a hand to smooth his rumpled hair and stepped into the yard. "She really means to leave."

"I must," I said to them both.

"You've a sennight, at least, before you need to depart," Jarom said. "Wait and travel with my family."

"That is generous, but I can't wait."

"You can," Noah said.

I shook my head and looked at my brother. "It's like you said. I can't let him leave without knowing—without knowing how I feel."

Noah took a step closer and slung an arm around me. After a slight hesitation he pulled me into a hug, a very unusual thing for him. After a moment, he murmured into my hair. "Please."

I sighed, pulled away, and nodded.

CHAPTER 20

The waiting was terrible.

I had finally decided to go to him, and yet I had promised Noah I would wait and travel in the company of his friends because they could offer me a safer journey. I had agreed to it anyway. Promise was such a strong word.

"Men of the Gadianton hide in these hills," he told me later that morning over the morning meal.

"It's true," Jarom said as he finished off the meat from a bone. "You'll be safer with us."

"I was safe the first time I went."

"You had Ethanim."

"But who are these men of Gadianton?" I asked.

The men exchanged a glance.

"You've not heard of them?" Jarom asked. "Noah, do you keep her shut up in a cave?"

I snorted. I considered myself pretty well-traveled by then.

"The Gadianton robbers are men who conspire against the

government, against religion, against God, and there are those among them who wouldn't think twice about carrying you off with them."

"And you mean to carry all your worldly possessions through the hills of these robbers?"

He grinned at me then turned to Noah. "You are right to betroth her to Lib. There could not be a more perfect match for him."

I didn't like his knowing look.

"Perhaps there is a more perfect match for me than Lib," I shot back.

"Oh? Was there someone else you were sneaking off to see before dawn?" Jarom returned.

I rolled my eyes, conceding. "There must be someone better for that darling Eve than you," I said under my breath.

Noah and Jarom laughed, and Eve sent me a smile from the other side of the yard where she was milking the goat, but Sasha didn't look as though she even listened, and Jared kept his eyes on his food and didn't even crack a smile.

He spoke suddenly. "Noah, may I take Miriam for a walk?"

Noah barely hesitated. "Of course, if she wishes."

Jared put down his dish and stood. "Miriam?"

I looked to Sasha, but she only offered me a weak smile and a small nod, so I stood too. We left the yard, and the others continued talking.

I was nervous. I didn't know what he would say. Noah had already told him he could not court me. What could he mean by this?

"Noah is leaving later today, and I mean to leave with him." The shadows and light played on his brown hair as we passed under the trees. He was pleasant to look upon, and I wondered why I had never taken much notice before.

"And you've a mind to go to the land northward," he stated flatly.

"I do."

He tucked his thumbs into the belt of his tunic. "I feel as though I'm missing something."

"Like what, Jared?"

"Or rather that I have missed something. You were always with Shad."

"I was," I agreed.

"If I had known you weren't going to marry my cousin, I wouldn't have held back so much."

"Did you think to take me from him?" I laughed.

Jared shrugged and bit off a smile. "I could have tried."

I tucked my hair behind my ear. "I think I see what you are saying, but I think, in the end, things would have been the same for me. I must go."

He nodded and let out a breath. "About your sister," he said. It's not that I don't like her. I think my words came out harsh before, with Noah. I thought I could consider the offer, but it doesn't feel right. Don't think I'm cruel."

"I don't! Of course I don't! I know you to be kind and fair. You would not be here at all if you were cruel."

He let out another breath. "Thanks," he offered awkwardly.

"No one thinks the worse of you." I thought Noah had made

that rather clear. "And Eve is right. There will be other men who will consider her—when she is ready."

"And perhaps that is just it—this business of being ready. I don't feel that she could love me, or even like me much at present."

We came to the main road of the village, but turned away from the huts and walked into the trees.

"I think you're right. I've been thinking it for weeks. It is not my place to counsel with my elders, but I fear Noah is too hasty. Sasha would resent any relationship right now—even the one she has with me. She needs time, and probably distance."

"I agree. I'm glad you see it, too."

I smiled sadly up at him. "I wish I saw more. I wish I could do more to soothe her heart."

"Believe it or not, I have the same wish. But, after meeting her and talking with her, I perceive that she needs more than I have it in me to give."

"I doubt that," I laughed and placed a hand on his arm. "You are all that a girl could want."

He smiled down at me as we came across another traveler on the path, just coming around a bend ahead of us. We slowed and Jared pulled me aside to let the traveler pass.

But nobody passed us.

I drew my gaze from Jared to nod at the passerby, but he was no longer there. I took a step forward. "Where did that man go?

Jared looked too. "He must have veered off into the trees.

But I looked in all directions and couldn't see him.

"You saw a man, right?" I asked. "My eyes aren't playing tricks on me?"

But my eyes were playing tricks on me. They had to be.

"I saw him."

At the risk of embarrassing myself, I sounded the very shrill call of the margay. I grimaced up at Jared's curious expression, but stayed silent enough to listen.

The return call came, but it was a distance away, and the caller never materialized.

"Do you know who that was?" Jared asked when we were on our way again.

"No." I shook my head. "I thought...I guess I don't." Needing to change the subject, I said, "Are you going to Zarahemla with Shad?"

"And how might you know about that?"

I shrugged. "I heard it somewhere."

"It seems my cousin cannot keep his counsel."

I laughed. "I didn't say it was him. Do you mean to go or not?"

Jared shook his head. "I don't. The offer was made, but after much consideration, I have decided against it."

Jared made no more offers to marry me, and he and Noah left shortly after he walked me back into Jarom's yard. Like with Sasha, his was a friendship I had missed out on—because I had fixated on Shad, because I was comfortable in my relationship with him and had become complacent, letting the relationship go on and on when I shouldn't have. Might other boys have approached me if I had not been so associated with Shad?

Or was it more terrible than that? Did I miss out on friendships because I was cold and unfeeling? I didn't notice others and their needs? I sought solutions rather than offered sympathy and charity and genuine friendship?

What had I offered to Lib but secrecy, even to direct questions? Hidden feelings, impulsiveness, impatience?

I offered to go for water, and when I was alone at the spring, I closed my eyes and tried to recall the nice things Hagoth had said to me. He had always known the right thing to say. I tried to put myself on the shore of the sea, near his boat and the sound of the gulls. And then I felt guilty because I should have tried to console myself with lovely things Lib had said to me.

I'm not good with the pretty words.

But that was a lie. He did perfectly well with compliments, with noticing small things about me, with showing that he cared for me.

You forgot to tuck your hair behind your ear. Drink slow, you'll have to strain the bark with your teeth. I admire the way you were with Corianton. You're better with geometry. I will always know where to find you.

It is there. Between us already.

He had been saying pretty words all along.

I wanted to jump up and run to the coast of the West Sea.

Instead, I filled the water jug and walked back toward Jarom and Eve's. Sasha was working alongside Eve, and I judged that they were becoming fast friends. I was glad of it, though touched with pangs of regret.

"Miriam."

Jarom was leaving the yard. "Would you like to walk to the tannery with me?"

I glanced around.

"Because you look like you're ready to run out of here on a straight course for the sea."

I laughed. "I'm not as bad as Noah makes it sound."

He grinned and started down the lane. "Well, as he's left you in my care, I thought I'd at least ask," he called over his shoulder.

"I wouldn't mind a visit to the tannery." I started after him down the lane, and when I caught up, I said, "I thought I saw Lib today."

"Here?"

"When I was out with Jared. And I think he saw me with Jared and turned around and headed north again."

Jarom frowned. "If it was him, I'm sure he wouldn't have made such a hasty judgment. If he's here, it's because he wants to see you."

I shook my head. "He's really busy. He likely has other business he meant to see to."

"Then he didn't hightail it north just because you were walking in the woods with another boy. He's seeing to what he came for, and he will come for you when he is able."

"You make it sound so straightforward. It's not as easy as that, as it is for you and Eve."

He shot me a look I could hardly interpret. "Miriam, Eve and I were apart for six years because I mistook something she said in her youth and couldn't forgive her for it. What she said made me doubt myself and envy my brother. Our walk together has not been easy."

I looked at him warily. He and Eve were so in love, not even a fool could fail to see it.

"Even now when we visit my brother, a part of me wonders if she does not wish his name had been on the betrothal contracts instead of mine."

I gasped. "Of course she doesn't!"

"I know that." He brushed a hand over his heart. "But you see what a misunderstanding can do."

"Are you saying Lib will not forgive me for walking with Jared?"

He shook his head as he turned off the lane and onto a smaller path that led through the trees. "Not at all."

"Then, Jarom, what are you saying?"

"That if he cares for you like I care for Eve, nothing will keep him from taking you to wife. And Miriam." He glanced back at me over his shoulder and winked. "The rumors I hear say that he does."

The mischief in his eye made me want to strangle him, but I held what he said close to my heart.

At the tannery, a young man and a girl were packing all manner of equipment into large sacks—tools, buckets, pelts, jars full of oils, blankets, small bags full of rivets and glues.

The girl looked up and offered us a bright smile. "I thought you'd laze away at home all day," she said to Jarom.

"I intended to stay home until you were done with the work, but it appears as though you are moving rather slowly."

She smiled at me and laughed. "Perhaps you are right. But I see you've brought an extra set of hands, so we should be ready on time after all."

I held my hands up. "Put me to work," I said. I was glad for the work she gave me, and glad to have two hands again to do it with. The work kept my mind occupied. I thought Jarom was glad for it too, because it kept me there in the clearing where he could keep an eye on me for Noah.

The girl introduced herself as Isabel, Jarom's sister, and the man was her husband, Kenai. She was a happy girl who teased both boys while managing to work quite efficiently. Kenai was quiet with watchful eyes, and he looked to be capable and strong. When he looked at his young wife, his eyes glowed with amusement.

When at last we were done and the men set off ahead of us with the large sacks on their backs, I said to Isabel, "I sometimes wish I was as close to my brothers as you are to yours."

She let her gaze follow Jarom for a moment before replying, "We haven't always been close. It's something we have grown into."

"Perhaps my brothers and I are still growing into it."

"Jarom and I have worked together for years now with much time together to talk. But I'm quite a bit younger than him, and we were not close as youngsters."

I nodded. "I'm much younger than my brothers, too."

"Younger than Lib, too, I think."

Her comment surprised me, but I nodded again. "Do you think that could keep us from being close? Our age difference?"

I expected her to deny it, but she was quiet for a moment then said, "Oh yes. But it doesn't have to."

"I am afraid his feelings for me are what he might have for a younger sister," I admitted. "He said he didn't think of me like a sister, but how could he not?"

Isabel actually laughed. Then she threw a smile over her shoulder. "If he says he doesn't, trust me, he doesn't."

"I'm sorry, but you couldn't know that."

She stopped on the path and turned to me. Her smile was sweet, and she looked into my eyes. "I am eight years younger than Kenai," she said. "There were many times I felt inferior because of my age and inexperience. Kenai was my brother's friend, and I had always thought of him as a brother, too, so of course I thought he saw me the same way my brother saw me. But when my feelings began to change, I didn't realize that his feelings might change as well." She took my hands in hers and squeezed them reassuringly. "I wish I could be of more help to you, for I can see you are distracted and worried."

"Oh, Isabel, you have helped. Perhaps Lib no longer sees me as Noah's little sister, but how do I know that?" I sighed and turned to continue down the path.

"Has he kissed you?" Isabel asked and then giggled as she skipped along beside me and saw my face. "I can tell by your blush that he has. Miriam, dear, men don't kiss their sisters like that."

"How do you know what it was like?"

She drew me to a stop again, put her hands on my heated cheeks, and looked me in the eye. "Calm your mind so you can hear the words of your heart. You're letting something interfere with what you already know to be true."

Don't let my inadequacies and your insecurities ruin what we already have.

I dropped my eyes and after a moment, I nodded.

"Come on now," she said. "Chin up. It is darkest before the dawn."

Later that night when I was alone in my bedroll staring into the darkness, I was grateful both Eve and Isabel would be going on this journey with me. I liked them both very much. And knowing they would be there with their wise words and their loving smiles helped me to stay put and wait to travel in the safety of the group instead of setting out on my own.

The week passed quickly because we stayed busy making preparations to leave. Eve and Jarom and the other families in the small village welcomed both Sasha and me as if we belonged with them. They were kind and helpful, and they were not judgmental of Sasha, something that brought me particular relief. I felt the pain and rejection when Jared left, even if she was too numb yet to feel it for herself.

The evening before we were to leave, the village gathered at the main fire for a farewell and a celebration. It was an evening filled with both excitement and sadness. These people had been friends for many years and through many trials, the same as the people in Orihah. Being there with them made me think of all the people I was leaving and would never see again.

I had hugged my mother tight, but I wished my father would have been in Orihah so I could have said goodbye. I would miss Esther and Beth. I would not get to say goodbye to Ethanim. I would never see Adreana again, and even that made me sad.

And then there was David. I wished I had gone to see him one last time. I wished I had taken him a hundred meals so I could be assured he would eat well.

But the more I thought of them, the easier it got. They were all a part of my past, and there was only one person for certain who was to be part of my future.

Lib had seen kisses he shouldn't have seen. Maybe they shouldn't have happened at all, but I had learned something bittersweet from each of them, something dear I could not regret. Shad and Hagoth, even Ethanim and Jared, were like islands dotting a sea, safe places to moor to for a time, to rest and learn and be nourished. Places to leave when the tide was high and the weather was fair.

I had to go. I had to go to Lib right then and explain.

I nearly rolled out of my bedroll in that moment, but clear as day, my mother's words came into my mind.

Let him come to you.

I shut my eyes, but the tears leaked out anyway as the Spirit elaborated on my mother's words.

Open your heart, and let him come to you.

And somehow, when it was whispered to my heart by the Spirit of God, I knew Lib was not the only one I had been walling out.

Ye shall seek me, and find me, when ye shall search for me with all your heart.

Such pretty words.

I had chosen the pieces of my heart I would give to God, keeping back the parts that were vulnerable and untried.

Likewise, I had chosen the pieces I would give to Lib, my admiration and my journey to the sea, but kept my trust in his reciprocated love hidden behind a fear that he would not give it because he could not give it.

But he did love me, and the how of it did not matter because it, Lib's love, had already happened. It was a ship that was already sailing, and if I did not jump from the shore onto the deck, I would miss it. I would be left behind.

Well, that thought made me want to get up and run to the sea, but I smiled, and my heart was calmed, and I slept.

CHAPTER 21

At last it was time to leave, and it was done without much fanfare. The people had said their farewells the previous night and their provisions were ready to go.

The group employed several large men to help carry the provisions, but everyone carried as much as was possible, including Sasha, though her load was considerably lighter than many of the others. Mothers carried their babies, and several young children toddled along at their feet, when they were not riding their fathers' shoulders.

When it was full light, we stopped for a rest.

Sidling up to Isabel, I asked, "Where are Gid and Keturah? I thought they planned to come."

Isabel glanced back toward the south. "The last missive we had said they were still undecided whether or not they would go."

"Oh," I said dumbly.

"It's a big commitment," she said. "And they may never have

the means to return. Gid's family is staying here."

We rested in silence a moment before I asked, "Do you think Gid doesn't want to come because of Lib's presence?"

"No," she said immediately. "I know Gid harbors no jealousy toward Lib."

She spoke as if she really did know it, and I had to believe her.

"There are many considerations for every family who goes north," she said.

I gave her a small smile. "Here is your Kenai," I said and gestured to the man approaching us. "I will go see how Sasha is faring with her load."

My sister appeared to be fine. She was smiling and actually seemed to be happier than I had seen her in many months, so I sat on a rough fallen tree and waited for the party to be ready to go again, thinking how much faster I could get there if I were alone.

That night we camped deep in the woods, far off the main road.

"I'll go for water if you'll show me where it's at," I said to Jarom as he was setting up a tent for Eve and Sasha.

"Yonder," he said and gestured to the northwest.

I took several containers and followed his vague direction. But the direction was good enough because I walked straight to a fast stream. Kneeling at its edge, I filled the containers quickly and wiped the outsides dry with the hem of my sarong.

Something caught my eye. There was movement in the trees.

"Hurry! We were supposed to be in the city tonight. The assassination is to happen within days."

"I know that. We'll say we were delayed."

The first voice laughed. "We just won't say who delayed us."

I looked up in time to meet the eye of a man through the trees. He grabbed his friend's arm and turned him to see me. They both grinned and started in my direction.

I fingered the small knife at my belt and wondered if I should call for help. Normally I wouldn't have thought to reach for a knife when meeting strangers, but hadn't one of these said something about an assassination? Surely I hadn't heard wrong.

Both men knelt for a drink.

"I forgot there was a stream here," said the darker one.

"There is plenty for all," I said and offered a smile.

"Indeed," he said. "I'm Elias." He put a slightly wet hand on my shoulder. "I'd stay and make your lovely acquaintance, but we're in a bit of a hurry."

I nodded. "I am traveling as well."

He took a last drink and got to his feet. His eyes flicked over my shoulder.

"Well," he said with a wry grin, "keep an eye out for danger."

The other man offered me a polite enough smile, but when they were on their way again, I heard them laugh boisterously. I thought they might have been inebriated.

I heard a sigh behind me and a step in the grass.

"Guess I won't be needing this," Jarom said, and I turned to see him return an arrow into the quiver at his back.

"I didn't know you were there," I said.

"You don't think I take my commitment to Noah seriously?"

I tucked my hair behind my ear. "I didn't know anyone took Noah seriously."

He grinned. "Ready to go?"

When I nodded, he stepped forward and lifted one of the jugs.

"Thanks for coming," I said, sincerely touched that he had. "They might not have been as nice as they seemed."

"They probably aren't."

"Well, we shouldn't judge them. They did not prove otherwise."

He just grunted.

Though the progress was somewhat slower than I could have traveled alone, I found I was glad to be traveling with others. The company of the other women was a comfort as my mind was filled with questions and doubts and my heart was filled with impatience. The protection of the men was a comfort also, as I knew I couldn't have been on my guard at all times had I been journeying alone.

On the third evening as I prepared the evening meal with Leah, a couple walked into our camp from the south. I took note of Leah's smile and turned to follow her gaze. I stood suddenly and stared as Ethanim and Adreana walked into the camp, Ethanim returning hearty hellos and Adreana looking exhausted. When she finally caught my eye, she smiled.

I smiled at her too, but when I approached them, I went into

Ethanim's outstretched arms.

"I'm so glad you're coming," I breathed out.

He held me back from him and took a good look at me.

"Don't cry," he said.

I wiped the corners of my eyes where small tears had barely formed. "I'm not crying." But when I looked back into his face, I started to. "I can't do this without you," I said.

It was Ethanim who had always had faith in me and my promptings. It was Ethanim who had taken me under his wing. He knew Lib so much better than I did. He wanted the best for his friend, and still he took me to meet Lib.

He gave a slight nod, but I knew he understood what I couldn't say. Then he gestured to Adreana who was waiting to embrace me.

"My wife," he announced proudly.

I smacked him on his arm and then turned to embrace Adreana. "Why did you not invite me?"

"It was very simple," he said, and glancing at Adreana with a dubious smile, he added, "And perhaps a bit rushed."

I nodded, understanding what he could not say, that he had wanted to have the thing done before they went off into the unknown.

From that point on, the trip was happy and my heart felt much lighter. If Ethanim was here with me, surely he would see that everything turned out right. And perhaps he would care for me if Lib would not.

"Don't even think what you're thinking," Ethanim said late that night as we sat on the first watch together. Jarom sat opposite us, but at a look from Ethanim, he turned his back and moved a distance away into the shadows.

"And how do you know what I am thinking?" I teased.

He gave me a wry smile. "It is written on your face as if it were a book."

I sighed and looked up at the stars for a moment. Then I looked back into the fire. "I think he was in Melek," I admitted. "And I think he saw me with Jared."

Ethanim was quiet for a moment, and off in the shadows I heard Jarom shifting around.

"What did he see?"

"I'm not sure."

"Miriam. I cannot form an opinion based on such a scant description."

"We were walking together. That's all."

"But you were laughing, having fun. Is that it? Flirting perhaps?"

"I am a happy person," I defended.

"You think Lib doesn't know your character?"

I hadn't thought of it that way, that Lib might know and understand things about my character.

"I think he may have misinterpreted, that is all."

"Why would he?"

"Why wouldn't he?"

"Give him a little credit."

"He took one look and darted away without an explanation."

Ethanim shrugged infuriatingly.

Jarom shifted again out in the darkness.

"You might as well just come back to the fire," I called out to him.

In a moment, he returned with a sheepish smile.

"I tried," he said with a shrug.

I nodded my thanks.

Jarom sat and spoke to Ethanim. "Would you just tell her not to worry already?"

Ethanim glanced at me. "I have no way of knowing what Lib is thinking. Miriam is right. If he was in Melek and saw her there, he should have stopped to say hello. At the very least, he should have sought her out later. He is not a rash person, but I fear," he glanced at me again, "that when it comes to Miriam, he does not think entirely straight."

"What is that supposed to mean?" I demanded, trying to keep my voice low.

"He has come to accept the idea of taking you to wife. He told me as much himself, but he has little experience with women, as far as I know, other than his time spent guarding Keturah."

Jarom whistled softly through his teeth.

"Not every man has your ability to flirt." Ethanim elbowed him in the ribs, and I stuck my tongue out at him.

Jarom laughed.

I was beginning to understand what he meant for me to see, but it was not new information. "The way Lib shows love is by serving me." I let my mouth feel out the words as I said them. "Is that what you're saying?"

Ethanim regarded me in the firelight for a long moment. He

gave one deep nod. "Use the knowledge wisely, young Miriam."

Soon, other men came to guard the camp through the night, and I crawled into a tent next to Adreana and fell fast asleep and slept better than I had in a long time.

By noon the next day we could see the city of Ammonihah in the distance. I could be to the sea by evening! But I knew the men planned to stay in Ammonihah and replenish travel supplies and purchase things at the market that they hadn't wanted to carry, specifically building supplies if they could find them, so we could build homes when we arrived in the land northward which was said to be barren of timber.

"I want to go on alone," I said to Ethanim when he caught me staring west that evening. "I don't want to meet up with him, to have this confrontation, with all these people looking on."

He put an arm around my shoulders. "Wait until morning?"

I didn't want to, but I nodded. "Of course I will."

I waited for morning, but I didn't wait for full light. I caught Ethanim's eye in the shadows as I crept out of camp. A smile tipped the corners of his lips and he gave me a small salute. By the time full light hit, I was in the gorge that led to the sea. Its walls were high, and they kept me in the shade for much of the time. I could see a path of debris, and the water was high and fast. I feared it had recently flooded, and as I scampered quickly over logs along a trail that was barely visible, I had the ominous feeling it might happen again. I knew that the men would carry the provisions along the higher route. Though that route was longer, the pathway was wide and flat. But I feared some of the children would want to come down through the gorge. I glanced back over my shoulder and prayed that God would warn his people to stay away from here.

I almost started skipping when I saw the ship in the distance, so happy I was to be back near the rippling waters and the gulls overhead. If I hadn't known my true feelings and desires before, I knew them now.

A long dock had been built, and the ship was floating in the deep part of the bay, just as Hagoth had long ago shown me it would be. When at last I stepped onto the dock, I had to keep myself from running. I called up to the deck, and a burly sailor's head appeared over the side.

"You'll want to be boarding down there, young miss," he called down and pointed to the far end of the dock where a new ramp connected the dock to the ship. I nodded and started to move in that direction. "Is Lib aboard?"

"Well now, I don't know."

"Is Hagoth aboard?"

"Oh, aye." He nodded vigorously and disappeared, replaced a moment later by Hagoth.

I waved. "Hagoth!"

A grin split his face. "Miriam!"

He gestured with a thick arm toward the ramp, and before I could start to climb it, he was at the bottom. For an awkward moment we started at each other, both breathless, and then he pulled me into an embrace.

"So, you've come to sail with us," he said as he took a step back.

I nodded and looked up at the big ship.

Hagoth touched my shoulder. "He's not here."

I would have asked who, but the word stopped half-formed on my lips when I looked into his face. "Where has he gone?"

His smile had an old touch of sadness in it. "He went to find you. He wanted you and his father to be here, to sail with him, so he went to find you both."

I looked back over my shoulder. "When?"

"Weeks ago, Miriam."

I bit my lip.

"He'll be back." He paused. "Would you like to see the ship? You can wait on board."

I offered him a smile. "Yes, of course I would like to see the ship." As for waiting, I wasn't sure if I could. What if Lib was looking for me? What if he had seen me in Melek with Jared and decided against bringing me? What if he had decided to stay with David? What if I was on this ship and it sailed and Lib was not on it?

Wait for him to come to you. My mother's words again brought temperance to my heart and urged me to be patient. But perhaps I should come to him as well, perhaps I should meet him halfway.

"It is surely the most beautiful ship on the sea," I told Hagoth sincerely when he guided me around the deck.

He laughed and tried to be humble, but I could see he was proud of the finished boat, of the large hold where provisions were stored, the small cabins near the captain's, and the passenger bunks below. He showed me how much timber had been loaded and how its weight had been distributed. He showed me the oil and lanterns and the food stuffs that were packed safely away. And when he showed me the relatively large captain's quarters I had stayed in, my eyes took in all the beautifully carved details.

"Did you do this woodwork?" I asked as I ran my hand over the molding at the door. But my eyes were on a painted mural on the far wall.

"No. We had many fine craftsmen on the work crew." He rested both hands on the sturdy looking table and pressed down as if to test its strength. "Some are even sailing with us."

"How many intend to sail?"

"Many. So many we will have to come back for a second trip."

I dragged my eyes from the colorful painting. "There will be a second chance to go?"

His eyes held understanding. "Many chances," he said. "We are colonizing the north, Miriam. We already have rudimentary governments and laws in place. Cities are being planned and built. There will be infrastructure there when you arrive."

I walked over to the small window and looked out. All I could see was blue sky and bluer water.

"You don't intend to stay," I said. "In the city. You don't intend to live there."

He came up behind me. "I'm a sailor," he said simply. After a few moments he dipped his head to see out the window too. "Have you brought provisions? I'll have your trunks taken to Lib's quarters.

"I...ah..." The words got stuck in my throat. I couldn't stay there alone with Lib. I didn't even know if he would make it back in time. And if he did, would he want me in there?

Hagoth chuckled. "Where are your things, Miriam?"

I swallowed. "I traveled with friends. My things are packed on their pallets."

"And where are these friends?"

"They are a day behind me, at least," I admitted. "I couldn't wait to be back."

I couldn't wait to see Lib is what I meant, and we both knew it.

Hagoth laughed again.

I swallowed again. "How long until you sail?"

"On the morning tide, two days hence."

"I need to go after him."

"Don't. He will return."

I turned to him and realized how close he stood. "Will you wait for him, before you sail?"

He shook his head slowly. "No. The departure has been publicized. Passages have been sold and booked for months, many months in some cases. We cannot wait for one man."

But they would come back for more passengers.

"Stay onboard," he said again.

I nodded because I was supposed to, and giving one last look at the sea through the window, I stepped back and let Hagoth show me the rest of the ship.

"You must be busy," I said. "With so much to do. You can trust me to be alone."

Hagoth shook his head. "Everything is done. The only

thing left is to orient the passengers, and I have employed men to do that."

I didn't know if that was true, but he stayed with me the rest of the day, taking me into town for food, and showing me the main docks where all the other ships had already set sail.

At the evening meal, he introduced me to a young couple. "Tec and Chloe are from Melek," he said. "You might know their family."

"My father is Hemni," she said.

"Oh yes!" I exclaimed. "I traveled here with him. He is but a day away."

"And my mother?"

"Indeed, I think the whole family tree is here," I told her, much to her delight. But when she looked to her betrothed, I could see there was trepidation in her eyes too.

When she got up later and walked to the rail to look out over the land, I watched Tec's eyes follow her. She had a slight limp in her gait, and I wondered what kind of harm had befallen this daughter of Hemni, and I wondered why she was alone here with her betrothed. I had heard her family speak of her but once.

"She is young," I remarked.

His eyes shot back to me, embarrassed perhaps for having been caught watching her so intently. But he said, "And wise for her years."

When morning dawned, I knew I still had a day before Hagoth sailed. I didn't have enough time to get all the way back to Melek, but perhaps I could inquire of travelers on the road as to whether they had seen him. I just needed word of him, I told myself. Then I would be calm and patient.

Chloe was looking over the rail again when I made to leave.

"You should go out to meet them," I told her. She acted like she had already been shut up on this ship for a while.

She smiled somewhat sadly at me. "I don't get around as easily as I used to, but perhaps you are right. It's, well, it's more complicated than that, though."

I studied her for a moment, wondering if I should pry farther into that statement, if she wanted me to. In the end, Tec came up behind her, and so I waved to them both and left.

I decided to take the Sea Road as there would likely be more travelers on it. It was scenic and held a view of the sea almost constantly. The view reminded me of the view from the top of the hill Lib and I had climbed that day I had become ill. From there one could see the narrow way, and I thought perhaps I would visit it one more time before I left. I would travel half a day on this road and then come back, and the next day, if I got an early enough start in the morning, I could visit the hill.

That thought brought calmness to my heart and I set along my journey in hopes of some word of Lib. I talked to everyone I passed. Most said they had not seen any man with the golden hair like mine, but some said they had. Unfortunately, it had been some time ago, and he had been traveling in the other direction.

I stopped to eat a late midday meal, and just as I was preparing to leave and return to the ship, Keturah and Gid came around a wide bend in the road. They were with two others who, to my surprise, appeared to be Lib's friend, Seth, and his wife. I waited until they were closer, rising slowly and brushing the dust off my clothing. I slipped back into my sandals as I waited, and when they noticed me, I raised a hand in greeting.

"Miriam?" Keturah asked with a beautiful grin. "What on this earth are you doing on the Sea Road alone?" She looked around as if she expected to see someone else.

I glanced at the others. "I wanted word of Lib. Have you seen him?"

Seth and Noel shook their heads, but Keturah and Gid glanced at each other before Keturah took another step toward me.

"He was in Orihah not long ago. He came out to the farm."

Of course he had gone looking for Keturah. I looked down to hide the look on my face. I sensed Gid step forward too.

"He was looking for you," he said.

"Is that what he told you?" I bent to collect my satchel, and I put it over my shoulder before looking back at them.

"That is what I know," he said firmly. I applauded his effort.

"Are you traveling to the sea? Do you mean to set sail with the others?"

"Aren't you going?" Keturah asked, and I might have imagined the alarm in her voice.

"I don't think so," I said. If Lib was not there, I had no reason to be either. And if he did not love me, I would be a fool to sail away after him. "But you can travel back to the village with me. It's been…" I sighed. "It's been a long day."

As we traveled, Gid fell back in with Seth and Noel as he and Seth carried most of their provisions on a pallet between them. Keturah let Gabriel walk for a time, and she and I fell behind the others.

I could see it was her plan, so I sighed and asked, "Did he really say he was looking for me?"

"No." The gentle reply was immediate. "He said he came to tell us goodbye."

I almost snorted.

"But that wasn't why he came." She glanced at me slyly. "He was fidgety," she said. "He couldn't sit still. He kept running his hand through his hair, and it looked like he'd been doing that a lot of late."

I bit back a smile. I could imagine it all too well. "Are you sure it wasn't your ravishing beauty making him nervous?"

Her laugh sounded up through the trees. "That is all done, Miriam. Let it be. We certainly have." She gestured ahead to Gid. "And your Lib has as well."

I grimaced. Maybe I was being unfair. Maybe I was being a big, immature baby.

She put a hand on my arm, then immediately removed it as she made a grab for her small son to keep him from wandering off the path and into the wilderness that surrounded us.

"I hope you'll reconsider sailing with us."

I turned my eyes north and smiled.

CHAPTER 22

After I had come aboard with Keturah and the others, I asked Hagoth to show me the head of the trail that led to the top of the hill.

"I want to see it one more time before we leave," I told him.

"Aye, it's a pretty sight."

Early the next morning, he led me down the ramp and along the dock. When we passed his small hut on the beach, I confided, "I had thought to stay here instead of sail. To wait, I mean."

He only nodded, a deep frown creasing his brow. "You would be welcome."

I took his hand in one of mine and his arm in the other and squeezed. "You are a good friend to me."

He groaned, and I laughed.

"Will this fog delay the departure?" I asked, perhaps hopefully.

"Nay. It will roll out before we sail."

He left me at the start of the trail with a very brief goodbye.

I didn't remember any of the scenery that surrounded me as I hiked alone along the trail, up and out of the fog. I recalled how very sick I had been that day so long ago and wondered that I had made it to the top at all, for it was very steep and somewhat rugged, and even now I had to stop frequently to catch my breath. It didn't help that the brisk wind seemed to be sucking my breaths away.

Though Hagoth had told me the ship would not sail until mid-morning, I felt a small comfort each time I turned back and could still see the ship through the trees. When I was high enough, the trees no longer blocked my view of it and the fog had indeed dissipated into the sunlight.

An eagle flew overhead and drew my attention to the last rise above me. I looked around and knew I must be at the place where Lib had made the willow bark tea that lowered my fever long enough for me to view the narrow neck of land—or as I had come to call it, the straight and narrow path. It led to a land of refuge where survival would depend upon the Lord.

Gathering my strength, I set out for the top of the mountain, my sandals scuffing the gravel and sand.

The view of the land that snaked its way through the dark seas was more breathtaking than the climb had been. It was beyond beautiful, one of the Lord's masterpieces, surely.

I stayed there as long as I dared. If Hagoth would not wait for Lib to return, he would certainly not wait for me.

I turned toward the ship. I had let the men move my belongings into Lib's small cabin. My family was staying in

Melek, and my head still told me I should stay in the beach hut and then return home. But my heart told me to board the ship and sail away.

I paused when I heard voices below me on the path, and in a moment two men crested the rise. One man was dark as a panther at midnight. The other was golden yellow like the sun on the sand. But they looked very much alike.

The three of us were startled for a moment, and then Lib looked at his father. David took a small step back. He clapped Lib on the shoulder and then turned to leave.

"David! Wait!"

They both turned to look at me, David with a kind curiosity in his eyes, Lib with…annoyance? Or perhaps impatience.

The wind came up as I looked between them. I tucked a strand of hair behind my ear but it didn't help—my hair wouldn't be tamed. Gesturing behind me, I said, "You've not yet seen the isthmus."

David looked from me to Lib and back again. "I've seen what I came to see." He smiled at me, his eyes crinkling at the corners.

"David."

"Oh, alright," he grumbled as he and Lib approached the top, and standing together, the three of us looked out at the sea and at the path before us.

After a moment, David took a deep breath. "I'll see you children at the ship."

"Father," Lib called before David disappeared below the rise.

David turned back.

"Thank you."

The two shared a look, and then David turned and left us alone.

Long moments passed. We looked at the isthmus, the sea, the trees, the sky, our sandals—everything but each other.

I knew David hadn't planned to leave Orihah. I wanted to ask Lib about it, about how they had come to travel here together. But I didn't want to talk about David—not really. Instead, I said a quick prayer of thanks and breathed a sigh of relief. How could they have possibly thought to separate themselves from each other?

Finally, when Lib still had said nothing, I looked up at his expressionless face. "Hagoth said you were gone."

Lib glanced down at me from the corner of his eye. "Aye, I was."

I kept looking at him, studying his face. Was he upset? Why wouldn't he talk to me? As I watched, his ears turned red. Maybe he was angry.

I was about to tell him he might as well just leave with his father if he didn't want to be here when he looked down and said, "I was looking for you."

I was able to search his eyes for a moment, but I could read nothing of his intentions there. I pursed my lips. "I'm sorry to have missed you."

"Sorry to have—" He grabbed me by the shoulders. "Miriam! Is that it? You're sorry to have missed me? As if we were nothing more than ships that passed in the night?"

Do not let him think for one moment that you do not love him. Hadn't Noah warned me of this? Hadn't Ethanim? Even Shad. I cringed.

Lib's nostrils flared in anger, something I had never seen before. He wasn't someone who let his emotions overrun him.

When it comes to you, he does not think entirely straight.

He let go of my shoulders, frowned, and gave a small nod. He clenched his fists and turned back to the sea.

The wind made my eyes water. I took a small step toward the boy I loved and slid my finger against his palm, pulling his hand toward me.

He looked down at it.

"I missed you desperately," I whispered. I tried, but I couldn't get the words to come out louder, and I was afraid the wind would just whip them away.

He looked up from our hands but didn't speak. I was sure he hadn't heard me until at last a very small smile lit his stormy eyes, and he said, "How desperately?"

I breathed out. "You make me feel safe," I told him.

His brows knit and he cocked his head to the side.

"And you make me feel on fire," I blurted. "And when you leave, it's like there is no wind in my sails, no magic."

He moved closer to me and touched me lightly on my cheek. "Come now," he said. "I explained lift to you. You're good with geometry. You understand it is not magic."

I smiled wide. "And surely you understand you cannot explain away feelings with your science."

He feigned a skeptic look. At least, I hoped it was feigned.

"You cannot explain, for instance," I said, "that moment when the wind first catches your sails."

He shook his head slowly and moved even closer, putting both hands to my face, his thumbs stroking my cheeks.

"No," he murmured. "But I can recreate it."

And with slow moving lips, confident now, and salty from the spray of the sea, he really did.

"Why are you crying?" he asked when he pulled back.

So many reasons. I was leaving my family. But I was becoming part of a new one.

A stricken look crossed his face. "You didn't come to sail." He put his hands in his hair and backed up. "You came to say goodbye, and I… You came because—"

"I came to be with you. If you sail, I will sail." I made my words firm. "I love you. I was prepared to beg you."

He laughed. "Why would you think you had to beg to come with me?" But he sobered and answered his own question. "I haven't been the easiest person to love, have I?"

I twisted my lips, trying not to smile. "I am not so very easy to love either," I consoled.

He scoffed and took my hand, leading me back down the path without a backward glance at the two gulfs which pressed in upon the isthmus. "I'm still not sure when it was—the moment I saw you asleep in the coils of rope, the day you told me my calculations were wrong, or the day you scrawled the angles on the ship's rail and left Noah to eat your dust—but you were very easy to fall in love with."

"So soon?" It couldn't have been. And I had thought all

those things were impulsive and bordered on rude.

"Truthfully, I think it was the day I carried you down this mountain."

I looked around and felt the steepness of the way below my feet, and I wondered that he had had the strength to do it.

I couldn't pinpoint when I had started to love Lib. I hoped he wouldn't ask. But maybe seeds of it had always been there—when I was seven, when I had watched him leave the village with the other striplings, when I heard his father talk of him with so much pride in his words.

Had David been matchmaking even then? Had he known all this time? Had he looked at a gangly ten-year-old girl and hand-picked me for the boy he told such valiant stories of? Had he been preparing me for life with his son?

Love might have crept up on me, on us, but I did know the first moments I felt the magic like the wind in my sails. It was the day we had carried Corianton together. It was the day he had first kissed me. It was the day he had started down the lane to Keturah's but never made it there.

We had struggles yet to overcome. We both knew that. But we had the Spirit, and we had David, and we did have love, new and tender and burgeoning as it was. And if that all failed, well then, we had mathematics.

Suddenly, Lib whisked me up into his arms. I laughed as the world turned around and my feet were swept into the air. But it all turned right again as I settled next to Lib's chest, where I could feel his heart, and where I knew I belonged.

PLEASE ENJOY THE FIRST CHAPTER OF

Follow WHERE HE LEADS

A Stripling Warrior Novel

CHAPTER 1

The darkness was overwhelming, and there were things in it—scratching, scampering, biting things—that made it nearly unbearable.

"In here." The whisper was so soft and unexpected, I thought I imagined it, but then three shadows crept through the doorway of the decrepit old house. I froze, still as stone. I was already nervous tucked into the back of the darkest corner of the room with the rats and spiders and snakes, but my heart beat so loudly when the men came in I was sure they could hear it.

They waited for a moment. All was still and silent but for breathing, and then I heard it. The Nephite patrol was approaching.

"I hate this part of the city," one man sneered as they passed. "The mangy dogs are disgusting."

Oh, if only they were dogs.

No sooner had the patrol passed and disappeared into the dark than the three dark shadows stole out of the building. I didn't know who they were, but I wished I was with them.

I waited in the heavy silence until the rodents started moving again. Something scampered past my foot. I closed my eyes and let slow tears roll down my cheeks, but I would not make a sound. I would not make a move. I could not be found here.

I didn't know how long the shadow had been in the doorway before I noticed it. When I did, I betrayed myself with a soft intake of air. It seemed to be the confirmation he needed that I was there in the darkness.

"Are you okay?"

His voice was soft, but he wasn't whispering.

Something scampered past when the man moved through the door. I tried to bite back a gasp, but I flinched.

"Come here," he said.

I shook my head jerkily, then realized he couldn't see it. "N-no."

He stilled. "Do you live here?"

"N-no."

He was silent for a moment. "Can I help you home?"

"No!" I couldn't go there.

"I see." More silence. "Are you hungry?"

I wanted to say no, but I couldn't and my silence spoke for me.

"Come on." He was moving closer. "I have food. You don't need to stay here with the lizards."

Lizards? They were rats! Gigantic, disgusting, terrifying rats!

He went to his heels in front of me, and I could see the reflection of light in his eyes and on his hair. He was handsome. But when he reached out for me, I flinched again.

His hand stilled before it touched me. "I'm not going to hurt you," he said. "I heard you when I was here before with my friends. I took them to safety. I'll take you to safety—if you'll let me." When I didn't say anything, he said again, "I'm not going to hurt you."

I pressed my lips together. Go with this stranger—trust this strange man who dodged the patrols in the middle of the night—or stay here with the rodents.

"Okay," I said. I hardly recognized my voice I hadn't used it in so long. "But don't touch me," I said when he reached out for me again.

He stood and stepped back. "Let's get you out of here."

I got to my feet. My muscles were aching. The man, to

my surprise, didn't reach out for me when my knees buckled and I nearly dropped to the ground again. He just stood there, large and silent and still, until I had my feet under me and I was steady.

He paused at the door, searching the dark street. Then he said, "Follow me," and he slipped out into the night.

We kept to the shadows. He moved slowly, and I thought it was deliberate so I could keep up. He didn't say anything, didn't try to ask me what I was doing in the derelict part of the city, only gave me terse instructions as we made our way through the streets. We moved generally west until we were in the very nice part of the city, the part where I had lived until a few weeks ago. Inexplicably, I looked down at myself in the sparse moonlight and felt embarrassed at my appearance. Not that the man had yet looked at me. But he would. And when he did, he would exact a price for his protection.

There was only one way left for me to pay, and I was so hungry I thought I would pay it. I had held out as long as I could. But I would have to pay it. I was starving.

Finally, he ushered me into a small hut. I stood in the darkness until he lit a small lamp, and then I stood trembling as he turned to look at me. I watched his eyes as he took me in. I was a sight, I was sure. Ragged, filthy clothes, flea bitten skin, unkempt and tangled hair, frightened eyes blinking in the sudden light.

After a moment he gestured to a stool. "Sit. I will prepare some food. It will be simple, but it will nourish you."

I nodded slightly and sat as he instructed.

"I haven't money to pay you," I said.

He glanced over at me. He might have blushed, clearly betrayed what he was thinking—but it was only what I had implied.

"But I will. Pay you, I mean. Do you have a basin I can clean up in?" I knew I looked disgusting and smelled worse.

He looked fully at me then, his eyes very hard.

"I don't want that," he said and after a moment he suddenly flushed again. "Or anyway, it is not mine to take."

I felt very foolish for offering, and if possible, I felt even dirtier than I was.

"The basin is there." He pointed. "I will haul in some water."

He left the hut abruptly and did not return immediately. I closed my eyes and leaned my head back against the wall. I didn't intend to, but I fell asleep there in the strange man's home. But it was clean—sparse actually—and rodent free, and despite how frightened I was, I somehow felt safe enough to sleep.

I woke alone in the morning on the lone pallet, and it was well past dawn, but the water the man had promised was in a pitcher beside the basin along with a cloth, a comb, and some opaque salve in a little jar.

I had finished with the basin and I was sitting stiffly on the bed when the man returned. In the light, I could tell he was young, not much older than me. He had hair the color of roasted chestnuts that fell into his eyes, and his eyes were dark like charcoal.

"I should go," I said.

"Do you have someplace to stay?"

What could I tell him? He had found me hiding in squalor. Would I have been there if I had any other place to be?

"Yes," I said, deciding on honesty. "But I can't go there." I wouldn't.

He didn't ask me why, just leaned back against the little table that was in the room and looked down at his sandals.

"We'll go into the market."

"No." I couldn't go there. I might be seen.

"Would you be safer outside the city?"

How did he know it was a matter of safety? And didn't he know it was not possible to get out of the city? Not with the Chief Judge murdered on the judgment seat and the army patrolling and enforcing the curfew and sealing the gates.

"I have a place I can take you, but I can't stay with you there." At my wary look, he added, "It's with my mother."

I shook my head, not to refuse the offer, but because I couldn't believe he had made it.

"She won't view it as an imposition, if that's what you're thinking."

I shook my head again. "I couldn't ask that of either of you. You don't even know me."

He regarded me for a long moment. "I know you have a need, and I know I have the resources to fill it."

But why? I wanted to ask.

"Get some more rest," he said as he came off the table. "You still look exhausted. How long were you hiding in that—?" He stopped, took a breath. "I'll go into the market alone." He paused at the door. His back was to me, but he turned his head. "Will you let me take you somewhere safe?"

He didn't even know my name. And I didn't even know his.

"I will." What choice was left to me?

He was right. I needed help. I needed food and shelter and a place to disappear, to hide.

And he was right about me being exhausted, so I lay back down on the pallet, curled up tight and fell asleep.

I thought he might come back with the Nephite guard, but he came back with a sarong and a soft new pair of long boots.

"I can't take those," I said.

I would owe him.

"Put them on," he said as if he hadn't heard me, though I knew he had. "You'll draw attention to us if you don't, and getting out is going to be tricky as it is."

"How do you plan to get out of the city?" The gates were locked. No one could get out.

"You're not the only one with secrets."

I guessed I deserved that.

He cleared his throat. "I'll wait outside while you change."

"I'm Olivia," I said before he could go through the door. "Livi."

"Get dressed, Livi. I want to get on the road."

The frustration of the past week caught up with me and I very suddenly wanted to scream that I didn't care about what he wanted. I cared about what I wanted, which was to go home—but that didn't even exist anymore.

Dutifully—because up until a month ago I had been nothing if not dutiful—I dressed in the clothing he had bought me and prepared to leave.

If he could get me out of the city, I could go anywhere. I would not have to impose upon this stranger's mother. I had never been outside of the city. I didn't know how to care for myself out there, but that didn't mean I couldn't learn. I would watch the stranger, and I would learn.

As we walked along the road in silence, I stole glances at the boy beside me. He was large like a man. Tall, strong, dangerous. I felt very small next to him. Weak and helpless. Why was I trusting him? I had taken my safety for granted my whole life.

But he had not hurt me yet.

For a time I thought he was taking me back to where he

had found me. I still didn't know how he had found me in the first place. I thought I had been hidden very well by the thick darkness of the night. But he didn't take me to the crumbling shack. Instead he turned north and eventually he cut back toward the west. I could hardly reconcile what we were doing—sneaking out of Zarahemla—with the beauty of the day. The sun was bright, air was calm, and the birds were chirping in the trees.

I didn't see it until we were on it, and even then I did not believe it. We walked over a place where the wall simply did not exist. It had been neglected to disrepair around what looked to be perhaps an ancient mudslide.

The man gave me his hand to help me up onto it, but after that he did not offer any more assistance or explanation.

When we were outside the city wall, heading west, I wanted to thank him. I wanted to share my relief at being at least temporarily safe from my life, but I said, "What was so complicated about that escape? Anyone could have walked over the wall."

He snorted softly. "Very few people know about that area of the wall, and fewer would dare walk over it."

"Ha!" I nearly laughed. "And why do they not dare?"

"It is guarded by..." He thought for a moment. "Some very dangerous men."

I hadn't seen any men. "Whatever you say."

"If my way out of the city does not please you, I can take you right on back," he said, clearly annoyed.

"No."

I couldn't go back. Not unless I wanted to live the way he had found me, and in that condition, I wouldn't live much longer.

He stopped walking, took a deep breath and let it out,

and surprised me by saying, "Sorry."

I had walked a few steps past him, but I turned when I heard the sincerity in his voice.

He caught my eye, looked away, then made himself look back. "Sorry, Livi. I did not mean to make your safety conditional upon...upon anything." He adjusted his satchel. "You are safe with me. You don't have to agree with me, be kind to me, or even like me."

I didn't believe that for one moment. At the first sign of his temper I would be gone, but until then, I really did need his help.

"What is your name?" Something I had been wondering for hours and too afraid to ask.

He was squinting into the distance, but he looked back at me. "Shad. Let's stop for a short break."

We stepped off the road together.

"And how far away is your mother, please?"

"My parents live outside of Orihah. You've heard of Melek?"

"You've a father?"

"Of course I've a father," he said, affronted. "Don't you?"

I opened my mouth to speak. Then I closed it. What to say to that? So I glared at him and raised an eyebrow.

"Okay. Dumb question," he said under his breath. It wasn't an apology.

I sighed. "It wasn't dumb. It's only, I don't feel like answering it."

"Alright." He cracked his knuckles, and heaven help me, but he noticed when I flinched.

Shad stared at me for a moment. Curious. Confused. Then he raised his hand and to my humiliation, I cowered when all he did was wipe the sweat from his brow with the back of his forearm.

"Liv—" He shook his head and reached for his water skin, the only water we had between us, and held it out to me at arm's length. "Drink," was all he said.

With shaking hands, I took the water skin.

"I'm sorry," I said when I passed it back.

He didn't reply. I couldn't tell if he was angry. He looked angry when he reached for the water, but he didn't hit me. He hesitated before he took the water skin, and in that moment I had a vision of him hitting it from my hand in a rage. But in the end, he took it almost gingerly and replaced it at his belt.

I backed away—slowly, so maybe he wouldn't notice.

"Is it time to go?" I asked into an awkward silence when all he did was stand there and do nothing.

He gave a curt nod I might have missed but for watching him so warily and moved back into the road.

We spent much of the rest of the day in silence, which was fine by me.

I had heard of Melek, but I had no idea where it was or how long it would take us to travel there. When Shad had offered his mother's home as refuge, I had assumed it was a small abode within the city or in one of the outlying villages. But we had passed the villages and this was starting to look like travel, like a lengthy journey.

With a boy.

When we finally stopped for the evening, he was careful not to touch me. He didn't even come near me. If there was something to hand me, like the water skin, he set it down and moved away. He was so deliberate about it, I almost smiled. Almost.

"Sit," he said when he had pushed a log up to our cook fire. "Have you been eating?"

He had been giving me things to eat all day. I hadn't been

throwing them on the ground.

He must have seen my confusion because he said, "I mean before today."

I looked into the tiny flame. "I left home a week ago." He was silent so I said, "I took what I could."

"How old are you?"

"Seventeen."

He frowned.

"How old are you?" I dared to ask.

"Older than that."

Something about his answer made me smile.

"You're not married, I take it," he guessed.

"No."

"Not betrothed?"

"No." Not exactly. I had disappeared before that could happen. Had Shad noticed my hesitation?

"I see."

He had noticed it, and I was afraid he did see. What must he think of me?—cowering away from nothing. I was pathetic, and I knew it, and now he knew it. But I thought of the way he had found me, and of course he had known from the first how worthless and pathetic I was.

I had allowed my fear to overcome my honor and I was sure that even if Shad could not read my dishonor on my face now, he would be able to if he looked at me for very long the way he was.

I hoped he would let it go—maybe be uncomfortable asking such questions—but he didn't.

"Why did you leave home?"

Couldn't he guess? There was really only one reason a girl might run away. A hundred words for it, but one reason.

"Olivia."

"An unwanted betrothal."

He scoffed. "Is that why you flinch from my hand?"

I shook my head slowly.

"Your father thought he would force your obedience."

I gave a nod.

"He has hit you before."

I realized what he thought had happened. "Oh, no. He didn't hit me. He wouldn't." But then, he hadn't stopped it from happening either.

Shad scoffed again.

"You don't have to believe me," I said. "My acceptance of your help is not conditional upon that."

A quick smile split his face.

"Okay. I guess I'm prying. I just need to know if there is someone who will be coming after us."

"Apparently not," I said, surprised to hear the glumness in my voice. I looked up at Shad. "I mean, no one will suspect for a moment that I am not still inside the city. It is impossible to leave."

He raised a brow. Obviously, it was possible to leave.

"Maybe you better just tell me why I found you hiding in the worst part of the city. You fled your family, but why?"

It hadn't taken me very many days without shelter, food, or money to realize I needed help. Shad was offering it. I was afraid, but I had to trust him.

"When I refused the betrothal, the man my father wants me to marry hit me." I took a breath. "A lot. And my father let him." And that hadn't been the only time.

"I see."

And now I was sure he did see.

ABOUT THE AUTHOR

Misty Moncur wanted to be Indiana Jones when she grew up. Instead, she became an author and has her adventures at home in her jammies with her imagination and pens that she keeps running dry.

Misty doesn't like to read as much as you might think. She hates bookstores and gets creeped out in libraries. She likes to Netflix-and-chill, stare out the window, and hang with her family. She lives in a swampy marshland and spends her evenings swatting mosquitoes.

Misty is the author of *Daughter of Helaman, Fight For You, In All Places,* and other novels in The Stripling Warrior series. Her stories are filled with tenderness and humor, and her characters are real, endearing, and memorable. Her LDS fiction titles will inspire you and your teen reader.

95949495R00188

Made in the USA
Columbia, SC
20 May 2018